"I have to get you to a hospital. Have you got this?"

"Yes. I'll be ready in a minute." He said, his head swaying dangerously.

"Okay. I've got to run get dressed and get my car keys. You wait for me here. I'll be right back."

She left him then, and hurried to her room.

Erika quickly struggled into the jeans and sweater she had on earlier. Grabbing her nightshirt, she yanked off the brooch and stuck it in her pocket. Grabbing her purse, she hurried back toward the open door.

So far, so good. Her heart pounded and adrenalin swirled through her veins. She would have Jonathan to safety and would have plenty of time to worry about 1837 and Charles later.

Stepping into the hall, she froze. Then fell back against the door. The muddled sound of voices and music filled the house.

The steady ticking of the grandfather clock drifted up clearly.

"No!" She cried and dropped to her knees in tears.

TWIST OF FATE

TWIST OF FATE

THE BECQUERELS

KATHRYN KALEIGH

To learn more about Kathryn Kaleigh, visit

www.kathrynkaleigh.com

PROLOGUE

Along the banks of the Mississippi
1714

"If you're going to kill me, do it now."

Lightning flashed and thunder shook the earth. Vaughn Dupre cowered among prickly brambles beneath the branches of a hickory grove and squinted through the blinding rivulets of rain washing over her.

An ancient white-bearded Indian dropped to his knees in front of her and stared into her eyes. His breath brushed her skin.

She clenched the valise holding her carefully folded wedding dress. She had been on her way to Fort Rosalie to meet the man who would marry her when they had been attacked.

As she had watched in horror, the Indians had killed those in her traveling party, one by one. Only her best friend and companion had lived nearly so long as she. But now she could see Mary's brutalized body several yards away.

"Please," she pleaded, "do it quickly."

The old man shook his head and spoke slowly - deliberately. "There is only one way you can possibly survive. You must travel - through time."

Vaughn took a deep breath, fear searing her throat. He spoke in French and she understood him. He was trying to help her. Though he was dressed like the Indians, his skin tone was lighter and his kindly features were more like those of the French familiar to her.

"I can run," Vaughn whispered, her throat closing as she spoke.

"It would do no good. The Natchee will seek you out and slice your throat as they did the others."

An image of her childhood home in the countryside of France flashed through her mind. It was followed by a memory of the orphanage where she had spent the last ten years of her life. There was nothing to leave behind and no one to miss her. The man awaiting her would find another wife easily enough. There were many more desperate girls on their way to take her place. She could only pray to God that they would fare better than she and Mary.

Though it was incomprehensible that she could be sent to another time by this man or anyone else, the alternatives were bleak, at best.

She knew only one thing - she did not want to die.

"I beg you, do whatever you can to help me."

Now that he had her permission, the old man hesitated. "There is no guarantee. I know not where you will go or for how long. You may not even live through it."

Looking back at the carnage of her friend and former traveling companions, she grasped his sleeve, ready now, to have it done. "If you don't try, I am certain to die."

"I have seen strange things since I've lived with the Natchee." He spoke slowly, as though his native language fell unfamiliar on his tongue. "Very well. I think I can help you, but we must act quickly.

"Once the rip in time is made, it may take centuries for it to heal itself. Not only you, but those of your blood may pass through it and possibly without warning. I warn you to be prepared."

"How will I know?"

"You won't."

Suddenly the French Indian lifted his arms and stretched toward the Heavens. He chanted words she couldn't understand and didn't want to. The wind whipped around them in a fury. He held his arms high and yelled indiscernible words to the sky.

Vaughn looked around her. The Indians would find them now. There was no doubt. The old man's incantation had to work.

The wind picked up and howled around them. The clouds swirled angrily. Thunder crashed over their heads. He was unaffected by the rain or the wind. His robe made of deer hide swirled around him, but he stood firm.

Vaughn closed her eyes. She was going to die. She should never have come to this new world. Should never have listened to the call of adventure in her blood. Only by a twist of fate would that very blood not be spilled upon the ground of this untamed territory.

Her ears rang, blocking out the commotion. Then a curious sensation pricked her skin. It was sunshine. She opened her eyes. There was no sign of rain or wind... or the strange Indian.

Her clothes were soaked and her hair sodden. Her valise with the wedding dress was still in her hands. She stood up slowly and turned around.

She gasped. A young gentleman on a large black horse towered over her. He was smiling.

"You seem to have had some sort of mishap. My name is Nathaniel Becquerel. Perhaps I can be of assistance," he said, stretching his hand out to her.

CHAPTER 1

The minute she walked through the door, Erika Becquerel knew something was wrong. Chandelier lights reflecting off the polished mahogany floor blended with the musty odor of the house to bring back a deluge of jumbled memories.

But the silence struck her like a cruel blow.

The grandfather clock stood with a blank expression.

Silent.

"Jonathan?" she called out, but a rumble of thunder drowned out her voice. As the noise faded, she set down her bag and dripping umbrella and called out for her grandfather again - louder this time. "Grandpa?"

No response.

Frowning, she stood in front of the nearly black rosewood clock and looked up into the faded dial. Its case was decorated with ornate columns. The clock's face wore a battle scar from the Civil War in the form of a jagged rip between the Roman numerals six and seven.

The first thing Jonathan did each morning was wind the two hundred year old family heirloom. It was one of his prized possessions. His ancestors had brought it with them when they left France to settle in the colonies.

Something was wrong.

A sense of panic gripped her. Jonathan could lie here for days before anyone discovered him. He could die and no one would know.

She started toward the kitchen, but a sound on the stairs caught her attention. Relief washed over her. Jonathan was alright. She, however, was the victim of an overactive imagination.

She turned with a smile, but the smile quickly faded.

Stepping briskly into the foyer, a woman in a loose flowered kimono glared at her through a pair of narrow glasses.

"Who are you?" Erika asked.

"That's a good question. Who are you?" the woman echoed, folding her arms across her ample chest.

"Where is Jonathan?"

"I will not discuss Mr. Becquerel until I know who you are."

Erika took a deep breath and slowly let it out. Her leather ankle boots resounded as she walked across the hardwood floor toward the woman and stopped inches in front of her.

"Where is he?" she demanded, looking down into the woman's cold dark eyes.

The woman retreated back a step, her gaze darting toward the stairs. Erika immediately closed the gap between them. Her hands clenched at her sides as the tension and fear for her grandfather returned, stronger than before.

"I want to know who you are and where my grandfather is."

Jerking her head up, realization spread over the woman's face and her skin blanched to a deathly pallor. For a moment Erika thought she glimpsed fear in her eyes. Then she blinked and the harshness was back. "I'm Mable," she said, "Jonathan is upstairs in his bedroom. I'll bring your luggage in, Erika."

Erika didn't respond. The woman's sudden change worried her. Yet even more disconcerting was the fact that this stranger knew her name. She'd never known Jonathan to hire help.

Erika sprinted up the stairs, turned left, and stopped in front of her grandfather's bedroom. A weak cough answered her knock.

Pushing the door open gently, she stuck her head around the corner. Darting past her feet, Smokey, her grandfather's large gray cat, pounced onto the bed.

Jonathan Becquerel lowered the handkerchief from his nose. He blinked and a smile spread across his wrinkled face, lifting for a brief instant the veil of sadness in his silver-gray eyes. Almost immediately, it settled back into place. As she hurried to his side, he struggled to push himself up on the pillows.

"Ah, Erika," he said, "you do look so much like my Vaughn."

His words sent a stab of pain through her heart. Vaughn. Her grandmother - her friend.

"Are you sick?" she asked, kneeling on the floor beside the bed, pushing threatening thoughts of her grandmother back into the shadowed depths of her mind.

In the six months since his wife's death, Jonathan had seemed to grow old quickly. Instead of months, he seemed to have aged years. The sparse hair on his balding head was silver and his eyes were lackluster. Even his skin had taken on an ashen shade.

"No. No. Just a bit under the weather," he said with a smile that seemed more like a lopsided frown.

"Who is that woman downstairs?"

"Mable?"

She nodded.

"She's the one your mother hired to take care of me," he said, studying her curiously.

"Really?" Erika replied, forcing a calmness into her voice she didn't feel. She placed her wrist against his forehead. His skin was cool. "What do you mean she's taking care of you? What's wrong?"

"I can't seem to shake this darned flu. It's probably just old age settling in." He paused to squint into her eyes, as though to read her thoughts.

"I didn't know you were coming," he added suddenly. "You haven't been to see me since the... since Vaughn..."

"I know. But I'm here, now. I'll take care of you." She stood up and leaned over to place her arms around his thin, feeble shoulders. Swallowed the lump in her throat. He'd grown so frail since she'd seen him last at the funeral service. *I should have come sooner.*

He patted her back and reached for his handkerchief. "The doctor is coming on Monday. Until then I'll be ok. And Mable is here. Your mother and you and Bradley all have lives of your own. I don't want to be in your way." There was no self-pity in his voice. She knew he was just stating the facts as he saw them.

At Vaughn's memorial service, he had been in good physical condition for a man of seventy-three. The deep sadness in his eyes had been there, though. It had become a part of him.

"Maybe you could stay until Monday though," he said, his face brightening with the thought.

"I'll try," Erika said softly. She sighed. There was no need to tell him now; she didn't have to leave until Sunday afternoon. Perhaps with two days of her care, he would be able to get up and around.

He reached over to the nightstand and picked up a key. "Would you mind winding the clock for me? This silence is driving me crazy."

Erika smiled. "Of course."

Slipping the key into her pocket, she left him resting, and stopped by the room that had been hers since she could remember. Mable had been true to her word. Her luggage stood in front of the wardrobe. She felt a twinge of guilt at having the woman bring it in for her, especially in the rain, but she quickly shrugged it off. If she knew her mother, Mable was being paid well enough. If Erika had her way, Mable would be dismissed as soon as possible. The woman gave her an eerie feeling.

Something was wrong. But then nothing had been the same for the past six months. Looking up, she studied the portrait on her nightstand.

Her grandmother, Vaughn, had been so full of life. Even though the black and white photograph had been taken when her grandmother was still a young woman, Erika pictured her clearly. She saw the slender, beautiful woman staring back at her with a smile that spread upwards to touch her sea-green eyes and a fragile oval face framed with long midnight curls.

Except for her straight, shoulder-length hair, Erika was a mirror image of Vaughn Becquerel.

Her mind, still spinning in confusion, returned to the situation at hand. Who was Mable? Why didn't her mother tell her about hiring this woman? They talked often enough; surely she would have mentioned that Jonathan needed someone to help care for him. Determined to find the answers and confront Mable, she got up and started back downstairs.

Halfway down, she stopped on the landing. The dark clouds had drifted off toward the horizon, and a patch of pale evening sunlight streamed in through the wavy glass in the eight foot window. Placing one hand on the thick indigo French brocade draperies tied back on either side, she leaned her forehead against the smooth wooden frame and rested her eyes. Suddenly dizzy, she fought to steady herself.

The soft ticking of the grandfather clock drifted upstairs.

Clouds wafted over the sun and a cool wind whispering through a young oak tree lightly brushed her cheeks and played about her hair. At the sudden loss of the sun's warmth, she opened her eyes. Had the window been open moments before?

She shivered.

Beyond the well-tended garden area to the left, fields of sturdy cotton plants stretched to the horizon. There, a wagon stirred up a cloud of dust. Like mounds of new fallen snow, the gray-white cotton covered the land. Workers in straw hats, brightly dyed shirts, and burlap sacks trailing along behind them, bent as they pulled cotton from the open brown shells and dropped it into the sacks.

Dazed, Erika stared out the window. A movement to the right of the house caught her attention. A girl, not more than ten, sitting beneath an oak tree, was playing with a calico cat. A doll fell unnoticed from her lap. There had been no children here since Erika and her brother, Bradley, had grown up.

She was startled out of her daze by a flurry of activity below. A black horse cantered into view, chased by two baying red hounds. Coming to a halt beside one of the outbuildings, the tall dark-haired rider slid easily from the saddle and tossed the reins to a black boy who had run out to meet him.

Absently, the man brushed dust from his white cotton shirt, black riding trousers, and tall black boots. His arms and chest visible beneath his shirt, unbuttoned at the throat, revealed a healthy tan. He was a trim man, trim, yet sturdy. A stray lock of black hair, slightly faded from the sun, fell across his forehead.

He strode toward the house, stopped directly in front of the window, and stared up at her. The man held her gaze for a moment before his clear, intense eyes slowly slid down the length of her. A shiver tingled up her spine as the wind brushed a stray wisp of hair against her cheek.

A frown briefly crossed his features and he ran a hand through his hair, sweeping it off his forehead. He blinked and his eyes came back to hers; his lips slowly tipped up in an arrogant smile. Despite the arrogance, he was ruggedly handsome. Bowing slightly, he started toward the front of the house.

The contact was broken with a jolt. Erika's heart raced and her body trembled. She took a deep breath, commanding herself to be calm and in control. It had always worked in veterinary school.

It didn't work. She couldn't slow her racing pulse. She was at a loss to explain her trembling hands and light-headed feeling at the bold perusal of this man. This stranger who seemed familiar somehow.

What was happening to her? Did she know him? Of course not. He wasn't the kind of man a girl would easily forget.

Her heartbeat pounded loudly in her ears, blocking out the steady ticking of the grandfather clock. She leaned against the window frame and closed her eyes.

The feeling of light-headedness swept over her once again and then was gone. The silence of the house rang in her ears.

A door opened downstairs, jarring her back to her senses. She hurried down the stairs and turned just in time to see Mable step through the back door with her purse and raincoat. At least she and Jonathan would be left alone until morning.

Erika sighed in frustration and turned around to check the time. She stood face to face with the silent grandfather clock.

The clock!

Jonathan had asked her to wind it, but she hadn't.

She squeezed her eyes shut and thought back through the last several minutes. It had definitely been ticking. She knew the sound as well as she knew the voice in her own head. Reaching into her pocket, she squeezed the clock's key.

Suddenly she felt very tired. Maybe she shouldn't have taken on teaching that zoology class at the community college, but with just one more semester of internship before becoming a licensed veterinarian, she had decided not to pass up the school's offer. It was good experience.

This Thanksgiving holiday was the first time off she'd had since Vaughn's accident. All the hard work would pay off next summer when she could finally open her own clinic. She looked forward to specializing in cute, cuddly pets, not the large farm animals her employer catered to.

Trying to keep her thoughts focused, she wandered into the parlor and found herself in front of the arrangement of portraits displayed on the wall. Jonathan and Vaughn were there as well as her mother and father. She and Bradley were the last ones added to the group. At the far end were William and Abigail, the ones who built the house in the early 1800s. Scanning the row of faces, she paused somewhere near the center.

Feeling a tingle at the base of her spine, she focused on the man's familiar face. A face was far too familiar – yet shouldn't have been.

Of course it was familiar, she thought, frustrated with herself. She had seen these paintings hundreds of times. She used to come here as a child and study them. Then why did this one stand out now?

She warmed her cool fingertips against her palms.

Suddenly fear and disbelief collided in her mind.

It was him! It was the man on the horse. This painting was well over a hundred and fifty years old. How could she have just seen him, living and breathing?

Disconcerted, she went back up to the landing and stood in front of the now closed window. Wondering briefly who had closed it, she realized that if the rider had entered the house, she would have seen him. Taking a deep breath, she pulled the heavy curtain aside and peeked out.

Her grip on the soft fabric tightened and her breathing came in shallow, quivering gasps. Where were the rows of cotton that had been there minutes ago? Familiar pine seedlings and briars had taken over the fields that had been neatly plowed only moments before. One of the two remaining outbuildings had caved in and was no more than a heap of rotten lumber.

The child was gone, too, and there was no sign of the cat or the doll. But, the oak tree... The tree the girl had been sitting beneath was no longer a young sapling. It was a full grown tree with its limbs stretching skyward.

She turned and numbly continued to the top of the stairs. A breeze stirred and cooled her sweaty palms. It was like someone had flipped a switch and for a moment she had seen a page of history. Perhaps she had wished for things to be the way they had been when Vaughn was alive so much that she had hallucinated. She shook her head. Impossible. Her imagination was much too vivid.

At the top of the stairs, she stopped with one hand clutching the rail. Her vision wavered and she blinked, trying to regain focus. Her entire world careened in front of her and she grabbed the rail with both hands.

Then the world righted itself and was still.

A soft ticking sound drifted from downstairs.

It can't be the clock.

She had the key. In a panic, she reached into her pocket and wrapped her fingers around the small, silver key.

"Excuse me, Miss? You must have come in while I was out."

Erika whirled around, startled. A tall, heavy set man in a black cloak and hat towered over her. In a state of confusion, she studied his kind honest face and tried to block out the clock's incessant ticking.

With an embarrassed chuckle and a grin that flashed his white teeth, he swept the hat from his head. "I'm sorry, Miss. I just came in from the smoke house. We didn't expect you so soon."

This was not her imagination. She swallowed and closed her mouth, dry with the onset of panic.

"Who are you?" she asked, her voice cracking in mid-sentence.

A flicker of hurt swept over his face. "Don't you remember Villars? But of course, you're wore out from the trip. I'll show you to your room so you can rest."

The clock began to chime the half hour. Erika started and nearly tumbled down the stairs. Grabbing her elbow, Villars caught her as her left foot slipped off the top step.

"Be careful, Miss Sierra," he warned as he steadied her.

Erika leaned against the banister. The color drained from her face.

Sierra?

"Are you feeling all right, Miss Sierra?"

Erika looked up into that unknown face and fear suddenly grabbed at her heart. He had set out to confuse her in order to rob them or murder them - or both. She took a step backwards.

"What are you doing here?" she asked.

"I'm the butler, Miss," he said with a puzzled expression.

"Sure." She took another step backwards. "You're no more a butler than I'm Sierra."

"Please, Miss. Let me send some vittles up to you. We have some fresh bouillabaisse."

Erika turned and ran like a fleeing rabbit to her grandfather's room. Instinctively she wanted to protect him from this intruder. She slammed the door behind her and frantically turned the lock.

Leaning against the cool wood, she listened to her erratic heartbeat pounding in her ears.

She feared for them both. She had to warn Jonathan and call the police. Taking a deep breath, she turned with an explanation on her lips.

Her mind soundlessly screamed.

The bed was neatly made up. Jonathan was not in the room and there was no sign that he ever had been. She felt like she'd fallen into an episode of the Twilight Zone.

Loosening her grip on the door knob, she walked to the bed and sat down. What had the man done with Jonathan? Could he really be a butler? She didn't know what to think anymore. Her life had somehow crashed and lay crumbled at her feet, ripping reality to shreds in the process.

She looked out the bedroom window at the setting sun. There was the garden, then a row of frame shacks. The cotton fields spread as far as she could see. She definitely wasn't where she'd started when she arrived not much more than an hour ago.

She couldn't stay here in this room forever. She had to confront Villars - and whatever was happening to her.

Steeling herself, she went to the door and unlocked it. Villars stood where she had left him.

"Who lives here?" she asked, keeping one foot safely inside the bedroom.

Understanding dawned on Villars' face. "I'm sorry, Miss Sierra. I forgot you hadn't been here since you were a child. There's Mister Richard, and Mistress Rebecca, and Miss Andrea, and Mister Charles. You've never met Miss Andrea, but you remember Mister Charles, don't you?"

Glancing down at her sweater and jeans, she ran her hand along the fabric, convincing herself that they, at least, were real. Trying to appear casual, she stepped out into the hallway.

"What year is this?" she asked hesitantly.

"I believe it's 1837. But it could be 1836. I don't rightly know."

Erika had the fleeting thought that she had died. She glanced toward the bottom of the stairs, and released her breath in a jagged rush when she didn't see her body crumpled on the pale cream rug.

What difference did it make whether it was 1836 or 1837? In fact, he may as well have said 1436 or 1437. The only thought focused clearly in her mind was that Jonathan was sick and he needed her.

"Would you like to go to the guest room, now, Miss Sierra?"

"Yes, I suppose so."

Erika followed Villars to the closed door of her room.

"If you need anything, Miss, just pull the bell cord."

She reached for the doorknob. It seemed to take forever. Her head spun as she felt the knob's coolness in her hand. She grasped it in an effort to steady herself.

Upon opening the door, relief swept over her. Her luggage stood neatly next to the wardrobe. She turned quickly back to Villars, but instead faced an empty and silent hallway.

She ran down the dimly lit hall and threw open Jonathan's bedroom door.

Groggily, Jonathan opened his eyes. "What's wrong?"

Suddenly there was a lump in her throat and her eyes stung with tears. Sniffing, Erika shut the door behind her and wiped at her eyes. She didn't know what stroke of fate had brought her back, but she silently blessed it.

"Nothing's wrong. Are you asleep?"

"Not anymore." Sitting up, he switched on the lamp on his nightstand.

"I'm sorry. I just..." She faltered. What was she supposed to say, *I've been traveling through time? I've been back to the year 1837?* "I just wanted to check on you."

"I'm fine," he said, reaching over to scratch Smokey. "Are you sure you're okay? You're awfully pale." He picked up a jar of Mentholatum from the nightstand and dabbed some under his nose.

Erika sat on the edge of the bed and fought back the tears.

Her heart twisted in misery at the sight of his bald head and wrinkled skin. Why did people have to grow old?

When he hadn't been here a few minutes ago, she realized even more how empty her life was going to be without him. That emptiness was inevitable, and the knowledge left her with a heavy heart.

He knew she was troubled. He always knew. Yet she couldn't bring herself to tell him. The whole idea that she talked to a butler and saw cotton fields covering their land was preposterous.

She, Vaughn, and Jonathan had often walked around the grounds and halls of this big, old house and talked about the history of the once grand plantation and their ancestors. Jonathan told her the stories he was once told by his grandfather. Hadn't he mentioned a tall, kindly butler that worked for their family for an extraordinarily long period? Perhaps that had been Villars. She shook her head. She was a professional with a firm grasp on reality. She was tired, that's all.

"I'll go now so you can get some rest." She stood up and quickly hugged him, biting her lip to fight back the sobs. "What would you like for supper? I'll fix you something good," she said. Not waiting for an answer, she pulled away and started for the door.

"I'll see you in a little while," she said with forced cheerfulness over her shoulder.

"Erika? Wait."

"Yes?" She paused and, with considerable effort, lifted her chin and smiled.

"I want to give you something while I'm thinking about it."

She wiped at her eyes and took a deep breath before walking back toward him.

He opened the drawer to the nightstand and took out a

small square box. "After my wife, you mean more to me than anyone ever has in my whole life."

"You mean a lot to me, too." She returned to his side and sat on the edge of the bed, trying to ignore the sense of dread concerning what he was about to tell her.

"What I'm saying is, I don't want anyone else to end up with this. I want to make sure it goes to you." He placed the box in her hand, his bony fingers brushing her smaller ones.

"Why are you talking like this?" She cautiously lifted the lid on the box and recognized the cream cameo brooch that lay on black silk lining. Jonathan was frightening her. He was giving away his most precious memento of his wife - the wedding gift he had specially crafted for her. The cameo was a likeness of Vaughn.

She swallowed the lump in her throat and met his gaze. She felt the tears spilling from her eyes, but couldn't stop them.

"I can't take this from you," she said softly. "It was Grandma's. You should keep it."

"Nonsense. I've kept up with it for six months. It looks so much like you. I want you to have it now. Please. Make an old man happy."

"All right." Forcing a smile, she brushed at the tears and kissed him on the cheek. "I'll take good care of it."

"That's better," he said, patting her hand. "Keep it with you at all times. It'll bring you good luck and keep you safe. If Vaughn had had it with her that day we went fishing on the river, she wouldn't have... maybe she would still be here."

He yanked a tissue from the nightstand and hastily dabbed at his eyes, then loudly blew his nose.

It must have been hard for Jonathan to stand by and helplessly watch his wife's life end. She had tried hard to stay too busy to think much about the accident. Now was not the time to dwell on it either. She had to be strong for her grandfather.

"Okay." She placed the brooch back in its box. "Thank you. It's a gift I'll always cherish."

"You'll let me know if anything is wrong."

She tilted her head to one side. "Of course." *If it's possible.*

"You get some rest now."

"Jonathan..."

His deep gray eyes met hers. "Yes. What is it?"

"I love you!" She blurted and buried her face against his shoulder.

He patted her back. "I love you, too, Kitten. I'll be alright."

Fleeing from the room, she hurried down the hall to her own bedroom. She couldn't bear to see her grandfather like this. She would find a way to be here Monday when the doctor came.

Hanging her clothes in the tall cedar wardrobe, she decided to take a quick nap before fixing supper. She searched unsuccessfully through her things for a nightgown. Giving up, she chose an old red plaid flannel shirt. It came to about mid-thigh in the front and back, but had side slits that gaped open a little higher. After rolling the long sleeves up to her elbows, she removed her barrette and used her fingers to fluff her hair. Wistfully pinning the brooch to the nightshirt, she climbed into bed and closed her eyes.

Within minutes she had drifted off to sleep.

Noises from outside the room woke her. She strained, but couldn't make out what was going on over the music.

Music? She got up, walked through the darkened room, and stepped into the hall. Her shadow wavered beneath flickering candlelight as she made her way toward the banister leading to the stairs... and the increasingly louder music and voices.

And a faint ticking noise.

She stopped just below the landing and could see into the smoke-filled library off to the left. Finely dressed men stood there, talking among themselves.

The clock began to chime. She grasped the banister and breathed in sharply. It had happened again. This was no dream. No figment of her imagination. She was certain of it now. Shivering, she watched the pendulum swing back and forth as the clock chimed nine times, echoing throughout the house.

Erika slowly moved down along the banister until she could see into the parlor.

Playing a lively tune, a six-piece orchestra sat at one end of the room. Dozens of couples either waltzed about the crowded floor or watched from the chairs and sofas that had been slid up against the walls. Dressed in the finest fabrics she had ever imagined, they seemed to float on a delicate cloud of satin and lace.

Erika was so engrossed in watching the dancers, she didn't notice Villars coming up the stairs. He was now almost beside her.

"Miss Sierra," he said, backing away from her and studying her suspiciously. He cleared his throat and continued. "I'm sorry you're missing the dance, but Mister Charles say to let you rest. And that's good because I didn't know where you got off to anyway."

"What's going on?" she asked, leaning over the banister, one bare foot dropping over the edge. Why was his expression so odd?

"Why, it's the Harvest Moon Ball," he said proudly.

Of course, the annual ball. A Becquerel tradition that lasted all the way to World War II.

"I think you better go on back up, Miss. It wouldn't be proper for you to be seen dressed like this."

Villars had no more finished speaking when, as though in response to his words, the music drifted away in mid-strain and the whispering became louder. The violin bows grew still and the soft flute became silent. The dance room seemed to have frozen and there were entirely too many eyes turned in her direction.

Erika scanned the room of faces - faces she had never seen before. Several pale skinned women stared at her from behind their open fans and others from behind crystal goblets poised at their lips. A couple of men blew cigar smoke into the air as they watched her.

"Who is she?"

Their whispered words, spoken by voices unchecked, drifted clearly to Erika's ears.

"Hardly dressed at all."

"A man's shirt."

"Of all the nerve."

"You'd expect this kind of thing under the hill, but how did that hussy get in here?"

What were they talking about? Her eyes paused on a man in the back of the room whose darkly tanned face stood out from the others. His eyes locked with hers across the crowded room. She breathed in sharply.

It was him! It was the man she had seen riding up on the black stallion - the man in the portrait hanging in the parlor.

Once again he was staring at her with that intensity that made her hands quiver. The passion in his gaze frightened her. His eyes slowly caressed her body down to her bare feet and slid back up to imprison her eyes.

He weaved his way across the ballroom, then started up the stairs.

He spoke. But she couldn't make out his words.

CHAPTER 2

The room had suddenly grown warm - much too warm. Releasing her hold on the stair railing, Erika tugged on the sides of the flannel shirt, but realized with frustration that she only succeeded in lowering the unbuttoned neckline.

She was trapped. She shouldn't be here. All these people staring at her as though she had grown stripes made that clear enough. Villars, the only friendly face she'd encountered had gone about his original errand and left her here. Alone. She was on her own in this unfamiliar world.

She thought of Jonathan. Where was he? What had happened to his world?

She had to remember the stories he and Vaughn had told and the people they spoke of. That was the key to survival. Frustration built as her memory went blank, but her mind raced with frantic thoughts.

What now? She could flee this house, but there was no where to go. She couldn't even begin to imagine what unfamiliar terrain lay beyond the grounds of this house.

If she left these people, she would doubtlessly be far worse off than she was now. Most importantly, she had no money, no means of survival. Whatever their reaction and subsequent treatment of her, she would have to survive until she could get home.

She would have to make sure no one realized she was an imposter. Here, at least, she would have food and shelter until she could figure out what to do. This house was obviously the gateway to getting back to her own time.

If the gods were with her, she would soon be swept back to her own time. Yet, something was different this time. Things were... less hazy. But she couldn't worry about that now.

She had to stay in the house. There was no other choice.

The man stood next to her, now, studying her curiously. He shielded her from the gaping strangers.

"Put this on and come with me, Sierra," he repeated, placing his dress coat over her shoulders and gently placing his hand on her elbow, led her back up the stairs and down the hall. The coat, nearly dragging the floor, swallowed her. He must be nearly six feet tall.

She didn't resist and soon found herself upstairs and alone with the man.

"You're creating quite a stir down there. Villars told me your trunks haven't arrived. Why don't you wait in your room until I've spoken with Mother. She'll find something appropriate for you to put on."

Erika looked into his eyes and her breath caught in her throat. They were a clear slate blue. If it were possible, he was even more handsome up close.

Her disturbing thoughts were interrupted when a woman with silver-streaked, but still blonde hair, curled and stylishly piled high upon her head, came into the hallway. Erika recognized the woman from the portraits in the parlor. She regretted not bothering to learn the names of her ancestors when the timing wasn't so crucial.

"Charles," the woman asked, "what's going on?"

"Here's your Aunt Rebecca now," he said, releasing his hold on her. "It seems Sierra arrived before her trunks. Do you think you could find her something to wear?"

"Of course," she said, kindly, shooing her son away.

Erika watched as he walked down the hallway to rejoin the other guests. The music was playing again. Hopefully they had forgotten about her.

"*Mon ami,*" Rebecca said, "*J'sais vous?*"

"What?" Erika's history was bad enough, but her French was worse.

"Pardon," she said with a slight accent, "I'm sorry. But you do resemble the Creole. My dear, do I know you?"

"No," Erika said and began walking with her along the upstairs hall toward her room.

"Well, we both know you aren't Sierra. What's your name?"

"Erika."

"Erika," she echoed, seeming to test the unfamiliar name on her tongue. "Where are you from?"

They reached the guest room and went inside. Erika tensed as she watched the older woman, elegant and sophisticated in her mushroom brown ball gown. She liked her immediately, yet was afraid of her. Somehow she sensed that if she met this woman's approval, she would have no problem staying here. On the other hand, if Rebecca decided she wasn't welcome, she could give up any thought of remaining in the house.

Unfortunately, she was balanced on a precarious ledge. Rebecca, as well as all those stuffy guests downstairs, no doubt thought she was here as Charles' prostitute. Her curiosity about this man was increasing.

"Have you been here long?" Rebecca persisted.

"No," Erika answered, choosing her words carefully. "I only arrived this afternoon."

"You're a friend of Charles'."

"No," she answered swiftly, "I'm really not sure how I ended up here."

Rebecca looked immensely relieved. She sat down on the blue velvet settee at the foot of the bed.

"Did you come with someone?"

Taking a swift glance around the room, she swallowed hard. The only light came from a short, thick candle burning brightly on the nightstand. She hadn't noticed it earlier. Villars must have lit it while she was downstairs.

"No, but my grandfather told me to wait for him here." She didn't know how much more of this interrogation she could survive. Her stomach churned in knots of nervous panic. The primitive world outside this house terrified her. At least here, she had a chance to get back to her own time.

"Now, are you going to tell me who your grandfather is?"

"Jonathan Becquerel"

Rebecca frowned. "I'm sorry, Dear. I don't know all my husband's family," she said, now speaking in a gentle voice. "Enough of this, let's get you properly dressed so I can introduce you to our guests. I have just the thing for you."

In a whirlwind of silk, Rebecca was gone from the room. Alone again, Erika went to the wardrobe and opened it. It was empty. She had no clothes. She had nothing but this inane flannel shirt. And Charles' jacket, she was reminded, as its masculine scent enveloped her.

She was getting more than a glimpse into the past. She was being swept into these people's lives.

She was still staring into the empty cabinet, her mind in turmoil, when a knock came at the door. Closing the wardrobe she went back to stand next to the four poster bed. Her bed.

"Who is it?" she asked, clutching Charles' jacket around her.

"Elizabeth."

"Elizabeth?" Erika mumbled. "Pretty soon I'll need a program."

"I'm not dressed," she called louder.

Ignoring Erika's response, a young woman with creamy skin, a full mouth, large blue eyes, and long, light brown curls came into the room. Her deep blue ball gown was almost black in the dimly lit room. Elizabeth was as gorgeous as any twentieth-first century model.

"Who are you?" Elizabeth asked bluntly.

"My name is Erika Becquerel."

Elizabeth made a quick turn around the room and returned to stand in front of Erika. "Charles is mine, you know."

Erika swallowed a laugh, whether of humor or panic, she wasn't sure. How much more ridiculous was this going to get? She'd barely even met Charles and now his girlfriend was threatening her. Charles was handsome enough, but she wasn't sure he was deserving of all this mess. She wished desperately for Rebecca to hurry back. It would be nice to put on some clothes, especially if she had to entertain all these people.

"I'm Erika Becquerel. My grandfather is Jonathan Becquerel. I'm just waiting here for him." That response worked once, maybe it would quiet Elizabeth, too.

"Humph," Elizabeth uttered, her beauty only emphasized in her anger. "Surely you don't believe he's going to marry you. Men don't marry women like you. You're only here for his pleasure." Though her words were harsh, she spoke each word with a control that could have been attained only from breeding.

"I don't even know Charles. I have no more desire to marry him than to go to bed with him." She had grown tired of the loose reference these people were making of her character. Her fingers tightened on the carved wood of the tall poster. This was her bed, she thought with tears stinging the corners of her eyes. She had slept here since she was a child.

"You may be telling the truth, but in any event, the least you could do is to be discreet about it."

No longer amused, Erika was tired of being on the defensive. It was time to put this woman in her place. "My name is Becquerel. I am part of this family. I am not dressed and I would like you to leave this room."

"You may be part of this family, but what difference do you think that makes? Why do you think he has to sleep in the garconniere away from his own sister? Anyway, I saw the way Charles looked at you. He's still looking forward to having you for the first time."

Erika smiled tauntingly. If this girl insisted on slandering her, she would get it back twofold. "I bet you wish he still looked at you that way."

Elizabeth inhaled deeply, looking at Erika's button front shirt, slender body, and smoothly shaven bare legs. "I trust you do not plan to be here long," she said as she turned and stormed from the room.

CHARLES LEFT his guests and escaped out onto the veranda. Clenching an unlit cigar between his teeth, he grasped the rail with both hands as he gazed across the moonlit lawn. Even outside, the orchestra music was loud. Absently, he wondered if it could be heard from the landing on the river. Probably not, he thought. It would first have to pass through Perry Miller's thick woods.

He couldn't understand Perry's ideas. Why hadn't he cleared that land and planted cotton? Why was he holding onto those trees? Cotton produced a hefty crop every year. Even with the depressed market, he could hold his cotton until prices went up and continue producing.

When Perry's land became his, the first thing he would do is clear it and plant the acreage in cotton. Becquerel fields would then stretch uninterrupted to the river bank.

As the cool breeze swept over him, his thoughts drifted

back to Sierra. Why hadn't he seen her for so long? His interest piqued as he thought of the way she was dressed... or practically undressed. It was hard enough to get a glimpse of a lady's ankles, much less her legs. His first thought had been to protect her. Now, her sea green eyes haunted him. And on this, the night his engagement was to be announced.

Why was he damned with such a beautiful cousin?

"Have you been with her?"

Charles immediately recognized Elizabeth Miller's controlled voice. He knew her anger well. Turning, he faced his livid betrothed.

"What are you accusing me of?" he asked, clenching his cigar between his fingers, although he was certain he knew

"Really, Charles. You should be more discrete."

"Discrete about what?"

"Your cousin. I saw you with her. You seemed quite familiar."

"Although I don't owe you an explanation, I will tell you this. Contrary to widespread occurrence I would never bed my cousin."

Elizabeth stood close to him now. She knew her effect on men and obviously hoped to use her wiles on him. Unfortunately for her, Charles felt no more than an acquaintanceship toward her.

"How do I know it won't happen?"

"You don't, do you?"

She whirled on him, now using a different technique. Tears glistened in her eyes and Charles wondered how she could summon them so easily. "Charles, are you certain you want this marriage? I mean, you're so worldly. How can you stand to be tied down to just one woman?"

"I've told you before. Once I'm married I expect my wife to be willing in every way. I will have no need to seek comfort elsewhere. We'll be married only if you agree to those terms."

Elizabeth turned, angry at the humiliation she was being subjected to, and left him as quickly as she had appeared.

Elizabeth quickly vanished from his thoughts as well and he readily acknowledged his desire to see Sierra again.

Going back inside, he made his way around the waltzing couples and into the foyer. However, his mother intercepted him before he started up the stairs.

"Who is she?" she asked.

"Sierra?"

"Do you honestly believe that girl is Sierra?"

"Of course, Villars told me she had arrived this afternoon."

"First of all, Sierra isn't due here for another week. Second, she's from my side of the family. Granted, I haven't seen her in half a dozen years, but a blonde fair-skinned child doesn't blossom into a dark-haired woman, no matter how beautiful."

Charles felt his spirits lift at his mother's words. If the girl wasn't his cousin, that could mean only one thing. She was available to him.

"Her name is Erika Becquerel. I'm not sure how she's kin to your father, but I'm much more likely to believe that story."

Charles' hopes sank as quickly as they had risen. She wasn't Sierra, but she was still related to him. "I suppose Villars just assumed that she was Sierra."

"Then you don't know her?"

"No. I've never seen her before. Why would she come here wearing only a man's shirt?"

"Maybe she's lost. Her speech is educated and I don't think she's intentionally lying. She seems a little disoriented actually. Why don't you talk to her? I'll speak with your father and see if he knows anyone by that name. Then I'll send Dr. Alkin up to examine her. I've heard of people entirely forgetting who they are."

Charles wasn't so sure about the possibility of her not knowing who she was. There was one thing he was sure about though. He would find out who she really was. And what she was after.

REBECCA MUST HAVE FORGOTTEN HER. Exhausted, Erika curled up on the settee and leaned her head against the cushions. The candle sputtered in its pool of wax and went out. She felt lost, but relieved to be alone, in the darkened room.

She closed her eyes again and wasn't sure how long she lay there in a light slumber before the sound of footsteps jolted her fully awake. She sat up. At last, she would have clothes to put on. Although, at this point, she just wanted to be left alone to sleep.

Slowly the door creaked open and a tall figure, illuminated by the light from the hall, approached.

The man easily made his way through the darkened room to the window. He stood, leaning his shoulder against the frame, facing her. Erika could then make out Charles' features from the moonlight.

The seconds stretched into what seemed an eternity. Erika began to shiver and pulled the jacket tighter around her bare legs. It wasn't cold in here. What was wrong with her?

"Perhaps I can be of assistance," he said, moving quickly toward the wardrobe. Easily reaching on top, he retrieved a quilt and proceeded to drape it over her. He then half sat, half leaned against the settee.

"Thanks," Erika said hoarsely. He was close enough now that she could clearly see his face. It was not the cold that made her tremble. It was this man who was making her quiver with a mere glance from those dark, slate blue eyes.

"When did you arrive at the house?"

Erika groaned inwardly. Another interrogation. "This afternoon, just before I saw you through the window."

"Yes. That's what Villars told me. But where did you go when he looked for you?"

She found herself unable to meet his gaze for long. It was too intense. "I was..." *with my grandfather - over one hundred fifty years from now!* "I took a walk."

He frowned. He didn't believe her. Just what would he think if she told him the truth? It was ever so tempting. Then taking a walk would certainly sound like a reasonable explanation.

"Where is your mother? She was supposed to bring me some clothes."

"She'll be here soon enough. I wanted to make sure we understood each other."

"Excuse me?"

"You heard me. I can help you."

Now he was beginning to sound like some of the guys she had dated. This was something she knew how to deal with. "Forget it."

"Your little masquerade didn't work. I know you aren't my cousin, Sierra."

"Good. I'm tired of everyone calling me that."

She thought he smiled, then decided she had imagined it.

"So, Erika, what brings you here?"

"My grandfather asked me to wait for him here." She'd told this lie so many times she was beginning to believe it herself.

"How convenient."

"Why don't you tell me about Elizabeth?"

His eyes narrowed. "Stay away from her."

"Don't worry. I won't bother her."

"I wasn't worried about her," he said under his breath.

"Who is Sierra?" she asked, eager to learn at last who everyone thought she was.

"You mean to tell me you don't know? It seems you conveniently chose to masquerade as my innocent cousin." He leaned toward her when he spoke, and she smelled the liquor on his breath. "But you have been found out, my sweet."

The endearment was obviously meant for nothing more than emphasis, impersonal, yet, as though on their own accord, the words seemed to roll off his tongue like a caress.

The tension grew between them in the moonlit room as he stared at her. She wanted to look away, but couldn't. Then, before she knew what he was doing, he leaned close and pressed his lips on her cheek, against the corner of her mouth. Gently. Softly. Lingeringly.

She swayed. *Surely I'll wake and this will all be a dream.*

But her eyelids fluttered open and Charles watched her, his lips a breath from hers. His own eyes half closed. He lightly swept a fingertip beneath her chin. She gasped softly.

Footsteps echoed somewhere down the hallway, pulling her from the gossamer moment. They couldn't be seen together. Not like this. Not tonight. It would only prove what everyone had been saying about her.

"Don't," she said. "You don't even know me."

"I know what I want when I find it."

A rap at the door interrupted them. Without waiting for an answer, Villars entered. "Mistress Rebecca told me to bring these things right in, Sierra," he said, smiling at Charles.

"Do you mind if I get dressed now?" she asked, forcing her mind to focus, as she shrugged out of the jacket and handed it to Charles.

Villars left the mound of clothing on the bed and promptly left. Charles lingered another moment.

"I'll see you downstairs. Shortly. Besides, the gossips are having a wonderful time and we wouldn't want to disappoint them."

She couldn't help but smile. It was true. What should she care what those people thought anyway?

Suddenly she longed to feel his virile arms around her and his lips against hers again.

"Don't be long," he said with a wink. He started to turn away, then as though on second thought, reached out and pulled her up to stand next to him.

He tipped her chin up toward him and, bending down, he gently placed his lips against hers. Unprepared for this unexpected onslaught, she didn't attempt to pull away. The pressure of his mouth increased possessively and she responded without thinking. *It's like coming home.* Her hands found their way around his neck and her fingers tangled in his soft hair.

He released her abruptly, leaving her feeling exposed and wanting more. Without a word, he pulled away and stepped from her. She couldn't read his expression as he turned.

As he walked away from her, she felt faint. Her head spun dangerously. No man had ever affected her this intensely. She reached out for him, for something - anything to grasp onto, but there was nothing. The silence was interrupted only by the ringing in her ears. She squeezed her eyes shut and her reeling head became steady once more.

When she opened her eyes again he was gone. Erika's mind was numb, yet she would do as Charles had requested. It was impossible not to. She savored the still warm and trembling sensation of his kiss. She would quickly get dressed and join him downstairs.

She turned to the bed. The dress, the petticoats, all the things Villars had left were gone.

There was no music. No laughter. The house was quiet. Even the steady ticking of the clock had stopped.

Her suitcase stood next to the wardrobe. She dropped onto the bed and pressed her palms against her forehead. She felt an overwhelming sense of loss. Was a brief encounter all she was destined to have with the man who set her body aflame and her mind in turmoil?

Penetrating her thoughts, two urgent voices drifted from the hallway.

Quietly opening the door, she squinted into the bright light. Mable. Her voice was easy enough to recognize.

"We've got to hurry."

"What about our plan?"

"If we don't hurry, there won't be a plan. You've got to increase the amount of arsenic we're giving the old man before his granddaughter suspects something and fires me."

"All right. Mother. All right. Just don't get caught."

"Don't worry about me. Just be here Monday morning. And wear your white coat in case she's still here."

Erika didn't recognize the man's voice. Her heart pounded in her ears as she listened to their plotting. She was still a little sluggish from her encounter with Charles.

But there was no doubt about they were talking about.

They were poisoning Jonathan.

She had to get him out of here and to the hospital. *Now.* She couldn't risk even waiting until morning. From the way things had been going, she might return to the Harvest Moon Ball any second.

She bit nervously on one of her fingernails. She would have to get past Mable and the strange man.

She waited, holding her breath, until she heard them reach the familiar creak of the bottom step. Peering down the hall, she followed cautiously. She would have to make it to the parlor or the kitchen. As she started down the stairs, the back door slammed. Bounding down the stairs, she ran into the parlor and grabbed the telephone.

"Please be home, little brother," she muttered as she dialed the number.

"Hello," Bradley's sleepy voice answered.

Erika sent up a silent prayer of thanks. Again. This had been a long night.

"Bradley. Thank God you're home."

"What's wrong?"

"Jonathan's in trouble."

"Is he hurt? Is he sick?"

"No."

"Do you know what time it is?"

"No. Bradley. Listen to me." Her words tumbled out in a rush. "You've got to come here now. Jonathan has a woman staying with him. Her name is Mable. She's poisoning him - with arsenic."

"What? Slow down."

"There's no time. In case I'm... not here, you've got to stop them. The doctor who comes on Monday is a fake. He's Mable's son."

"This is crazy."

"I know. Believe me. I know. But I've got to go. My only hope is to get Jonathan out of the house while I'm here. Can you come tonight?"

"Yeah, but why wouldn't you be there? Where are you going?"

"Nowhere, I hope. Bye, Bradley."

Erika hung up the phone and breathed a sigh of relief. Turning around, she came face to face with Mable watching her from the doorway.

"Mable," she said, trying to smile. "I thought you left hours ago."

"You shouldn't have done that."

"Then why don't you explain to me what's going on?"

Mable glanced quickly behind Erika. Erika turned her head just in time to see a tall, skinny man approaching her with an outstretched strip of red cloth.

Without giving herself time to think, Erika grasped the first thing that caught her eye. Her fingers wrapped around the silver handle of the fireplace poker. She lifted it just as the man lunged for her.

There was a thud as the poker punctured his overcoat and a cracking sound as it hit a bone. The coat hung over his back like a tent. Drops of blood ran down the poker.

He had skewered himself on the poker. The cloth fluttered silently to the floor.

He stared at her, his eyes glazed. With horror, she pushed him away as hard as she could with her end of the poker and he fell backwards. He collided with an end table and an antique lamp crashed to the floor. Then he slumped to the floor, motionless. Mable cried out and ran to her son.

Erika backed away. It had all happened so fast. Turning, she fled from the room. She had killed a man. But there was no time to consider that now.

Running up the stairs, she threw open Jonathan's door. She had to get them both out of here. Mable would kill him now, for sure.

"Jonathan! Jonathan, you've got to get up."

Her grandfather rolled over and reluctantly opened his eyes. They were pink with infection. Why hadn't she seen the signs of the poison earlier?

"Maybe later," he said, bringing a hand up to shield his eyes.

Hurrying to his wardrobe, she grabbed a pair of slacks and a shirt.

"You have to get dressed." She stuffed pillows behind him until he was in a sitting position. After a moment's hesitation, she started unbuttoning his pajama top.

"If you don't get dressed, I'll have to do it for you."

"All right," he said, "help me up. Is the house on fire?"

Throwing back the covers, Erika grabbed his ankles and slid them off the bed. She flinched at his cold, clammy skin.

Jonathan finished unbuttoning his pajama top and was struggling out of it.

"I have to get you to a hospital. Can you finish by yourself?"

"Yes. I'll be ready in a minute." He said, his head swaying dangerously.

"Okay. I've got to run get dressed and get my car keys. You wait for me here. I'll be right back."

She left him then, and hurried to her room.

Erika quickly struggled into the jeans and sweater she had on earlier. Grabbing her nightshirt, she yanked off the brooch and stuck it in her pocket. Grabbing her purse, she hurried back toward the open door.

So far, so good. Her heart pounded and adrenalin swirled through her veins. She would have Jonathan to safety and would have plenty of time to worry about 1837 and Charles later.

Stepping into the hall, she froze. Then fell back against the door. The muddled sound of voices and music filled the house.

The steady ticking of the grandfather clock drifted up clearly.

"No!" She cried and dropped to her knees in tears.

CHAPTER 3

*S*urely she was not some figment of his imagination. He had held her and felt her soft skin - her warmth.

"Where is she?" Charles asked himself under his breath.

Upon reaching the door, he had looked back for one last glimpse. *Why did I turn back?* He only knew that it was at that very moment he felt his heart stop.

She was gone.

Going out onto the balcony, Charles leaned against the wide wooden rail and took several deep breaths. The lighthearted music mocked his darkened mood and his confusion. He was at a loss to explain her disappearance. She couldn't have left the room in that split second. He had called out to her and thoroughly searched the room. As far as he could discern, she had simply disappeared.

He clenched his fist in anger and hit the rail, hard. A trickle of blood oozed unnoticed from a small cut on his hand.

Where was she?

His lips still tingled from the kiss that he had been unable to resist. He swore even if he had to tear the house apart, he would find her. He couldn't explain it, but he needed to see her again - to hold her and kiss her.

And she was gone.

Searching for Villars, he rushed back into the house, through the crowded ballroom, and out toward the kitchen at the back of the house. Maybe Villars could find her while he dealt with his father.

There would be no engagement announcement tonight.

At the sound of approaching footsteps, Charles straightened his jacket and stuffed the still unlit cigar into his mouth.

"What did you do to Elizabeth?" His father asked, coming up behind him.

Taking the cigar from his mouth, Charles flexed his throbbing hand.

"Nothing," he lied smoothly. The fact that he had intentionally baited Elizabeth was the least of his concerns right now.

Before Richard could question him further, Charles heard one of the workers running through the house screaming frantically for help.

Overcome with a feeling of dread, Charles retraced his steps, leaped up the stairs two at the time, and hurried to the huddled form just outside the guest room.

It was her. Erika was on her knees, huddled on the wooden floor. She was dressed differently now, wearing man's pants.

He was no longer angry that she'd disappeared. There was a logical explanation. He had only to find it. Right now, all that mattered was that she had come back to him.

Vaguely, Erika realized someone approached her. Responding to his kind, whispered words, she went into his strong arms and he rocked her gently.

She had to get back to Jonathan. She had to save him from Mable. She shuddered at the memory of the woman's rage. Justified, no doubt. Erika had killed her son.

"I have to get back to my time. I have to go to my grandfather - to help him," she said, trying to push away from him.

"Your grandfather will come for you. Until then, you'll remain here."

Erika recognized Charles' voice, but his words meant nothing to her. "You don't understand. Mable will kill him."

Lifting her easily into his arms, he carried her into the guest room and gently laid her on the bed.

"Where is Doctor Alkin?" he asked the small crowd that had gathered around them.

"He had to leave," someone said. "there was a buggy accident in Natchez."

"Leave us," he commanded, "and close the door."

When they were alone, he took her hands in his. "How do you know your grandfather needs help? Where is he?"

"He's not here. You don't understand. She's trying to murder Jonathan. I have to go to him."

"Damn it, girl," Charles said, grasping her by the shoulders. The gentleness was gone. "If I'm going to help you, you have to start making sense."

His fingers biting into her flesh, he searched her face. She couldn't meet his gaze. Her mind was in turmoil. Somewhere out there, her grandfather waited for her. She had to get back to her world.

She had to find out what triggered her passage through time. Nothing added up. Nothing made sense. Something had to be triggering it.

Suddenly releasing her, Charles took a step back. His expression changed to one of suspicion. She hadn't spoken aloud, had she?

"Tell me," he said softly.

Erika moistened her lips. "My grandfather is waiting for me. I promised him I'd come. But that woman is going to kill him."

"Where have you been?"

"Here."

"How do you know these things?"

"Because I... I saw her."

"You have the curse." There was a hint of fear, a distrust she hadn't seen in him before.

"Will you help me?" She asked, desperate now.

The crisp night air penetrated her senses and she felt some of her sanity returning. She had to remain in control. If there was a way to return to Jonathan, she would find it. If only it wasn't too late.

He hesitated, and she thought she had failed. But, when he spoke, the kindness had returned to his voice. "Get dressed. My father will want to see you."

She started to protest. She was dressed. She had on her jeans and a nice sweater. Then she noticed the pile of clothes Villars had left on the bed. She'd have to put on a dress to fit in.

She nodded and he went to wait outside the door.

Studying the pile of clothes on the bed, she picked up the corset, shook her head, and tossed it to the floor on the far side of the bed. She was only willing to go so far. Besides, she didn't need it. After slipping on the stiff petticoats and pulling the dress over her head, she carefully pinned the brooch to her bodice. The dress was dark green cotton with a cream and brown plaid pattern. The neckline was high and the skirt consisted of two layers, the top one falling to the knees. This was a lot like dressing for Senior Prom. Now, if she could find her feet beneath all this, she'd be ready to join Charles.

She had only one major problem. Hooks and eyes down the

back of the dress. Someone would have to fasten them. She couldn't even reach them, much less fasten them.

She paused at the sound of his voice just outside the room. He sounded annoyed. Footsteps receded down the hallway, then it was quiet again.

Erika had caught Charles off guard. The pieces were beginning to fit together now. Although he had never encountered it before now, he knew about the curse. He wasn't sure, though, that Erika knew about it. He could see the fear and confusion in her eyes.

She'd asked for his help. Some people would be afraid to get mixed up with the curse. But Charles wasn't afraid of anything. He would help her.

"Where is she?" Richard demanded, storming down the hall.

"Who?"

"You know damned well who. Stand aside."

Charles blocked the door. "She's getting dressed."

"Well, it's about time. She's the main topic of conversation at our Harvest Moon Ball which was supposed to be your engagement party."

"Don't frighten her."

"Do you know who she is?"

"She's Erika Becquerel. I assume she's related to us on your side of the family."

"Assume again. I've never heard of her. She's an imposter."

"Are you sure? She could be one of Uncle Zach's children."

Both men turned as Erika opened the door and stepped out into the hall.

Going quickly to her, Charles took her arm.

"Is it true? Are you a Becquerel?" Richard asked.

She lifted her chin. "I'd stake my life on it, Sir."

"Do you know who I am?"

She studied him briefly. "You must be Richard."

"Who's your father?"

A flash of pain swept over her features, then was gone. My father's name is Lance and my grandfather is Jonathan Becquerel."

Richard and Charles exchanged glances. Charles couldn't prevent the corners of his mouth from turning upwards in the beginnings of a smile.

She wasn't his cousin. There was no Jonathan in the Becquerel lineage.

Charles placed his arms around Erika and held her waist lightly, but firmly with both hands. His chin grazed the top of her head. "You're safe here," he said softly.

Richard watched them closely. He seemed to be in a quandary about how to respond.

ERIKA PRESSED CLOSER TO CHARLES. She trusted him to protect her - and to help her get back to Jonathan. His life was in danger and all she could think about was this man she'd only just met. She was in a web of confusion. She should be focused on getting to her grandfather.

"I think we have the answer to our question, Becquerel," The stranger's loud voice interrupted her thoughts.

"What is your meaning, Perry?" Richard asked angrily, turning to the man. Several of the guests, including Elizabeth had gathered behind him.

"Look at them," Perry said, gesturing toward Charles and Erika. "Are you a guest here?" He asked her pointedly.

Erika glanced around quickly, but there was no doubt he was speaking to her. She swallowed thickly.

"Yes, she is," Charles answered for her.

"What kind of question is that, Perry?" Richard added. "She obviously is or she wouldn't be here."

"I just want to make sure I have my facts straight," Perry said, "Now we all know why the wedding has been postponed. Charles has found himself a new playmate."

"No one said anything about postponing the wedding," Richard insisted.

"I just heard it from the bride-to-be, so I have it on strict authority."

"She's nothing more than a child," Charles said, "Can't you see that she's not much older than Andrea."

Erika couldn't help but wince. At twenty-seven, it was a little hard to accept being called a child. Especially if Andrea was the child she had seen playing outside earlier. That girl was no more than nine or ten. The only logic was that people used to age quickly and Erika always had looked younger than her years.

"Indeed, I could see a lot more when she was prancing around in your shirt."

Erika felt Charles tense, felt the anger radiating from his body. If they knew her gown wasn't even fastened, they would really get themselves in a bind.

"This is no business of yours, Perry," Richard said.

"This child is harmless, Perry," Charles added.

"I'm not a child," Erika couldn't help but mumble.

"Shh," Charles released Erika and took a step toward Perry. "Do you really want to know why I haven't married your daughter?"

A hush descended over the guests. A dog yelped somewhere outside and a door slammed downstairs.

"It's because she's in love with someone else."

Suddenly all eyes were on Elizabeth. A flush crept up her neck and over her face as she drew away from the young man standing next to her.

"No," she cried and delicately lifting her hem, she hurried to her father's side and grasped his arm. "Tell them it isn't so,

Father. I love..." She lowered her chin and brought a white lace handkerchief to her nose. "I'm afraid I'm destined to love someone who doesn't love me in return."

She lifted her eyes to Charles and sniffed delicately.

If they hadn't been so effective, Erika would have laughed at Elizabeth's theatrics.

"Come, come, Daughter," Perry said, glancing about the room and patting her hand awkwardly. "I think we've taken up enough of these people's time. Let's find our carriage."

Elizabeth ignored the young man she stood next to only moments earlier. Erika felt sorry for him.

Before descending the stairs, Perry paused. "By the way, Becquerel, our deal is off."

"Wait!" Richard called, starting after them.

Perry and Elizabeth hurried down the stairs and stormed out the front door. Richard followed close behind them.

"Would you like something to eat?" Charles asked. "There's plenty of food downstairs."

Erika suddenly realized she hadn't eaten since lunch and it must be near midnight.

"Would you help me first?" she asked, her cheeks burning as she turned her back to him. She couldn't see his face as he deftly fastened her dress and he didn't say a word. His fingers lingered over the last one, and she pulled away, unable to meet his gaze. As they went downstairs, she hoped her dress would meet everyone's approval, though it wasn't nearly as elegant as those worn by the other women.

Richard intercepted them at the foot of the stairs. The clock ticked steadily, the pendulum swinging back and forth.

"Look what you've done."

Charles stepped protectively in front of Erika.

"You've cost this family four thousand acres of land."

"How?" Erika asked, behind Charles.

"It was the betrothal agreement," Charles said, "between

Elizabeth and me. Upon our marriage, I would receive four thousand acres of his land."

Erika stepped around from behind Charles. "Mr. Becquerel, if you want the land so badly, why don't you just buy it from him?"

Richard's face turned a beautiful shade of red and if he had started to jump up and down, she would not have been surprised.

"Get her out of my sight," Richard said and stormed back toward the study.

The guests had slowly wandered back to the ballroom after the excitement, but seemed to have lost their desire to dance. Instead, they clumped into small groups and stood talking among themselves. What had happened here tonight would doubtless be the scandal of the season.

"Really, Richard, why don't you just buy the land from Perry?" Rebecca asked, coming to join her husband. There was a look of smug satisfaction on her face.

"Because the son of a bitch won't sell it to me."

"Everything has a price. Pretend you don't want it for awhile and he'll come around."

"Why doesn't anybody understand? Perry wants his daughter to have our name. He's not going to give that up for any amount of money."

"Exactly," Charles mumbled under his breath.

"Then find another access to the river. But don't sell our son's dignity."

"Dignity! The Miller's are a respected family."

"They're white trash and you know it. Why, just having them under our roof is a breach of etiquette."

"Stay out of it Rebecca. You don't know enough about business to understand."

"Indeed," Rebecca lifted her chin regally. "In that case, my dear, I shall have to relinquish running the household to you.

You manage the two hundred twelve workers, see to that we have enough food, but not so much that it spoils. You haggle and stretch our household allowance for needed supplies. See to it that the ice gets here on time for your parties without melting.

"No, dear Richard," she continued, "I know nothing about business. And while you're at it, you can knit the gloves and socks for your workers and sew their clothing." She turned away and disappeared into the parlor.

"Wait," Richard called after her. The blood had drained from his face, leaving him pale. "Wait. Rebecca. Let's talk." He followed her into the parlor, but was quickly intercepted by guests wanting the scoop on Perry and Elizabeth Miller.

Erika piled a plate with fruits and fish and fresh vegetables before allowing Charles to lead her to a quiet spot on the veranda.

"I was hoping you could avoid my father for a bit longer," Charles said as he opened a bottle of brandy.

"I think he's more bark than bite. Though I wonder that he hasn't had a heart attack or a stroke by now."

"He's a true Creole."

"Your father is French and your mother American. Isn't that unusual?" Why hadn't she paid more attention to history lessons? She had memorized facts for tests, then flushed it all out. There was so much that would have come in handy to remember now.

So much about this way of life that she now wanted and needed to know.

"Extremely rare at the time they married. But it is becoming more and more common. It seems we French can't resist you Americans."

Erika lowered her eyes and smiled at his easy flattery. She had been so wrapped up in school and now work, she couldn't remember the last time she'd had fun. Except for the memory of his passionate kiss and unreasonable demands in her room, she would have thought him the perfect gentleman. She was enjoying getting to know the many facets of his personality.

"It seems you got your father's dark looks and your mother's disposition."

"You're very observant. I think of myself as being half and half in both looks and personality. There is one thing to remember, though. I do have Creole blood running through my veins. Don't ever anger me."

Despite the smile on his lips, she knew he was serious. There was an unmistakable threat in his voice. She shuddered. Anger was one facet of Charles Becquerel she did not care to witness - or provoke.

"Where are you from?" he asked.

Erika considered his question carefully. She'd spent most of her childhood here around Natchez, but that could be hard to explain. It would be easier to be from somewhere distant. "Baton Rouge," she answered truthfully. That's where her home had been for the past three years.

"How did you come to arrive without your trunks?"

She frowned and picked at the fried catfish on her plate. "Jonathan and I were separated. After that, all I remember is being here."

"Was there an accident?"

"I don't think so." She answered hesitantly. She wasn't ready yet to limit her options. Unless she could get back, she would need to come up with a plausible explanation soon.

"I'm sorry. I know you've had a tiring day and I don't mean to interrogate you. When you've finished eating, I'll escort you to the guest room so you can rest. I'll make sure you're left alone tonight."

Erika breathed a sigh of relief. She didn't feel up to battling with anyone else. Besides, she never knew when she would be hurled back to her own time.

"What will you do now?" Charles asked suddenly.

As Erika gazed into his clear, blue eyes and considered her options, she felt tears welling behind her eyelids. She didn't want that question from him. She wanted reassurance from him.

There was no one else to confide in. She had already told Charles far more than she should have. Hopefully, he had forgotten her ramblings. "I really don't know," she confided, lowering her eyes.

"Well, let's get you up to your room. You're exhausted."

No one bothered them as they made their way upstairs. Erika moved slowly, maneuvering the full skirt up the stairs.

He followed her into the guest room, turned down the blankets, and lit a new candle on the nightstand. Then he stopped and studied her.

She wasn't sure what to say to him now. Not only was she dressed for the prom, she felt as awkward as a teenager on a first date.

"I don't think it's cold enough for a fire tonight. If you need one, just call Villars. Sleep well."

"You're leaving?" She asked without thinking. And immediately regretted the words.

He looked at her with a half grin, full of arrogance. Her heart thumped dangerously. "Turn around," he said.

"What?"

"I said turn around."

Hesitantly, she turned her back to him. Before she realized what he was doing, he had her dress halfway unhooked.

"Hey," she cried, pulling away "what are you doing?"

"Hold still,"

"I don't think so."

"Are you telling me you want to sleep in all this?"

Reluctantly, she turned back and allowed him to finish unhooking her. She held tightly to the front of the dress to keep it from slipping off. Then he gently turned her around and kissed her on the cheek. Her eyes fluttered closed.

"Good night," he said and closed the door behind him as he left.

Erika sat down on the edge of the bed and suddenly did feel chilled. Cold and empty. Charles was so alive. *It's a shame he's a life gone past, a life lost to the passage of time.*

He was caught up in quite a mess. She wished she could help him with Elizabeth, but for some reason his father was angry with her. It was almost as though he had recognized her. Recognized and hated her.

She started to undress, but remembered she had no nightgown. Deciding she would have to sleep in her clothes, she put her jeans and sweater back on. It seemed she'd done nothing but dress and undress since she got here.

That led her back to Jonathan. She had to get back to him. How could she have allowed herself to be distracted from getting back? Damn Charles and his whole mixed up family. She should be studying the house this minute, trying to find a door to the future.

Getting up, she went to stare out the window. The guests were still there, some of them scattered about the lawn, especially couples, even at this late hour. It would be best to stay out of sight until the house was quiet, she convinced herself, and crawled back under the blankets.

Maybe if she did go to sleep, she would wake up on her own firm mattress and box springs.

Having justified staying in bed, that perhaps sleep would get her back to Jonathan, she closed her eyes and immediately fell into a deep slumber.

"Stay away from her."

Charles was tired. After a full day in the fields, the events of the evening were wearing thin. As soon as Richard shut the door to the library, he knew the night would only get longer. "Father, she's harmless."

"She's a liar. And she's evil."

Charles dropped into a chair and stretched his long legs. "What would you have me do, burn her at the stake?"

"That's one option."

Charles ran a hand through his hair. "What makes you think she's so terrible?"

"I just know," Richard said, turning his back.

"What do you mean, you just know?"

"I have ways."

This was too ridiculous. A stranger shows up in their house and suddenly she was an evil witch. Nobody was that superstitious anymore. *Except Father.* "Just let her stay for awhile. She doesn't have anywhere else to go."

"She's cast an evil spell upon this house. Already, Perry and Elizabeth have walked out of our lives."

"Thank God."

"Damn it," Richard said, slamming his fist against the desk. "Listen to me. For once, just listen to me."

"All right, tell me."

Richard hesitated. "I can't tell you."

"Does this have anything to do with Vaughn?"

"No."

Charles was getting nowhere. His father could be the most exasperating man. "I think she may have lost her memory. Just let her stay until she figures out where she belongs."

"No."

"Fine. She can stay with me."

"That's not a good idea. Your sister is too inquisitive. It wouldn't make a good impression on her young sensibilities."

"What would you have me do? Throw her out with no where to go?"

"Damn," Richard said, "All right. I can't fight both you and your mother. But there's one condition. I want you to find her something to do. I don't want her staying here and not earning her keep."

"Very well. I'll let her knit some socks."

"No, that's not good enough. I want her to do something outside. Hell, let her clean the guest house."

"That place is filthy."

"I don't care. I want her to pay for what she's done to this family."

"Let the workers do it."

"We can't spare them."

Charles shook his head, but knew he had no choice. He could comply with his father's demands or he could toss Erika out. He knew what he had to do.

Erika would never survive on her own.

FINALLY ESCAPING FOR THE EVENING, Charles walked across the moonlit lawn, and down a wooded path. Someone else could deal with the lingering guests. He'd had enough of people for one night.

Hurrying onto the porch, he entered his bachelor's quarters. His mother hadn't liked the idea of his moving out, but that had been years ago. He supposed she'd gotten used to it by now. His garconniere had the appearance of a whitewashed cottage in the woods. It sat on the one acre of land that his father had agreed to leave wooded. Not only did the trees keep the house cooler in summer, but it allowed him unlimited privacy. His mother probably hadn't thought of that.

After tossing his jacket across the couch, he loosened his cravat, and poured himself a glass of brandy.

What had Erika meant by her time?

There had to be a logical explanation. As soon as she was able, he was certain Erika would explain it all to him.

She would have hell explaining how she'd disappeared almost in front of his eyes. So far, he hadn't been able to approach her with it. Maybe he was crazy. He emptied the glass and sighed. His father wouldn't be so patient. He would have to come up with a better explanation for him and quick. What could he tell him when he didn't know the answers himself? A woman who disappeared into thin air was rather hard to accept, much less explain.

He didn't know why he felt responsible for her, but he did. He was obviously attracted to her, but attraction was one emotion he allowed to go only so far.

Then there was the matter of the curse.

He shook his head and kicked off his boots. He was too tired to even think about that right now. Anyway, the immediate concern was his father.

What was wrong with Richard? They had taken in needy people many times before without question. In fact, it was Richard's rule that no one be turned away. A man should always be allowed to work for his food, he had said many times. Well, he was asking Erika to work like a man and worse, like a servant.

Erika was the strangest woman he'd ever met. And the most beautiful. Even her shoulder length hair didn't bother him. He didn't think Perry had fallen for that child act for a second. And he was surprised that his father had gone along with it. But then Richard had seemed distracted. He almost seemed to recognize Erika and hold a personal vengeance against her. Charles certainly hadn't seen her before. He would have to remember to question his father about it.

Richard believed everyone should pull his own weight. Even guests. But cleaning the guest house was too much. He would find something else for her to do. That shouldn't be hard. He had a few things in mind and the memory of her kisses was only the beginning.

He frowned. Why would she come here with nothing more than the strange clothes on her back? Suddenly he remembered the bag she brought with her and hurried to his bedroom. Villars had done as he had asked. It was there on his bed. He had been hoping she wouldn't ask for it, but he would have given it to her. In the meantime he was hoping to find some clue to her identity.

Examining the bag, he saw no opening. He shook it. There were definitely things inside. He assumed it to be her reticule, but how did one get into it? Noticing a small metal tab, he pulled on it gently. Suddenly there was an opening in the top of the bag. When he pulled the tab in the other direction, the opening resealed itself. Intrigued, Charles almost forgot to look inside.

There was a small glass rectangle box inside – a box that had no opening. The only identification on it was a half-eaten apple. It appeared to have no use. Disappointed, he set the box aside. Reaching back into her bag, his fingers closed upon a key ring and he immediately knew she ran a household, even if it was a small one. His mother had five times as many keys. If she did run a household, she must be married. His heart sank at the realization. But there had been no ring on her hand.

She must run her father's home, then, he decided. Or her grandfather's. He then felt pity for her. He could image a young woman running her grandfather's household, day in and day out. Never hoping to escape the drudgery. Never having time to go to parties or chat with suitors. Had she run away or had they lost their small home to debtors?

Putting the keys back inside and feeling he had intruded too far into her private life, he resealed her bag. How had she come to his home? The thought that she had come for money nagged at him. He would give it to her. But would she go away if he handed her some?

Perhaps.

He didn't want her to go away. So he wasn't willing to take that chance.

She could be some sort of sorceress. Someone who could disappear and appear at whim. Someone who carried strange bags that opened like nothing he had seen before. She wasn't evil, he told himself. Such an angelic face couldn't belong to someone evil.

If Erika Becquerel were evil, then he was a spotted dog. With wings.

CHAPTER 4

*E*rika woke the next morning to the chirping of birds and the barking of dogs. She hoped Jonathan's cat, Smokey, hadn't gotten outside. Erika was afraid that the dogs would catch her one day.

Rolling over, she squinted at the sunlight streaming in through the window. It was a beautiful day.

She stretched her legs out along the soft downy mattress. The sound of the grandfather clock chiming the hour drifted softly up the stairs and down the hallway to her room.

The clock.

No!

It hadn't been a dream after all. She turned and whimpered into her pillow. Now what was she going to do?

Mable had probably gotten to Jonathan by now. She had killed him just like Erika had killed the woman's son. A murderer. She hadn't meant to kill him - only to keep him away. But she was a murderer nonetheless. This was probably Hell.

She turned her head at a knock on the door. And froze. It could be anyone - Villars, Rebecca, or even that hateful

Richard. Pulling the blanket up to her chin, she called for the visitor to come in.

Or it could be Charles.

Freshly shaven, Charles opened the door and leaned against the door frame, his expression unreadable. He had on a pair on narrow slacks tucked into high black boots and a crisp, clean cotton shirt. Just as he had been dressed yesterday when she first saw him out the window.

If this were hell, she would plead guilty to whatever had brought her here.

"Good morning. I trust you slept well."

Erika swallowed and tried to silently clear her throat. "Yes," It was all she could trust herself to utter.

"Well, it's already daylight." he said, grabbing her foot beneath the covers and shaking it.

Though he seemed disappointed, she wasn't the least bit shocked by his action. Bradley used to wake her up that way every Saturday morning.

"Fresh water is on its way so you can freshen up. I'll wait for you downstairs. Don't be long. I have work to do."

When he was gone, she got up, quickly locked the door, and tried to straighten her clothes. Yesterday, this sweater was one of her favorites, but it was quickly losing its appeal. She hoped Charles would be generous enough to find something more appropriate for her to wear. She certainly couldn't spend the day in that ball gown, no matter how plain it was.

After Villars brought up a pitcher of warm water and soap, she gave herself a spit bath. It reminded her of life before her parents' divorce. The four of them used to go camping in a pop-up travel trailer, sometimes spending several days roughing it. No running water, no electricity. Even relatively speaking, that was roughing it. It hadn't been her favorite pastime, but she had dealt with it.

That was before her mother cried so much and before her

father spent days at the time away from home only to come home drunk - stinking drunk and mean. He had usually been off gambling away any money they might have had left after paying the bills.

She paused, staring at her reflection in the mirror. Her childhood seemed like light years ago. Taking a deep breath, she forced her thoughts back on the present and finished washing. She actually felt worse afterwards. She never had liked these spit baths. She wanted to climb into a tub of water and soak from head to toe.

She realized these people didn't bathe every day, but surprisingly thus far she hadn't come across anyone who smelled offensive. Well, she fully intended to set the precedent of a daily bath. However, at the moment, Charles was waiting for her and she hurried to join him.

If she hadn't known her way to the dining room, the delicious aroma of home cooked breakfast would have led her to it.

Charles, busy with a plate of eggs, bacon, biscuits, and grits didn't look up when Erika came into the room. She lingered near the door, wondering if she should go to the kitchen and pick up her food.

"Sit down," he said, motioning to the chair next to him.

"Where is everyone else?" She asked as she sat down. She was actually relieved that no one else was here. It was bad enough just to deal with Charles. A servant appeared with a plate heaped high with food and placed it in front of her.

Charles paused and watched her begin to devour her food, slowly at first, then hungrily.

"You didn't eat much last night," he said, "How long has it been since you had a decent meal?"

"Too long, I'm afraid," she said, her cheeks warming, and set down her fork.

"Everyone else has been up for hours," he said as he finished his meal. "All the guests are probably home by now."

Erika laughed. "Then I suppose we slept late."

"You did indeed. I've been up since before dawn."

Erika ran her fingers self-consciously through her hair. "I must look a sight. I need to wash my hair and put on some make-up."

When she got no reaction from him, she bit into the flaky buttermilk biscuit and chewed thoughtfully. Her grandmother, Vaughn, used to make biscuits this way. "By the way, have you seen my purse?"

Charles pushed back his plate and leaned back in his chair. "Your reticule? I'll check with Villars to see if he came across it."

Satisfied, she continued to eat, but remained silent and thoughtful as she tried to remember. She knew she had her purse with her the last time in the twenty-first century. But she had been so distraught she hadn't noticed if it came with her. She hoped desperately that it had. She could use some Blistex about now, she thought, flicking her tongue across her dry lips. She wondered if she had anything else in it that would be useful here. There certainly wouldn't be any cell phone service, she thought, and almost laughed.

Glancing up, she noticed Charles silently studying her. Self-conscious now, she set her fork down and wiped her mouth on the cloth napkin.

"Finished?" he asked.

She nodded and followed him out the back door to a small building several yards away from the house. They went up the narrow steps and waited for someone to answer Charles' knock.

A vine of miniature white roses trailed up the side of the wooden house. It was little more than a shack compared to the mansion they lived in.

"Who lives here?"

"No one lives here."

What unfathomable mood was he in now? Frowning, she turned back to the house where she had spent every summer she could remember as a child and adolescent, then countless weekends and holidays... and swallowed the lump in her throat.

She should be able to go inside and find her grandfather - and her grandmother. She always had. Up until six months ago, that is. They had never recovered Vaughn's body. Erika had never had the opportunity to say goodbye.

A middle-aged black woman with streaks of gray hair opened the door. She had a bright blue flowered bandanna tied around her head, a green flowered shirt, and a patched blue plaid skirt which accented her ample bosom and hips.

"Mister Charles," she said with a broad grin of gapped teeth as she pulled him inside. "You know you don't have to wait outside. You're always welcome here."

"Hattie, I want you to meet Erika. She's going to be staying with us for a while."

Erika stepped into a room that couldn't possibly hold another item. Except for a door covered with a sheet in the back, the walls were completely lined with shelves and the middle of the room was stacked high with boxes and bags of various objects for dressmaking leaving no more than a square walkway around the room.

The shelves were crammed with bolts of cloth in every color and fabric imaginable, boxes of thread and needles, rolls of ribbon and lace, coarse linen, straw hats, books of patterns.

Erika walked around the boxes stacked over her head in awe. A woman could become anything in this room - anything in the nineteenth century. Impulsively, she picked up a wide brimmed straw hat, placed it on her head, turned, and smiled at Charles.

He just watched, his face expressionless.

"Come on, Child. I s'pect we gonna start from the bottom," she said as she inspected Erika's sweater and jeans. "You like that hat? We'll put a wide ribbon around it and tie it on like this." She unrolled and cut off a section of pink ribbon, wrapped it around the hat, and tied a bow beneath Erika's chin.

"Oh, yes. We'll make her pretty, won't we Mister Charles?"

"Hattie, go to the shelf of coarse linen and make her a dress from it," he said, his voice a little hoarse.

The smile on Hattie's face turned upside down into a frown. She put her hands on her hips and shook her head.

"Mister Charles, are you sure?"

"Yes, Hattie."

"What a waste. What a shame," she mumbled as she ducked behind the sheet into the other room.

Erika studied Charles, standing at the door with his profile to her. Hattie seemed to like him, but what had he said to make her angry? And what had she done to make him angry, she thought as she watched the muscles in his clenched jaw.

Hattie came back with a tape measure and wrapped it around Erika's waist and then beneath her arms. The woman remained silent throughout the procedure and again disappeared into the back room.

Charles went outside and sat on the steps. Left to her own devices, Erika kneeled beside one of the shelves filled with books. She flipped through *The Ladies Cabinet* and *The Beau Monde*. Her imagination ran wild as she studied the fashion plates. Since the dress had to be made, she wondered how long it would take. While looking at the books, she could dream of new clothes such as a lovely riding habit or a conservative day dress. Either way, she was looking forward to fitting in again. She never had liked being different.

After what must have been about an hour, Hattie returned with a length of coarse brown material over her arm.

"Can the child have a camisole and a petticoat?"

Charles shot Hattie a warning glance.

"Well, I just wanted to make sure. You never know what an innocent child like this might of done to deserve such treatment. You go on back there, Honey, and put on this camisole and petticoat."

Hattie stuck her bottom lip out stubbornly and pulled a white cloth from one of the boxes. "And put on these pantalettes, too. I don't care what Mister Charles say, a white lady has to have on pantalettes."

Erika went behind the sheet and slipped on the camisole.

"Hattie," she called, peeking out from behind the sheet.

"What do you need?"

"Can I get some clean panties?" she asked in a whisper so Charles wouldn't hear.

The old black woman took the pantalettes from her hand and looked them over. "Are these dirty?"

"No. No. Panties."

"I don't know what you're talking about."

Erika unzipped and slipped off her slacks.

"Lordy mercy." Hattie said with a chuckle. "Where did you get something like that?"

"You don't have any?"

"No ma'am. I ain't never seen anything like that. Get them things off and put on your pantalettes."

Hattie examined the camisole and noticed that Erika had two sets of straps.

"What's that?" she asked.

"It's a bra," Erika said hesitantly.

"Let me see."

Her face burning, Erika pulled up the camisole and showed Hattie her bra.

"Miss Erika, I don't know where you got such things, but they ain't proper. A lady wouldn't be caught in such things. If I was you, I'd take that off, too." Hattie nodded her head emphatically and went back into the other room.

"What's wrong, Hattie?" Erika heard Charles ask.

"There ain't nothing going on that a gentleman needs to know about a lady."

If Hattie's reaction was any indication, people would be shocked by her modern clothing. Who's going to know, part of her argued. But she couldn't take a chance. With a sigh, she removed her bra and panties and replaced them with the camisole and pantalettes. Then she slipped on the petticoat.

Hattie came back in and slipped the dress over her head. The dress was not exactly what she had expected. In fact, her heart sank at the sight of it. It was coarse linen in drab brown. It appeared to have been sewn along the sides, leaving a hole for her head and two for her arms. There was also a tie for her waist so the dress wouldn't hang loosely and be in her way. It had a high neckline and buttons down the back. So this is what Hattie had been angry about.

Erika put on the woolen stockings Hattie handed her and then put on her short-ankle boots – her only item of clothing that hadn't drawn attention. Whatever would possess Charles to have her dressed like this?

Feeling somewhat exposed without her underwear, Erika gathered up her clothes and went back out to Charles.

He stared at her for several seconds.

Her face flushed at his perusal. All she could think was that he somehow knew she didn't have on a bra or panties.

Grasping her wrist roughly, he pulled her behind him from the shack. They followed a path until they came to another structure.

"This is the guest house," he said, "It would have been used last night except that it hasn't been cleaned since last year."

He opened the door and a musty odor drifted out. Going inside, Charles opened all the windows of the one room building. Erika waited outside for him. Her dress wasn't much, but it was clean.

"It's a mess," she commented as Charles came back to the door.

He didn't answer, but disappeared inside for a moment. He soon returned with a large wooden pail, a chunk of lye soap and a handful of rags.

"When you're finished, we should be able to move a table, some chairs, and bed in here," he said, handing her the supplies.

The pail was heavy in Erika's hand. "Why are you giving me these?" she asked softly, but she already knew the answer. She knew it and she didn't like it.

"If you're going to stay here, you have to earn your keep."

"Whatever happened to Southern hospitality?" She couldn't help but ask.

Charles frowned. "There is an alternative."

"Forget it," she said, "You know, there are a lot of things I can do that don't involve manual labor."

"Like what?"

"Well, like..." What could she do? "I can tend the animals."

"I doubt it," he said, looking her up and down.

"I know more about animals than you'll ever know."

"I suppose you know what to do when a cow is having trouble giving birth or when the hounds get the worst of a coon fight."

"I certainly do."

"Well, we'll see. You have to start here and work your way up."

Erika wanted to sit down and cry. Surely he didn't expect her to make this place livable. Her resolve threatened to break, but one look at his arrogant gaze and she raised her chin, ready to do whatever it took to prove to him that she could, indeed earn her keep - and keep what little respect he seemed to have for her.

"The way I see it," he said, "you have three choices. You can scrub this place from top to bottom, you can go back where you came from, or you can - you know..."

Narrowing her eyes in his direction, she walked past him and surveyed the empty room. The floor was liberally stained with tobacco juices. The only other evidence that anyone had ever been inside lay in a heap of empty liquor bottles next to the blackened fireplace.

"What kind of guests did you have in here?" she asked.

"Some of the neighborhood boys must have gotten in here."

"Then let them clean it up," she said under her breath.

He was the most impossible man she had ever dealt with. She would scrub this place down if it killed her. How hard could it be anyway?

"Does your father know about the third choice?" she couldn't resist asking.

"My father doesn't concern himself with what I do."

"Indeed?" She taunted. "He seems awfully concerned about who you marry."

"That's different." His eyes darkened and for just a moment, she was afraid of him. She didn't know this man well enough to taunt him. He could probably ravish her right now and no one would know, much less stop him.

Suddenly he turned and faced the window and she saw something in his expression. Something she knew well - pain.

"Where do I get water?" She asked, softly, not willing to intrude further on his private matters.

Silently, he led her outside to the well. It was a white bricked structure much like she had seen in pictures. A wooden bucket was attached to a rope connected to a crank.

Squaring her shoulders, Erika glanced determinedly at Charles and approached the well. Glancing down into the darkness, she remembered all the horror tales she had heard about people fallings into wells and dying. She would have to be careful.

Grasping the crank in both hands, she attempted to turn it. Unsuccessful, she tried to turn it the other way. It wouldn't budge. Stepping away, she looked accusingly at Charles.

With a raised eyebrow, he reached up and untied the rope holding the crank in place.

"Where did you say you were from?"

"Baton Rouge," she answered, grasping the lever again. This time it turned surprisingly easy and the pail dipped down into the black hole. The echo of a splash came up through the pit. She immediately reversed the direction of the crank.

"You use well water down there, don't you?"

No, she thought, frustrated. *We turn on a faucet and water comes out. We even have a choice, hot or cold. We don't have to go out and dig for it.*

"Of course we do," she replied, "Doesn't everyone?"

Charles didn't answer. He just shook his head slightly and continued to watch her.

"Ours is more of a cistern." She did remember getting water from a cistern before Jonathan converted to city water.

"I see," he said. And waited.

At last the bucket came into view. Erika smiled as it swung gently within reach. She had been careful to bring it up slowly, trying not to spill any.

She couldn't let go of the rope. If she did, the bucket would crash back into the well.

"Could you grab the bucket please?" she asked, irritated at Charles for not helping.

He didn't help; he only continued to watch her.

"Don't you have workers to do this?"

"We can't spare them," he said flatly.

"If you can't spare them, then this must not be very important."

It was hot and the air was still. Sweat trickled down her back. How did people live like this? She would have a bath tonight if she had to haul up every bucket of water herself.

"Charles!" she cried, exasperated. "Come get the bucket so I can let go of this rope."

"What are you going to do when I'm not here?"

"But you are here."

He shrugged and grasped the bucket. Dropping her aching arms with relief, she picked up the empty bucket he had handed her earlier.

"Set your bucket here," he said, indicating the ledge. He lifted the dripping bucket and tipped it over hers.

Erika, who had been so proud of her accomplishment, could only stare at the empty buckets.

"What did you do with the water?" she asked accusingly. The pail she had lowered into the well and so painstakingly lifted was empty. Only the outside was dripping.

Charles burst into laughter.

Erika put her hands on her hips and silently fumed. He had dragged her away from her breakfast, dressed her like a servant, watched her make a fool of herself when he knew good and well she was doing it wrong, and now this. He had the gall to stand there and laugh at her.

"That's enough," she said through clenched teeth. "I've had all of you that I can stand. I'd rather sleep on the streets than stand here and put up with you and your moods."

She turned around and started marching down the road. Anything would be better than this. She glanced back once, but he was watching a group of workers in the field.

He let her go at least thirty yards before she felt his arms around her waist. He pulled her backwards into a grove of trees.

"Stop it!" she demanded, trying to break loose of his grip.

He set her on the bed of leaves, none too gently. When she

tried to get up, he clasped his hands around her upper arms and held her down.

"Just listen to me, all right?" he said. "I won't hurt you."

She nodded. Though she wasn't sure she should trust him, she currently had no choice. She should run and run fast, but his hold on her was too tight. Even if she did get away, he would catch her.

Releasing her arms, he ran his fingers gently though her hair.

She could have slapped him, and she might even could have gotten away at that point, but his eyes held her prisoner. She should at least scream. She should claw at him; do anything to get away. He was dangerous. She had felt his kiss before. It had been like a drug, dulling her senses.

She mustn't let him kiss her again.

He placed a finger beneath her chin and tilted her face toward his. Lowering his head, he pressed his lips against hers. Softly, ever so softly. A warmth shot through her.

She mustn't let him stop.

Before she realized what he was doing, his mouth covered hers and his kiss became urgent. He forced her lips apart and his tongue swept against hers. The embers burst into flames and everything but Charles, the feel of him, the taste and smell of him, was swept out of her mind.

Distantly she realized she was no longer held prisoner. Reaching up, she gently placed her fingers at the back of his neck and pulled him closer. Her fingers caressed his silky black hair. It was soft, downy, and reminded her of the mattress she had slept on last night.

Downy mattress. Jonathan.

Suddenly, she pulled away from him. How could she waste time like this? Jonathan needed her. Here she was cavorting with a perfect stranger.

And her grandfather's life was in danger.

CHAPTER 5

$\mathcal{L}$ooking into Erika's wide green eyes, eyes that outshone the deep emerald of the fall foliage, Charles forgot what he was going to say. His heart pounded dangerously in his chest, so loud, it was deafening in his own ears.

Dress her in rags and she's still beautiful, he thought. He hadn't wanted to treat her that way. But it was the only way he could convince his father that she was in need of their charity. It was the only way he could keep her here.

When she pulled away, he let her go. This girl had no more drawn water from a well before than a two year old. Perhaps she had stolen the keys. She had lied about being his cousin, Sierra. She could be a liar and a thief.

Even his little sister, Andrea, could draw water from the well and she was as spoiled as humanly possible. Anyone who carried the keys to a home had drawn water from a well. Swaying slightly, she stood up and brushed past him. He wanted to stop her. Wanted to pull her back and take her into his arms. But first he had to find out what she was after. He loved his home too deeply to risk losing it to her - to anyone.

"I'm sorry, ma chérie," he said. But if you go back and clean the guest house, my father will allow you to stay here." He said to her retreating back. "He will grant you food and shelter and you will otherwise be treated as a guest. For some reason, he needs proof from you. I don't know why."

I also need proof. Proof that you aren't another Elizabeth, only much more dangerous. You're after not only my land and my name, but you're after stealing my heart.

ERIKA SQUARED her shoulders and continued walking. She didn't want to admit it, but he was right. She had to do whatever it took to remain here in this house. She had never backed away from a little hard work. Besides, there was always the possibility that she would never get back to Jonathan even if she tried.

Refusing to think about Jonathan for the moment, she went back to the well and, this time, brought up a bucket of water.

Charles walked past her toward the stables, not bothering to look in her direction, much less acknowledge the fact that she had drawn water - without him.

A few minutes later he stormed from the stables on his black horse, and galloped across the rolling acres of fields. The chanting songs of the workers paused as he reached them, then resumed.

Either he fully expected her to remain here at the plantation and clean that house or he didn't care whether she left or not. It had been foolish of her to walk away. She felt sick as she realized that if she left here, she would most likely never return to Jonathan or her own time - her way of life.

She wouldn't allow anyone to force her away. Walking back to the guest house, with the bucket of water, a building on a rise in the distance caught her attention. It was a small cottage standing apart from the slave quarters. It was larger than those around it and was freshly whitewashed.

A woman stood on the porch, watching her. Despite the warmth of the sun, she was wrapped in a hooded cloak and her face was shadowed. A chill scurried up Erika's spine. She hurried inside and quickly closed the door behind her.

Now that the room had aired out some, it really wasn't so bad. She would have to wash down the walls, scrub the floors, and do the windows. Without furniture, it couldn't take too long.

Erika was a little surprised at herself for even considering doing the job. She was a professional. If she wanted floors cleaned, she hired it done. But this situation was unusual.

She thought of her mother. She spent her life, hour after hour, day after day, doing things that made no sense. When she was gone, who was going to know or care whether her floors had been spotless? Erika wanted to do something that would make an impact lasting long after she left this earth.

People benefitted from what she did. Her life's work was important. Only now she was at a loss. She doubted anyone around here had any use for a veterinarian, especially a female. Her skills were useless. And so was she, Erika thought painfully. There was nothing here that she could do.

She couldn't claim to be a seamstress; she couldn't sew. She had never done needlepoint or embroidery. She couldn't knit and had no desire to learn.

No desire. That was her problem. She was not domesticated and women of this era were domesticated. Domesticated and dominated.

What would Charles really do if she didn't clean this house? His father would probably make good on his threat and throw her out. Then she would be destitute. No money and no viable skills.

Assuming she did clean these quarters, what then? Would

Charles think he could command her to do his every bidding? And would it be so terrible if he did? To her it would be degrading. To him it was expected. After all, she was a woman.

Erika took a deep breath and squared her shoulders. She would show these people. She would show them that a woman of the twenty-first century could scrub floors with the best of any nineteenth century woman. She would do it and do it well.

SEVERAL HOURS LATER, after the sun had started its downward path, Erika sat back on her heels and lifted her eyes past the black boots, the trousers, past the slim waist, and over the now dusty white cotton shirt of the man standing in front of her.

She dipped the rag into the pail and squeezed it out.

"You've done well," Charles said, leaning against the door casing.

Surveying her work, the sparkling clean walls and floors, she couldn't help but smile inwardly with a sense of accomplishment and pride. She had tied her dress up above her knees and rolled up the sleeves. Her knees were raw and her hands bleeding from the soap and water, but she had done it. She had hauled every bucket of water herself and cleaned this house.

"You can finish the floor and do the windows tomorrow." He said. "It's time to go in to dinner."

"All right," she said, standing up. That was reasonable enough. Then she would have earned her stay here, hopefully for long enough to get back to her own time.

"After you've finished here, you can do the gazebo in back."

Erika's mouth dropped open. "You mean this isn't enough?"

"This is only the beginning. As long as you're staying here, we can find you something to do. Can you knit? Of course you can. The workers need socks for the winter."

"Then perhaps someone best knit a pair for me. It seems I

have become a slave myself," she replied, threw down the rag, and stomped to the door.

He blocked her path.

"Do you mind?"

"After you." He stepped away with a gallant flourish of his arm. "My lady." He added when she had passed.

She rolled her eyes and walked past him in silence, trying to ignore his masculine scent of horse and tobacco.

"You might want to untie your skirts," he said, to her back.

Biting her lip, she reached down and untied her dress. In the 1990's it was sexy to show off the knees, but here it was something women didn't do, especially red, raw knees. She may have been here only a day, but the customs didn't take long to grow accustomed to.

The house was quiet, and pausing at the doorway, she saw that the parlor was empty. She went to stand in front of the familiar row of family portraits. She found Charles' and his mother's and father's. She didn't see one of Andrea.

Next to Charles was a painting of another man. They had the same eyes and the same strong jaw. They were similar, yet they were different.

Charles was without a doubt, arrogant, but the other man had softer features. He looked kind and gentle. They could easily be brothers.

She was startled by voices coming toward her from the back of the house. She mustn't let anyone see her like this.

Running up the stairs, she went straight to her room, and closed the door behind her. Then she paused. How did one get a bath?

Walking over to the bell cord, she gave it a yank. When nothing happened, she yanked it again.

Within seconds, Villars appeared at the door.

"Villars," she began and tried to put confidence in her voice.

She only hoped she was making a reasonable request. "I'd like a bath, please."

"Of course, Miss," Nodding, he went off, she presumed, to get the necessary items.

Erika sighed with relief. Thankfully, she hadn't given these people another reason to question her. Even if she had, a bath would be worth it.

A few minutes later a couple of workers had helped Villars bring up a bath tub, fresh towels, soap, bubble bath, and steaming buckets of hot water to pour into the tub.

A young black girl named Sadie offered to help with her bath, but Erika refused, preferring to enjoy the bath in private.

Erika could hardly stand still while the bath was filled and everyone was satisfied she had everything she needed. She hadn't had a bath in two days and could barely contain her anticipation. Finally she was alone.

Shedding her damp, sweaty dress and underclothes, she climbed into the hot water. She lay back, closed her eyes, and relaxed with the aroma of crushed rose petals.

She couldn't remember ever having enjoyed a bath so much. She lathered her hair and rinsed it out. It was such a wonderful feeling to be clean again.

Her thoughts wandered to Charles. He constantly contradicted himself. She saw flashes of kindness in his eyes, but he seemed intent on hiding it. He hid behind a facade of arrogance and nonchalance.

She knew it was a facade because she had seen his kindness and felt his kiss. His kiss had been gentle, even tender. Yet the touch of his lips had burned her with a passion she had'd never known. Even the mere thought of his body against hers set her insides aflame.

She felt the heat rise to her cheeks as her thoughts worked backwards to last night. He had been kind to her, holding her gently in his arms and he had protected her from Perry and probably alienated his own father for her sake.

Thinking of fathers, Erika reflected on her own parents. For years after her father walked out on her mother, she watched her mother deny the divorce. She denied it to her family and friends, and worst of all she denied it to herself. After ten years, she still refused to think of herself as a divorcee and always set a place for her husband at the table.

"No," Erika vowed to herself once more. Fall in love was nothing to aspire to. The only guaranteed result was pain - pain and heartache.

Erika stepped out of the tub and used a soft cotton towel to dry herself off. It was only then that she realized she had nothing clean to put on. Someone had removed the evening gown during the day.

After wrapping the towel around her and securing it beneath her arms, she went over and pulled on the bell cord. Within seconds a knock came at the door. With only the towel around her, she hoped desperately that it was Sadie and not Villars.

It wasn't Villars, but then neither was it Sadie standing at the door. It was Charles.

"Did you need something?" he asked, seeming not to notice her state of undress.

"What are you doing here?"

"Why, surely you would allow me to have dinner with my family." He walked to the window and seemed intent on the view.

"I mean, what are you doing in my bedroom?"

"I'm sorry. I thought you rang the bell."

"I did. But I rang for a servant."

"They are all busy at the moment. I, however, am always at your service."

Erika frowned. Her hair hung in a mess around her

shoulders. She hadn't even had the chance to comb it out. Her cheeks flushed.

"It seems I have nothing clean to wear," she said, growing desperate.

"I rather like your current outfit," he said, turning and studying her as though he hadn't already noticed she wore only a towel.

"Charles, please find something for me to put on. It's getting cold in here."

Suddenly, he was standing near her, much too close. Then she was drowning in those clear eyes of slate blue.

"I have just the thing for a cold fall night." Charles murmured and wrapped his arms around her.

Erika began to tremble, but she was no longer cold. He lifted her chin and pressed his mouth against hers. The now familiar excitement began to race through her veins again. She liked the feel of his strong arms around her. She liked the taste and texture of his mouth.

Then, still clutching the towel to her, she wrenched her mouth from his and took a step backwards. Her blood was racing and her hands trembled.

Charles lifted an eyebrow and folded his arms across his chest.

"What brought you here?" he asked again suddenly.

"I... I..." It was a question she had asked herself a hundred times over. What had brought her here? If she knew, she could probably get back. As it was, she had to survive in this unfamiliar time period. "I don't know what you mean."

"Don't be obtuse."

"It must have been fate."

She watched the play of emotions across his face and could only wonder what thoughts were behind those unfathomable eyes.

"I gave you a dress this morning. What's wrong with it?"

"It's all sweaty and I just had a bath." She self- consciously ran her hand down the length of her damp hair.

For a moment he didn't answer. "You mustn't let my father think you ungrateful," he said.

"No." She said quickly, looking away. Why was he doing this to her? She had only asked for something clean to put on. Surely it wasn't too much.

"We'll see you downstairs for supper," he said, his voice kind. He closed the distance between them, and pressed a kiss on the top of her head.

Erika's eyes fluttered closed. *Another glimpse of kindness.*

He turned away and halfway out the door, he stopped and turned back. "Make sure you get to bed early. Your day will start at dawn."

Erika watched the door slam behind him and immediately felt bereft. She dropped to the side of the bed and sat shivering on its edge, tears welling in her throat.

Suddenly overwhelmed by the events of the past two days, she did cry - deep wracking sobs that shook her body. She lay back on the bed and muffled the heart-wrenching sounds in her pillow.

She feared for her grandfather. *I need to make sure he's safe. How can I live with myself knowing it's my fault he was harmed by that horrible woman, Mable? I told him I would be right back.* Was he looking for her now? She didn't want to cause him pain, but knew he would be heartbroken if he couldn't find her.

If he lived.

She longed for her mother - for the security of home. As a child she had taken her way of life for granted. Even after her father left, her life hadn't changed that much. She'd still had her mother and her brother, Bradley.

Bradley. Had he gotten to the plantation in time? Or had he come upon disaster? She and her brother were close. They shared a special bond that only siblings could experience.

He would never stop looking for her. She knew that. But he would never find her. She had dropped though a time door, one that seemed to have slammed and bolted behind her.

Why had this happened now? She had spent a fair portion of her life wandering around the estate.

Her tears dried and she wiped her nose on the pillow case. Perhaps she'd been sent here for a reason. All she had to do was find it.

With new purpose, she reluctantly put on the soiled brown linen dress, and short ankle boots. Her whole body was beginning to ache from the day's hard physical exertion. She probably wouldn't be able to crawl out of bed in the morning, much less do it all again.

She washed her face, went to the dresser, and combed out her hair. She'd catch pneumonia walking around in the cool night air with wet hair. But there was nothing she could do to dry it.

She couldn't face the Becquerel family over dinner with these bloodshot, red rimmed eyes - and this horrible smelly dress. She would go for a walk and find something to eat after everyone had gone to bed.

The upstairs hall was empty and she made it down the stairs unnoticed. Avoiding the dining room, she slipped out the front door. It squeaked as she slowly closed it behind her.

Her heart pounding wildly, she stood on the porch and waited, listening. It wouldn't do for Charles to carry her thrown over his shoulder into dinner. She had no doubt that he would do so if it suited him.

But no one followed and she hurried down the front porch steps. A light drizzle filtered down and covered the land and everything on it with a damp mist. She was cold. But she had to get away, had to collect her thoughts and compose herself.

With no destination in mind, she started down the road. It

might be fascinating to see history in the making if it weren't so dangerous.

In twenty four years, the country would be torn apart by war. She hoped she would be gone by then. Yet there was no guarantee she would ever return to her own time. She could grow old and die here. A stranger in her own home.

She was startled back to reality by the sound of horse's hooves galloping toward her. She turned and only then realized she had walked too far. She was no longer in sight of the house and except for a sliver of moonlight, it had grown dark.

She ran off the road behind the trees, frantically searching for a place to hide. Coming to a large oak, her feet sank into a puddle, coating mud over her boots, stockings, and skirt hem.

The thought flashed through her mind that she would have to wear this dress, sweaty and muddy, for the rest of her life.

Standing very still as the horse and rider approached, she peered out from behind the tree. She was close enough that she could see his face. The breath caught in her throat at the straight, arrogant profile that had become so familiar to her.

Though Charles sat tall and straight on the horse's back, he rode with an ease that could only be obtained from a lifetime of riding. She had assumed he would be having dinner with his family right now. Whatever had caused him to come out in the rain?

And it was raining now. She could hear the drops landing on the leaves and splashing into the puddles. Once Charles had passed without seeing her, Erika began to pick her way out of the murk.

The mud oozed over her short boots and the muddy water seeped down to her toes. Her feet were sucked into the mud at each step.

Suddenly she stopped dead still.

There was something beneath her right foot and something was thrashing in the mud at her feet.

The clouds seemed to hesitate in torture before drifting on past the moon. The pale light was enough for her to clearly see that it was no stick she was standing on.

In horror, she jumped backwards and inadvertently dropped her other foot on the snake.

She screamed unconsciously from the bottom of her lungs.

The last things she remembered were the sounds of a horse galloping in the distance, the yellow eyes of that water moccasin coming toward her in the darkness, and a piercing pain in her right leg.

"It must have been fate." Erika's words rang in Charles' ears.

Those words frightened him. He had tried to be angry with her. Tried to be angry because she invaded his home without explanation. Angry because of the feelings she caused in him - the burning desire. Angry because she made him discontented with his life, especially his betrothal to Elizabeth.

He had to marry Elizabeth. It was the least he could do for his family.

Charles had stood at the door to Erika's bedroom and listened until she quieted. Always susceptible to women's tears, Erika's sobs had especially touched him - he had caused them. He was the cause of her pain and he felt like a brute.

Only his pride kept him from rushing to her side to comfort her.

Why couldn't he trust her? She'd never done anything to him except lie, masquerade as his cousin, and set his passions aflame.

But he still didn't know why she was here or where she came from. He couldn't trust her. He mustn't trust her.

He went to the dining room door and stood there. His

mother was laughing at something Richard had said. His sister, Andrea, was laughing, too. They were such a happy family.

Charles was a thirty-one year old bachelor. He should have a wife and child of his own. They must think him a complete failure in life.

He frowned. Whatever caused him to think like that? He had always prided himself on being elusive to women. He had always had his pick of the belle of the moment. He had never wanted to choose just one and settle down.

Now it all seemed empty and futile. Love and family were the only things that really mattered in the end.

"Charles," Richard said, spotting him. "Come on in. We waited for you."

"Are you hungry, Dear?" Rebecca asked.

Andrea turned and smiled that innocent little girl smile on him. Brahe, her doll and constant companion sat on the table next to her.

He had to get away. He had to get out.

"Go ahead," he choked out. "I'm going for a ride. I'll eat later."

Turning, he strode out the back door to the stables and saddled his huge black roan. He did it quickly, with a practiced hand and was soon riding out the stable doors.

With only the thought of getting away by himself, he started down the main road. The cool mist helped to cool his fevered thoughts. What was wrong with him? He had allowed a stranger he had met only yesterday to upset his entire life.

His mother and father were unusual. Married people rarely loved each other like that and enjoyed each other's company so openly. Marriages were arranged and agreed upon for the sake of convenience. He should have already married Elizabeth and gotten on with his life.

Marry Elizabeth? Christ, he had gone insane. His sense of honor had gone too far.

He was about to strike the reins and urge the horse into a trot when he heard a scream behind him.

His heartbeat quickened. It was a woman's scream of terror.

He yanked on the reins and turned back toward her. The night was deathly quiet, but the scream echoed in his ears.

CHAPTER 6

Her body soaked with perspiration, Erika groaned and kicked at the unwanted weight of the heavy blankets.

Someone placed a cool cloth on her forehead and she relaxed a little only to become acutely aware of a dull throbbing in her right leg.

She drifted off again and sometime later sunshine streamed through the window and touched her eyelids, drawing away the drugged-like sleep. The daylight was warm and welcomed, but it was much too hot in this room. It was as hot as any summer day.

She turned her head, and found the source of the unwelcome heat. The flames of a fire greedily licked at the fresh stack of wood and sent sparks spiraling up through the chimney.

Someone stirred on the bed beside her and a cool hand pressed against her forehead. Erika slowly turned and blinked. She immediately recognized the dark tousled hair and sun-kissed face. Those dark blue eyes peered questioningly into hers. She was still in the midst of that same dream - with

Charles Becquerel in 1837, but was too tired to fight it anymore.

She closed her eyes and told herself to wake up. But she was so tired... so tired.

She opened her eyes again and he was still there, stretched out atop her blankets. His upper lip was beaded with perspiration from the heat and his face was covered with the evening shadow of the morning after. His head propped on one elbow, he watched her, his brow creased with concern.

Concern? She struggled to open her eyes wider. It was there. There was genuine concern on his face. She swallowed thickly, her tongue swollen, and he quickly turned his back to her.

She had been wrong. Why would he be concerned?

"Good morning," he said, turning back to her.

Slipping his arm behind her head, he shifted her shoulders to rest against his chest.

Holding a glass to her lips, he tilted it slowly until she took a sip.

"What happened?" she asked, feeling her body relax against his stronger one. Her forehead rested comfortably against his chin. She was too weak to even think about trying to move away.

"How do you feel?"

She allowed her eyes to fall shut again and felt her pulse pounding against her right ankle.

"Awful. Where am I?"

"You're safe." He pushed a lock of damp hair off her forehead. "You're home," he added gently.

Home? She didn't have the strength to think about it right now.

"My mouth tastes like I ate something vile."

Charles chuckled. "You did. It's the whiskey."

She wanted to see his expression - the smile she heard in his voice. Twisting to see his face, her head reeled from the effort.

They were so close. She could feel his breath against her lips. Her confusion at his mood changed to chagrin as the memory came flooding back of his lips pressed against hers. Her face felt warm as she imagined the sensations again and an unbidden longing to feel his body pressed against hers crept into her mind.

She hastily lowered her eyes, certain he could read her thoughts. How could she think such things especially when she couldn't remember what she was doing in bed with him.

"What happened?" She asked again.

He ran a hand along her arm and the feel of silky material was soft against her skin.

"What do you remember?" He asked.

She certainly didn't remember why she was wearing a silk nightgown - or why she had been drinking. He was being far too kind. She didn't dare trust him. She tensed and tried to pull away, but he held her close and she was too weak to resist further.

"What have you done? Where did I get this nightgown?"

"Settle down. You're going to wear yourself out. We've been like this all night. And your virtue is still intact, though I dare say it's with some regret on my part." There was an unmistakable hint of humor in his voice. He was enjoying this.

Realizing her struggle was futile, she relaxed against him again.

"Who changed my clothes?" she asked, voicing the one thought utmost in her mind.

She couldn't see his face, but she felt his smile.

"Also with some regret, it wasn't me. It was Sadie."

She closed her eyes and felt his strong heartbeat against her cheek. She tried to remember what had happened to bring her here. She remembered being on the road and seeing Charles on his horse. Why had he been there? Her head was beginning to ache.

"How does your leg feel?" he asked.

She'd been trying to ignore the throbbing near her ankle, but now she allowed herself to focus on it.

"It hurts."

"How much do you remember?" he asked again.

"Did you bring me here?"

"Yes."

"It's throbbing and it itches."

She felt him take a deep breath. "You were bitten by a snake."

In a flash, it all came back to her. She was walking through the mud, then there was something beneath her feet. Yellow eyes coming toward her in the moonlight.

Charles gently stroked her hair and his arms tightened around her.

"Was it poisonous?"

"Very. It was a water moccasin."

"Will I live?" She felt her stomach twist in panic. If she died here in this God forsaken time, no one would ever know what happened to her. Just like her grandmother, Vaughn. Jonathan was too weak to survive another loss.

If he lived.

"You'll be fine. Your fever has broken. You were lucky, though. It bit right through those leather shoes and you didn't get much poison. It was more exhaustion and exposure that made you sick, I expect. And you were lucky that I happened by."

She lay still, watching the blue flames playing among the logs in the fireplace. If Charles hadn't happened by, she probably would have died. It had been foolish of her to go out alone at night. It had almost cost her her life.

"You saved my life," she said quietly.

"It's what any gentleman would have done," he said in a strained voice.

His closeness was intoxicating. Impulsively she turned her head and brushed his cheek lightly with a kiss.

He moved away and lowered her gently back onto the pillow.

"You have to rest now. You'll be fine," he said and tucked the blankets around her shoulders.

"Close your eyes," he said.

She did, but she felt empty without him next to her.

When he left, she opened her eyes and stared at the closed door. She wanted him to come back. She wanted him next to her.

Within minutes, though, he returned to sit next to her on the bed. She closed her eyes and immediately fell asleep.

The next time Erika woke, she was grateful for the blankets. The sun had gone down, as well as the fire, and a cool breeze drifted through the open window. She felt less lethargic now and the throbbing in her leg was no more than a dull ache.

She turned her head to study the face that had become all too familiar. He was still there. There was a certain comfort in waking to find him by her side. It was something she could get used to, she thought, and then immediately brushed the thought aside.

Charles had fallen asleep on top of her blankets with a quilt pulled up over him. Even with a full day's growth of beard, he looked boyish and vulnerable.

She reached over and gently swept a dark strand of hair off his forehead. She longed to touch his cheek, but didn't want to risk waking him.

She jumped at a knock on the door and quickly dropped her head on the pillow, closing her eyes.

"Mister Charles?" Villars called in a low voice.

Charles stirred and immediately checked Erika's forehead.

Villars came in without waiting for an invitation. He carried a tray laden with steaming food.

"What time is it?" Charles asked irritably and checked his watch on the nightstand.

"Villars, what are you doing in here at 5:00 in the morning?"

"Sir, if the young lady is going to get her strength back, she has to eat something."

Erika's mouth watered at the smell of hot bacon and fresh biscuits. Villars was right. She was starved. She fought the urge to sit up and attack the food.

"Open your eyes, Erika," Charles said. "I know you're awake. According to *Dr. Villars*, it's time for you to eat something."

She opened her eyes. "How did you know I was awake?"

He took the tray from Villars and positioned it across her lap.

"You can't keep anything from me," he said.

Villars furrowed his eyebrows and rolled his eyes.

Charles helped her sit up and supported her with pillows. She grasped a blanket and pulled it safely beneath her arms.

Charles scooped up a forkful of buttered grits and brought it to her mouth.

"I can feed myself, thank you very much," she said and grabbed the fork from his hand.

"You're welcome, very much," Charles said, laughing.

And she did. She hungrily began to devour the fried eggs and bacon, buttered biscuits and homemade jam, hash browns, and grits.

While she ate, Villars puttered about the room, picking up discarded towels and glasses. Then he stoked the fire and added a couple of logs to it. Finally, he pulled a feather duster out of his back pocket and with painstaking slowness, swept it over the dresser, the bureau, and last, the nightstand.

Charles stared at his servant, obviously none too pleased.

"Villars, do you want something?" he asked.

"No Sir."

Hardly noticing them, Erika took a sip of the rich, cream laden coffee, then after cutting the biscuit in two, added bits of bacon and strawberry jam to its center.

Villars finished dusting and straightened Charles' boots that lay discarded on the floor next to the bed.

"Don't you have something to do?" Charles asked him.

"No Sir."

"No Sir?"

"I'll just take back the tray when Miss Erika's finished."

"When she's finished, I'll set the tray aside and you can take it away later."

"Yes Sir," Villars said, but continued to stand, looking straight ahead, his hands behind his back.

Charles sighed. "Go on. She's safe with me."

Erika paused and looked up. Villars didn't seem the least bit threatened.

Charles continued to glare.

"Oh, all right, Mister Charles," Villars said reluctantly and left.

"Why did you do that?" Erika asked.

"He was just standing there, watching us."

"Maybe he just wanted our company."

"He's trying to protect you."

"Protect me? From what?"

"From me."

She studied him over her cup of coffee. Except for being a bit gruff, he didn't appear threatening. Except that he was in her bed. The only thing about him that really frightened her was her feelings toward him.

For the first time, she studied her surroundings. She could see grass and flowers from the window. Two squirrels scampered playfully past. She didn't remember a bedroom on the first floor of the house.

The curtains were brown and definitely masculine. A razor and strop were on the washstand next to the porcelain pitcher and basin. A long sword hung on the wall.

"Where are we?"

"In my garconnaire."

"Your bachelor's quarters."

"You know French."

"Not really."

It suddenly occurred to her that this was highly improper. Why had Rebecca and Richard allowed her to stay with him unchaperoned like this?

Unless they didn't know.

"Charles," she began, setting her fork down. "What does your mother think about my staying here with you?"

"She doesn't think anything."

"She does know, doesn't she?"

"How could she not know?" he snapped.

"It seems highly improper."

"I have to go into the fields today," Charles said, throwing back the quilt and jerking on his boots.

Erika watched him warily. His kind face had been replaced by the angry one. What had she done this time to anger him?

He stomped out the door without even a glance back.

She suddenly felt sad, as though she had lost a friend. He had stayed with her all day yesterday. She knew that was quite a sacrifice for him. He had cotton to harvest. Still, she had hoped it would never end.

Today, she would get up. She was tired of lying useless in bed. Throwing back the blankets, she examined her leg. Charles had been right. It had been a mild bite. There were two marks, barely noticeable, just above her ankle, and the area was only slightly puffy. At least it had gotten her out of scrubbing floors.

She swung her feet over the edge of the bed and almost

changed her mind when her toes touched the cold floor. After searching for her dress, she found it hanging, clean, in the wardrobe.

She went over and pulled the bell cord. It was time for a bath.

CHARLES PULLED his hat lower over his eyes to shield them from the morning sun. His workers had done well yesterday without him, but he felt much more comfortable being out here with them.

He could see the overseer in the distance. He knew the man resented him. No overseer wanted interference in day to day activities from the plantation owner - or even his son.

At the sound of a horse running toward him, he twisted in the saddle. He recognized the rider as Albert's manservant. Something important must have happened for Albert to send a message this early. His friend usually didn't bother to get up before noon.

"Curtis, what the devil's wrong?" he asked as horse and rider came to a halt beside him.

"I don't know, Sir," Curtis said. "Mister Albert said to get this to you right away. He done threatened me six ways to Sunday if I don't get back before noon with an answer."

The man's large eyes were an indication that he believed the threat.

Charles managed not to smile. He and Albert were of the same school of thought on many things, one of which was they didn't mistreat their workers. But Albert didn't mind threatening his. Curtis had been with Albert for years and still expected to be flogged by the hot headed Creole any day.

Charles quickly read the note. He wanted Charles to come in to his office - immediately.

"Damn." Charles uttered. Another day lost. "Tell him I'm on my way ."

"Yes Sir. I'll tell him right away."

After the man had ridden out of sight, Charles made a quick stop by the house to change his shirt and reluctantly followed Curtis toward town.

He reached Albert's home in less than two hours and was promptly admitted into the library where he was working.

Albert sat at his desk engrossed in one of his thick bound law books. He looked up with tired, bloodshot eyes. It was still a good two hours before he was normally up and about.

Charles dropped into the chair across from the desk.

"Well?" he asked.

Albert leaned back and locked his hands behind his head.

"Pour yourself a brandy."

Charles raised an eyebrow. "It's a little early. Of course I wouldn't expect you to know that since you don't normally engage in mornings."

"Suit yourself," Albert said and began searching through the papers on his desk. He found the folded sheet and slowly opened it, glancing at Charles over his wire rimmed spectacles.

"Have you talked to Elizabeth?" he asked.

"No. I've been busy," Charles was fidgeting in his chair. Daylight was burning and he had cotton to pick.

"With your new diversion, I presume?"

"What new diversion?" Charles asked absently.

"You know, what's her name?" Albert paused, scratching his chin. "Erika."

"She's a guest in my home."

"She means nothing to you?" Albert asked.

"Of course not," Charles said, frowning.

Albert swallowed his brandy. "How are your parents?"

"Come on, Albert," Charles said jumping from his chair. "Why did you call me here? What's so damn urgent?"

"All right. All right. Just sit back down."

Charles sat and glared at his friend.

"This came this morning," Albert told him indicating the creased parchment.

"Perry Miller has filed a petition denying you access to the river," he said quickly and waited for the explosion.

It never came. Charles stared at him for what seemed like minutes. The tension was almost tangible.

Then Charles leaned back and howled with laughter.

Albert dragged his spectacles from his face, frowned, and crossed his arms over his chest.

His laughter spent, Charles stretched one leg out and propped it on the edge of the desk.

"He can't do that," he said flatly.

"I'm not so sure," Albert said. "That's what I've been researching."

"He can't deny me access to the river. He has to grant us an easement."

"Have faith in me, Charles. After all, I did go to law school."

"And?" Charles prompted.

"You have to have access to the river, but it doesn't have to be across his land."

Charles jerked his foot off the desk and it slammed against the floor. "Goddammit."

"Perry's land runs along the center edge of your property. But you have land that overlaps other properties on each end. And if I'm not mistaken, your land actually touches the river at one point."

Charles stood up, turned his back to Albert, and ran his hand through his hair.

"All because I wouldn't wed his slut of a daughter."

"Why do you insist on calling Elizabeth that?" Albert asked, his voice strained.

"Everybody knows it." Charles said absently, walking to the

window. "Do you know how far it is to that little peninsula of land that touches the water?" he asked, biting his lip. "It's miles. Isn't there something in there about causing undue hardship?"

Albert shrugged his shoulders and drummed his fingers against the edge of the desk.

"Find it, Albert. Find it." Charles said, picked up his hat, and started toward the door.

"Are you sure Erika means nothing to you?" Albert asked.

Charles paused and turned back to his friend. "Why would she, Albert? What do you care? Doesn't Elizabeth keep you busy enough?"

Without giving Albert time to reply, he turned away, walked outside, and mounted his horse.

Making his way along the streets of Natchez on his way home, Charles passed people on the streets, but he hardly noticed them. At first he had been angry enough to tear Perry Miller in two. Now he had just lost interest.

Albert would take care of it. He could always count on Albert. They had always been friends, ever since they were toddlers. They had sat through classes at West Point together. Then, Albert had gone off to law school and Charles had come home to be a planter. It was what he had always known he would do. Through it all they had remained the best of friends.

He reached into his pocket for a cigar, but he was out. Green's General Store was a block ahead. He would stop and get some there.

Only then did it occur to him that Albert shouldn't have known about the petition before he did. Perry must have just decided to save time, knowing Charles would take it to Albert anyway. Still...

He walked through the door and the smells of a thousand different things that could only belong to a general store took his mind off Perry for the moment.

He chose a box of the best cigars, knowing they wouldn't be

as good as the ones he and his father rolled themselves, and was about to approach the counter when a small porcelain box caught his eye. The lid was delicately painted with tiny pink flowers and a couple of butterflies. He lifted the lid and it began to play soft music.

Smiling to himself, he thought of Erika. She had one of these, a strange one called a Nikon, but it seemed to be broken. He would have to remember to give her things back tonight. It wasn't fair to keep them from her, especially after all she'd been through.

Picking it up, he walked to the counter with both boxes.

"Just put these on my account," he told the clerk.

"I'm sorry, Mr. Becquerel. I can't do that."

"Pardon me?"

"I have strict orders that you're to pay cash for any purchases."

"My family's credit has been good here for fifty years, since the day this place opened."

"I'm sorry, Mr. Becquerel."

"What reasoning is behind this?"

"I don't know, Sir. I just take orders from Mr. Green."

They could both go to hell, as far as he was concerned. He didn't need the man's cheap cigars anyway. Then Erika's image drifted across his mind. Her large green eyes looked back at him and suddenly he realized he would do anything to see her smile.

"How much?" he asked through gritted teeth. Pride was a bitter thing to swallow.

"A dollar fifty."

"A dollar fifty? Why that's highway robbery." He said, but reached into his pocket and pulled out a bill.

He waited patiently for the man to count out his change. But the longer it took, the angrier he got. What right did they have to deny him, Charles Becquerel, credit! It wasn't like he needed it; it was merely for convenience.

"Is there a balance on my family's account?" He asked after he had tucked the music box under his arm.

"You owe ten dollars." The man said after quickly scanning the ledger.

Charles threw a ten dollar bill down on the counter.

"Consider my account closed. And make sure you tell Mr. Green that it will be a cold day in hell before I or a member of my family set foot in your store again."

He picked up his box of cigars and the music box, stomped out the door, and climbed onto his horse. That was one bridge he hated to burn. His father would be furious. But what had they done to warrant such an action? They always paid off all their accounts when the cotton money came in.

Maybe Mr. Green was hard up for money. Charles tended to forget that the South was in a depression.

He should have gotten Andrea a gift. He always brought her something back from town. Well, he wasn't going back into the store after one.

What had come over him? His every thought seemed to lead to and come back to Erika. She had bewitched him. First she disappeared into thin air. Then she wormed her way into his mind. Definitely a witch. But an intriguing witch.

He still didn't know why she had come to them or what she wanted. But when he had found her lying in the mud with the snake coiled at her feet, he didn't care what she was after. He had beat the snake to a pulp and gently carried her back to his house.

He hadn't wanted anyone else to touch her. He had treated the snake bite himself, then reluctantly allowed one of the workers to clean her up and change her clothes into one of his mother's nightgowns.

He had then sent everyone away while he held vigil at her side.

Although he still wasn't sure why, Rebecca had left them alone together without argument.

He had stayed with her, watched her every breath until the fever had broken. Then, when she opened her eyes and looked at him, he had wanted more than anything to take her in his arms and kiss her.

But he knew she had reason not to trust him. He didn't even trust himself around her. He had been wrong to go along with his father's inane plan to make her clean the guest house. There had been no logical reason to treat her with such disrespect.

He didn't understand his father's harsh reaction to her. It hadn't been anything like him. Charles did know, however, that it wouldn't happen again. He would make it up to her and wouldn't allow anyone to ever mistreat her ever again.

He didn't know what twist of fate had brought her into his life, but whatever it was, he gave it his blessing. Heaven help him, he was falling in love with her.

CHAPTER 7

*E*rika had spent the morning in the library of the big
house. She had been fascinated by the old books that
were so new. There was an autographed copy of *Pride and
Prejudice* by Jane Austen and an original copy of *Wuthering
Heights*. English classics were nestled among Greek and Latin
literature. A New Orleans *Picayune* was spread out on the
coffee table.

She had purposely avoided the other members of the
family. She hadn't seen any of them since the Harvest Moon
Ball. The little girl, Andrea, was outside playing. She could see
Rebecca out back, dipping candles. She had toyed with the idea
of going out to help her, but didn't know if Charles' mother
knew she was still here, much less if she would welcome her
inexperienced assistance - or her company. She didn't know
where Richard was, but hoped he had ridden off somewhere.

Suddenly tired of being cooped up inside, she slipped out
the front door and started down a deserted path. The sun had
dried the ground and leaves crunched beneath her feet.

Where was Charles now, she wondered? The cotton
harvesting was finished, so he wouldn't be in the fields. Then

again, he was probably preparing the ground for next year's crop.

At first she didn't notice Andrea approaching her. The little girl had her head down and didn't see her either.

Erika stopped and, smiling, greeted the child. "Hello Andrea."

Andrea stopped abruptly and stared wide eyed at Erika. She didn't answer.

Erika felt like some sort of criminal trying to speak to a frightened child. Determined to dispel the feeling, she continued to smile.

"I'm Erika."

"I know."

"You look worried. Is something wrong?"

Andrea watched her with wide smokey blue eyes. Eyes full of passion for life, so like her brother's.

"Father said I should stay away from you," Andrea said.

"Okay," Erika said. "I understand. But I promise I won't hurt you."

"Yes, I know," Andrea said. "Charles likes you."

Erika's heart warmed.

"Charles likes me?" she asked, trying to sound casual.

Andrea brought a hand to her mouth and giggled. "Of course. It's just like when Jeremy put the cricket down my dress."

Of course, Erika thought. She wanted to whirl around in a dance of joy. But she didn't, of course. He liked her, but he wasn't supposed to. She was forbidden. That's why he fought it so hard. All she had to do was give him enough rope to hang himself.

"My cat's sick," Andrea said, her mouth turned down into a pretty pout.

"Where is he?"

"Her. Can you help her?"

"I can try. Do you know where she is?"

Andrea nodded, reached up to take Erika's hand, and led her toward the stables.

Erika felt as though a weight had been lifted from her shoulders. There was a lightness in her step that hadn't been there for months.

Charles likes you.

Three little words from a ten year old child. Yet the impact couldn't have been more profound if Andrea had told her the meaning of life.

She still didn't know why she had been sent back in time, but the confusion and uncertainty would be tolerable somehow, knowing Charles didn't completely detest her.

She didn't know why she cared. She didn't know why it mattered what Charles thought. She only knew that she did care and it mattered a great deal.

Andrea led her behind the stables to a stack of hay. Burrowed into a warm, dry cavern of hay was a pathetically thin, short-haired tabby cat.

Andrea reached in and dragged the cat out by her front legs.

Erika's heart lurched at the sight of the cat's protruding stomach and swollen mammary glands.

This cat was not only sorely undernourished, but was about to have kittens.

"Andrea," Erika said calmly. "Go to the kitchen and ask for a bowl of milk. And see if somebody will give you some scraps of food."

"But Father says Mittens should feed herself. He said rats are the only food she should eat."

Erika swallowed hard. She was appalled. How could anyone, even Richard, mistreat an innocent animal this way?

"When Mitten gets sick, she can't chase mice. If you want Mittens to get well, you go find her something to eat and some milk."

Andrea quickly hugged Mittens and darted toward the kitchen without another word.

After quickly examining Mittens, Erika gently placed her back in the warm cocoon. She spent the ten minutes or so that Andrea was gone scratching the kitten's head and speaking softly to her.

When Andrea came back, she had half a bowl of milk, as the other half was on the front of her dress. She didn't seem to notice or care about the mess. Erika rescued the two bowls and placed them in front of Mittens.

The cat hesitated; but only a moment passed before she was eagerly lapping up the milk and tasting the chicken scraps. She and Andrea glanced at each other and Andrea giggled at the cat's loud purring.

"Mittens was starving," Andrea said, looking up at Erika with a new respect.

Erika kneeled down and looked into the child's now trusting eyes.

"Do you like kittens?" she asked.

"Oh, yes."

"Mittens is going to have kittens and be a mommy. But we've got to help her. You've got to bring her food and water every morning and every evening. Can you do that?"

"Yes, but Father won't like it."

"What would your mother think?"

"She would say that we should help Mittens get well."

"Then if Father won't understand, we won't tell him."

Andrea struggled a moment with the dilemma before she made her decision. "I want Mittens to get well."

"Then promise me you'll feed her twice a day."

"I promise."

Erika smiled, realizing she had made a friend. At last, someone in this century trusted her.

"So... you're using animals and small children to plot against my father."

Erika turned at the familiar deep voice. Charles leaned against the corner of the building, almost camouflaged against the natural colored hay and the whitewashed wood. He was close enough that she could see his eyes, deep blue and smoldering. But smoldering with what? She would have thought with anger, but after her conversation with Andrea, she was no longer sure.

His attention didn't remain on her long, however. Andrea cried out his name and ran to hug him. He bent down and grabbed her up, holding her small form easily in the crook of one arm.

His own expression changed to an unguarded adoration. There was no doubt as to the extent of his love for his sister. His whole face was alight with naked affection. In that instant, Erika would have given anything to have him look at her that way - just once.

"Miss Erika's going to make Mittens all better," Andrea said.

Closing the distance between them, Charles turned his attention back to Erika.

"So I heard," he said, keeping his voice emotionless.

"She's going to have kittens," Erika said.

Charles nodded, speaking to Erika now. "Do whatever you can to help. If Father says anything, I'll back you."

Erika smiled. She'd just taken one more step in the right direction.

"Come see Mittens," Andrea said, scrambling down from her perch.

After watching them persuade the cat to leave her warm cocoon, she decided to leave the sibling alone. Slipping away, she turned and continued down the path.

The trail forked and she started down a familiar path toward the cemetery. It passed in front of the cottage where she had seen the old woman when she was cleaning the guest house. She paused in front of the house and a curtain fell back into place.

That woman had been watching her again.

Erika started running and didn't stop until she reached the grassy knoll where the cemetery was. She stopped and caught her breath in the shade of a young oak tree, ignoring her tender ankle.

The woman in the cottage spooked her. It was almost as though she watched her every move.

Erika's eyes filled with tears as she stared out over the cemetery. It was much smaller than in her own time, but she knew it would expand as people came into the world, lived out their lives, and finally came to rest here.

Someday her grandmother would lie here among these people.

But I may be here long before Vaughn is even born, she thought, with tears springing to her eyes.

Even now, Jonathan may be lying in this cemetery, somewhere far into the future.

"Why the sad face?"

Erika jumped, but she recognized the voice and looking up, she knew she would see Charles standing there. His dark wavy hair had fallen beneath his open collar. He leaned carelessly against a tree, one foot propped behind him.

"You don't know these people," he observed.

"I was just thinking about my grandparents."

"Have they passed away?"

"My grandmother has, but I hope... I hope my grandfather is okay."

"His name wouldn't by chance be Jonathan, would it?"

She jerked her head up. "How did you know?"

"The night of the party, you mumbled something about helping him."

Erika watched him carefully. What else had she told him in

her delirium? She was fairly certain that Villars had seen her fade into her own time. Even now did he know she was from another time?

She wanted to tell him the truth. Maybe his family would accept her into its fold, or banish her and get it over with.

"Have you ever had something happen to you and you didn't understand why it happened?" she asked, going to stand next to him.

"What happened to you Erika?"

"I don't know how I got here. I'm not from here."

"No, you're from Baton Rouge."

"That's not what I mean."

"You were separated from your grandfather."

"Oh, yes. I was separated from my grandfather, my brother, my mother and father, my cat, my home, my way of life. And I can't tell you why. I can't tell you because I don't know why," she said, clenching her fists.

Charles took her hand and led her to a fallen log.

"Sit," he said. "I don't want you passing out on me."

She sank gratefully onto the log, but she was only getting started. Now that she had started, she couldn't stop.

"Do you hear what I'm saying?"

He nodded. "What would you have me do, Erika? What can I do to get you back to your family? I'll give you as much money as you need."

"Money! All the money in this world couldn't get me home."

He sat on his haunches, laid his lower arm across the log, and looked up into her eyes. He was trying to help her, but he couldn't. No one could.

"Then what?"

"I don't know."

"Why don't you start at the beginning and tell me what happened."

She stared at him for a long time, then with a smile at the corner of her lips, she answered him.

"I was born on February 6, 1981."

"You mean eighteen eighty... eighteen...," he faltered, struggling with the numbers.

"No, I mean 1981."

"That's impossible," he stated.

"Exactly," she said seriously. "Why do think I was dressed in those pants and that sweater? That's how we dress in 2008. That's where I left Jonathan - 2008."

She watched his face for a reaction. She had no desire to be sent to an insane asylum - or burned as a witch.

"You're telling me you came from the future?" His face showed no expression.

"Yes," she said tentatively.

"How did you get here?"

"I was in my grandfather's house, your house, one minute and the next second I was here. Same house, different time."

If felt so good to get it out, to tell someone, she had stopped caring if he believed her.

"Can you prove it?"

She looked out across the tombstones. Did those people who had lived and died have the answers? She certainly didn't. A squirrel chattered in the tree above them and part of a shredded pine cone hit the ground at their feet.

"If I had my purse, I could."

"I know where your bag is."

"My purse! You know where it is?"

He held out his hand, pulled her to her feet, and they started back toward the house. He didn't release her hand.

"Why didn't you give it to me already?"

"I was afraid it would only confuse you further.

"Do you think I'm crazy?"

"Yes."

She decided it was best not to question him further. Right now, the most important thing was getting her purse back.

Stepping into the garconnaire, she waited patiently for Charles to rummage through a trunk. The house smelled of cigars and there were clothes lying about on the floor. It seemed man hadn't evolved very far over the years.

When he finally produced her handbag, she grabbed at it and quickly located her tube of Blistex and applied it to her dry lips. He watched her closely, but remained silent.

All her belongings were there - her keys, her wallet, even some make-up. Charles waited as she tried to decide what to show him.

She tossed her keys aside, not bothering to consider them, but Charles seemed quite interested in them.

"Are these the keys for running your household?" he asked, picking them up and counting them.

She remembered seeing Rebecca's huge key ring. Everything had to be locked up from silver to clothing to candles to flour. Things had to be rationed to the workers.

"I live alone," she said.

He was surprised, but she thought he hid it well.

"Neither my mother nor my father would want me to live with them. It's customary that when children, even girls, get to be a certain age, they go to work and move into a place of their own."

"Considering my father, that custom sounds appealing."

She smiled at the image of a twenty-first century man in his thirties living with his parents. He wouldn't exactly be admired for it. In fact there had a movie about just that very situation.

"However," he continued, "I wouldn't want to leave them. We can survive only if we stick together and help each other. Running a plantation is a lot of hard work and one person could never do it alone.

A shiver ran up her spine. He was right and she envied their close-knit family.

"Do you have any slaves?" he asked.

She was surprised at the question. Charles saw slavery as cruel and unnecessary. But was it wise to tell him about the future? Would she change the course of history? She didn't know of any established rules for this game.

"No. My family doesn't believe in slavery."

"Neither do I. Actually, my grandfather freed the slaves he inherited from his grandfather, giving them land and a house. And they stayed on."

Erika nodded, relieved that they were in agreement despite their different worlds.

She sat quietly and studied her date book. She had an appointment today with a realtor. They were supposed to look for a building to house her new pet clinic.

That all seemed so distant now and so futile. She looked out the window. It was so peaceful here. No stress.

"Tell me what happens."

She closed the date book and placed it back in her purse. She didn't want to answer him. It was too scary.

"Is there a war?"

She studied him closely. "What makes you ask that?"

He shrugged. "There's been unrest for some time."

"Why do you believe me when I say I'm from the future? You should think I'm insane."

He reached out and gently placed his hand over hers. "I don't know if I believe you, but I think you believe what you're saying. Sometimes people have a reason for what they believe."

She looked away and blinked back the tears.

"Now, just in case, when does this war happen?"

Taking a deep breath, she told him what she could remember about the Civil War. She wasn't worried about changing history. She did good to remember the basics. She knew it began sometime in 1860 or was it 1861?

TWO HOURS LATER, Erika started back toward the main house. She was exhausted. Charles had to take care of some business and had suggested she go to the guest room for some rest. She wasn't certain she would be welcome there, but Charles had assured her that no one would object.

She had hardly gotten inside the door before a shadow fell across her path. She gasped and her hand flew to her throat. Her eyes wide, she turned. Speaking of Richard, she wasn't up to confronting him. He would probably send her out to scrub something.

It was Villars.

"Miss Erika, what are you doing still up? You should be off that foot, getting some rest."

Didn't he make sounds when he walked? Her heart pounding quickly, she took a deep breath and exhaled slowly.

Villars stood a moment, watching her, a strange expression on his face.

He knows, she thought again. She only hoped he kept it to himself.

No, she thought desperately. He wouldn't tell because they'd think he was crazy.

"Hattie wants to see you out at the sewing house." He was saying. "I don't think you should go. I don't think you're well enough. I told her that, but she said Mr. Charles wanted you to have this new dress she's all but finished."

A new dress! At last she'd have something different to put on. Hopefully, it wouldn't be as drab and childish as this brown one.

Ignoring Villars' protestations, she hurried out the front door and down the path to Hattie's sewing house.

As she stood waiting for someone to open the door, she spotted Charles astride his black horse. She thought he watched her, too, but the distance between them was too great to be certain.

He said he thought she was crazy, yet he listened intently. He was probably going to use it all against her at the first opportune moment. She stopped herself, however, from thinking about that too much.

Once she was inside, Hattie made a fuss over measuring her from head to toe.

"Mister Charles, he sets quite a store on you, Child." Hattie said.

"He does?" Well, if he did, she'd probably talked her way out of it this afternoon. How could anyone like a crazy woman who claimed to be from the future?

"Oh yes, ma'am. He come barging in here yesterday and ordered up only the best for you. And he wants it ready this afternoon. I've estimated your size, but you're a bit thinner than most."

For the first time in days, she felt a smile tug at the corners of her mouth. She would have something new to wear to dinner tonight. Perhaps she could entice Charles into letting her do something besides clean floors. Then he only had to convince his father.

When Hattie had finished measuring her, Erika went back to her room and took a nap on the daybed. When she woke, there was a pile of new clothes on the end of the bed.

The dress was made of folds and folds and folds of pale pink silk. The only thing even remotely comparable in quality that Erika had ever owned was a little black silk dress. The bodice of the gown dipped down and was bordered with hand woven lace, light as a spider's web. Exactly what she had wished for.

This dress must have cost a fortune!

There were also pantaloons, a whale-bone corset, silk stockings, crinolines, and a pair of matching soft leather shoes.

She ran her hand along the silk gown again. How could anyone make her scrub on her hands and knees one day and then turn around and give her a gift like this the next? Maybe it wasn't a gift, she thought suddenly. Maybe it was just for her to wear.

Or maybe it was payment for something she hadn't done yet. Charles would probably even do this to get her into bed. Probably even listen to ranting and raving about being from the future. Poor Elizabeth. Perhaps she had reason not to trust her fiance.

She forced herself to focus back on her goal of staying in the house. Now that she had this dress to wear, her plan to make Charles fall in love with her just might work, she thought with a smile.

Sadie came in and helped her dress. Everything would be perfect tonight. She found a fingernail file in her purse and gave herself a manicure. For once, she was glad she carried so much junk in her purse.

She didn't have any base make-up with her, but did have powder for her nose, lipstick, and mascara. Sadie came in, helped her put on the new dress and all the undergarments that went with it. She used tongs she had heated in the fireplace to add curls to Erika's shoulder-length hair. They made her a little nervous, but Sadie assured her that she used the tongs all the time - on both Rebecca's and Andrea's hair.

She then swept it up and tied it with ribbons at the back of her head in a shorter version of the style Elizabeth had worn at the party. Looking in the mirror, she caught her breath at her own reflection. She floated in a world of pink silk. Apparently hoop skirts weren't in style yet, but the dress was held out by the petticoats, stiffened around the bottom with horsehair padding.

Her eyes fell on the cameo Jonathan had given her. She picked it up and carefully pinned it to the bodice of her dress.

Jonathan would be proud of her now, just as he was proud of his heritage. Her appearance was worthy of having her portrait hang with those in the parlor.

The breeze had cooled considerably and the afternoon shadows were growing long when Erika began her descent down the stairs. She made her way slowly, careful not to trip over her dress. She stopped outside the parlor and listened before entering.

Her heart raced like any girl's on a first date at the sound of Charles' voice. She took a deep breath. She had to remember - he was the one who was supposed to fall in love; not her.

CHAPTER 8

"Just wait, they'll admit Texas to the Union. It'll not only be admitted, but it'll turn out to be a strong Southern state. You'll see." Charles said.

"I don't know," Albert replied. "There is absolutely nothing out there. What can a man do with land that has no trees?"

"What do you mean? He's already saved himself a year by not having to clear the things off."

"You sound more like Christopher every day."

Erika took a step forward and peered into the parlor. She could see Charles' profile as he stared out through the window, seeing something only he could see. He wore that same haunted expression she had seen before. Whatever his friend had said touched on a painful subject.

Seeming to sense her watching him, he turned. He blinked, smiled into her eyes, and held his hand out to her.

Erika, awkwardly manipulating the full skirt, stepped into the room.

She felt a smile playing at her lips. Whether he was frowning, smiling, or wearing that far off expression, he was by far the most handsome and virile man she knew.

He was wearing a deep black tailcoat and trousers. A pleated blue cummerbund was fastened around his slim waist and a blue cravat was carelessly tied over his white cotton shirt. His clothes were clean, yet his appearance was one of studied negligence.

Most men would have seemed stiff and uncomfortable in the formal clothes, but Charles wore them with the ease of his black work trousers and white shirt.

He stepped forward to gently take her gloved hand. He laid it on his arm and covered it with his own. His eyes held hers captive. She barely heard his whispered words, "you're beautiful" over her own heart pounding in her ears.

"No wonder you couldn't go through with it," Albert mumbled.

"Albert, this is my guest, Erika."

"The pleasure is mine," Albert said bowing over her free hand.

"I'm pleased to meet you," she replied, giving him no more than a quick glance as her eyes were drawn like a magnet back to Charles.

"Albert will accompany us."

"Where are we going?" she asked.

"My apologies for not telling you. We're going to a dinner party at the Alkin's. Mother and Father have already left.

"Oh, but..."

"That is, of course, if you feel up to it," Charles said, his voice suddenly full of concern.

"Yes. I'm fine," Erika said quickly. "I just had no idea. I thought we were having dinner here."

She hoped she masked her disappointment. She had been looking forward to a quiet evening of having Charles' attention. Now, it seemed, she would have to share it with his friend.

Albert retrieved his and Charles' black top hats and canes

from pegs near the front door and followed Erika and Charles out the front door.

The three of them went out to the carriage and with Charles' assistance, Erika placed a foot on the carriage step. With her weight, it tipped slightly in her direction. With a gasp she dropped her foot back firmly on the ground.

"What's wrong?" He asked, looking inside the coach. "I don't see anything."

"It almost fell over on us."

Charles watched her curiously. "It won't fall over. Albert, would you get inside the coach first?"

With comprehension, Erika watched as Albert got into the coach. It leaned in their direction, but certainly didn't tip over.

"I'm sorry, Charles. You must think I'm terribly foolish."

"Not at all. You're still skittish from the snake-bite. I'm being selfish in taking you out so soon," he said and brushed his lips against her forehead.

"Come on, you two. We're gonna be late," Albert called from inside the coach.

With Charles' hands firmly and reassuringly on her waist, Erika climbed into the coach and somehow managed to get all her skirts in with her. She was disappointed that Charles sat with Albert opposite her, but her skirts took up most of the bench on her side.

She watched Albert closely, but his expression showed no sign that her trepidation about the carriage had surprised him. It was going to be a difficult task not giving herself away.

"That's a lovely dress," Albert commented.

"Yes. Hattie seems to have done a fine job," Charles said, glancing peevishly at Albert.

"It's a perfect fit," she said. Because of the tight corset Hattie had insisted she wear, she had to breath shallowly. No wonder women were so delicate and were always fainting. They couldn't get enough air.

"It was made for you," Charles said. "No one else would ever do it justice."

Erika almost forgot they weren't alone. But Albert was watching them closely. Too closely.

"Do you live nearby?" she asked Albert, trying to divert his attention.

"My father owns a plantation south of here."

"I see," she said and adjusted the folds of her dress.

"Do you?" Albert asked.

"Do I what?"

"Do you live nearby?"

"I'm from... ah... Baton Rouge."

"Will you be staying long?"

She glanced uncomfortably at Charles and truly wished that she hadn't started this conversation. He shrugged slightly.

"I don't really know yet. I'll stay until my grandfather comes for me," she answered, falling back into her original story.

"Your grandfather dropped you off and left you unchaperoned?"

Why was Albert looking at her like that? If only it were something so simple as a lack of chaperone.

"Of course," she said, trying to sound casual. "You see, Charles and I are distant kin. Besides, Rebecca is a wonderful chaperone.

It wasn't a lie. Charles was her ancestor, after all.

"Who is your grandfather?" Albert persisted.

"Jonathan Becquerel."

Albert asked entirely too many questions.

Charles seemingly had lost interest in them and was staring out the window. His mood seemed to have blackened. Even that was better, though, than that far off, painful expression.

Albert stroked his chin and watched the passing trees for a moment. Then he turned back to her, perplexed. "I don't remember ever hearing of a Jonathan Becquerel. Are you certain you're related to Charles?"

"Albert," Charles interrupted. "I realize you don't spend much time in the company of ladies, but you're being rather rude."

"Charles and I went through West Point together, you see, and ever since then he thinks he's had the upper hand. West Point attracts women like honey. There was this one girl, why I believe he'd have swum the Mississippi itself. Of course, it was a different girl each week."

"Albert!" Charles threatened. "I believe you have bored the lady quite enough."

"Of course. My pardon."

Now Erika turned her attention to the window. The last of the evening sunlight glistened across the cotton blanketed ground to the horizon. If she closed her eyes just enough, it was almost like flying in an airplane over the clouds on a clear afternoon.

But she wasn't in an airplane. She was in a carriage and it was 1837. And the man sitting directly across from her swept all rational thought from her mind. Except now, his friend had managed to take some of her romantic ideals about him and try to trash them. She didn't need to know that he was popular with the ladies. Anyway, he was with her now.

Why on earth had Charles brought a friend along tonight of all nights? There was something about Albert's unblinking eyes that caused her spine to tingle unpleasantly.

They had traveled about a quarter hour when the coach came to a halt. The conveyance swayed as the driver suddenly jumped up and began yelling at the top of his lungs.

Erika's heart lurched. They were being attacked. She looked out the window, but couldn't see beyond the dense canebrakes. Her eyes wide, she turned back to Charles. He showed no alarm. In fact, he didn't even seem to notice the commotion.

She glanced at Albert. He, too, sat quietly, pulled his watch from his pocket, checked the time, and replaced it.

"Charles, what is going on? Are we being attacked." Maybe there were Indians. Weren't there still Indian attacks in 1837?

"Attacked? No. It's just a bad curve in the road." Charles replied with amusement.

"Has he gone mad?"

"He just wants to make sure that no one is coming around the curve before he starts around it. You see, it's a very sharp curve."

"Oh." She sat back and took a deep breath. The coachman sat back down and they rounded the curve uneventfully.

Erika leaned against the leather seat and closed her eyes. She truly was at a loss as far as expectations went for this as yet untamed land. Maybe Charles was right. The snake had made her even jumpier.

"What does your grandfather do?" Albert asked as though she hadn't left his thoughts.

Erika turned back to him and tried to put a pleasant expression on her face. She could feel Charles watching her again.

"He was a banker."

"Was?"

"He's retired."

"What does he do now?"

"He does whatever he wants. He's retired," she said and turned away from him with tears in her eyes. She only hoped Jonathan was still alive to do whatever he wanted to do. Why didn't Charles make his friend stop? She glanced at his face. His jaw was clenched, but otherwise he showed no expression.

"I take it his son owns the bank now?"

Erika opened her mouth to tell him that her grandfather never owned the bank and shut it as she realized that they wouldn't understand. They would see Jonathan as nothing more than an overseer.

"No," she said. "My father is an architect. He - he designs houses. So - a good friend of my grandfather's is in charge of the bank now."

At her response, Charles' expression darkened.

"Intriguing," Albert said. "Has your father designed any homes in this area?"

"No. As I said, we're from Baton Rouge. And anyway, he works mostly back east." The story was at least partially true. Her father did design homes on the East coast. She hadn't seen him in years.

Albert opened his mouth to ask another question.

"But enough about me. Tell me about you," she said abruptly.

Albert began to chatter about nothing in particular. Charles frowned and turned back to the window. Erika relaxed against the seat and let her mind wander. At least the man had stopped asking questions. She frankly didn't care to know anything about him.

The carriage wheels rolled along steadily, then slowed, dipped through a hole, and started up a driveway. Erika leaned over and looked out the window. The sun had gone down completely now, but the driveway was well lit with torches. A few minutes later they came up in front of a Greek Gothic style plantation home comparable in size to the Becquerel Estate. There were several other coaches moving about and a few guests standing out on the stairs and the porch.

"Do you expect Aime to be here?" Charles asked as they slowly made their way around the circle drive.

"I certainly hope so," Albert said. "In fact, I'm counting on it."

"You can always dance with Elizabeth," Charles said.

"Do I have your permission?"

"You have my blessing."

"How do you expect to get away with this?"

"Don't worry. I fully intend to pay the price. I said you could dance with her. Just don't get overly attached." Charles said, glancing at Erika.

"Well, I hope you can afford the price," Albert said beneath his breath. "Because the price will doubtless be steep."

Charles continued to gaze at Erika beneath his lashes. "It will be a bargain. Whatever the price, I can assure you, it will be a bargain."

Once they had alighted from the coach, Albert disappeared to look for his friend Aime. Erika and Charles both relaxed visibly.

"He can begin to grate on your nerves, can't he?" Charles asked. "I don't know what's gotten into him. He normally shows a lot more restraint."

"I'm sorry," Erika said. "I was trying not to be impolite."

"My dear, you have the patience of a saint," he said, then abruptly changed the subject. " This house belongs to Dr. and Mrs. Alkin. About every other month or so they give a dinner party," Charles said as they climbed the steps leading to the porch.

They went into the house and Charles handed the butler at the ballroom door a card. Two long rows of tables were set up in the middle of the room and most of the chairs were already filled with elegantly dressed guests. The room was alight with what must have been hundreds of candles.

"Mr. Charles Becquerel and Miss Erika Becquerel."

A hush fell over the guests as they entered and then a murmur, louder than before, rose.

"My dear," Mrs. Alkin began as she took Erika's hands in hers. "We are so honored that you could come. Indeed, I wish my son, Alexandre were here. He would find you to be a lovely companion. Charles never even hinted that he had such a lovely cousin."

Cousin? Erika blushed as she realized there could be a vast and varied amount of rumors floating around about her. This dress was certainly different from the shirt she had worn last time in front of these people. She was, however, certain they hadn't forgotten.

"I'm honored to be your guest. Everything is so beautiful."

The woman beamed as she turned to Charles. He took her hand and bowed slightly as he brushed a kiss across it.

"It's kind of you to have us here, Mrs. Alkin."

"Please, Charles. My home is yours. Don't let anyone make you think you aren't welcome here tonight," she said pointedly.

Charles nodded and Mrs. Alkin moved on to the next guests.

"Why did she say that?" Erika asked as Charles led her toward their seats.

"I'm afraid you'll find out."

He seated her in a stiff high backed chair and sat down in the chair next to hers.

It wasn't long before Erika found out what he meant. When she turned to the person sitting on her opposite side, the woman glared at her through her narrow spectacles, sniffed, and turned away.

No, they hadn't forgotten - or forgiven.

She was about to question Charles, but paused at his expression and followed his gaze. Albert sat on the opposite side of the room between two women. One, she assumed to be Aime and the other she recognized as Elizabeth.

Charles and Erika sat quietly through most of the meal. Following the main course, the dishes were taken away and the table cloth was removed.

Erika could no longer keep silent.

"What did we do that was so terrible?" She leaned over and whispered to Charles. "Aren't these people your friends? How can they ignore you like this? You haven't done anything."

He set down his fork and turned to look into her eyes. At the moment there was no kindness on his face and she wondered if she had angered him again.

"Some of these people are friends, like the Alkins. Fortunately, this is their home. A good many of the people, though, are merely members of our social circle. They are extremely closed minded and workers of tradition."

He paused and looked across at his father. Erika could almost feel the tension between them as the two men locked gazes.

"You see," he said, turning his attention back to her. "My father insists that I marry the woman of his choice . Elizabeth. You met her. Elizabeth, however, insists that I led her on and trifled with her affections, which I did not."

He quickly finished his dinner and sat back.

"Do you plan to marry her?"

"I'm afraid I have an obligation."

"I can see why you would. She's beautiful," Erika said honestly. Trying to keep her voice steady.

His eyes seemed to bore into her very soul.

"She is beautiful, but I don't love her. No matter what my father says, I don't want to marry her."

"What will you do then?"

She watched as the pain passed briefly over his features, but he quickly had it under control. "I will have to make a bargain," he said.

"I see," Erika said and shoved her food around with her silver fork. Though she really didn't see.

"I don't love her, Erika," he said.

She studied her hands folded neatly in her lap. Whatever woman he gave his love to, she was convinced, would be the luckiest woman alive - in the past, present, or future.

"I don't understand," she asked looking back at Richard. Why did he look at her with such hatred? She wasn't the reason Charles hadn't married Elizabeth. And it didn't matter anyway, because he was going to do as his father wished anyway. Swallowing the lump in her throat at his declaration that he would marry the other woman, she forced herself to focus on her task - staying alive long enough to get back to her time.

After dinner was finished, a desert table was set up in one corner of the room and the dining tables were cleared out. An orchestra set up their instruments at one end of the room and dance cards were handed out.

"What do I do with this?" Erika asked. There were twelve dances listed. It was going to be a long night.

Charles took the pencil and the card from her hand and quickly signed his name in each of the twelve slots.

"You spend the evening with me," he said.

She smiled at him. As long as he was with her, he wasn't dancing with anyone else. "What about Elizabeth?"

"Let me worry about her," he said. "How's your wound?"

"I had forgotten about it."

He swept her hair back and pressed his lips against her forehead. She closed her eyes and for the moment, short as it was, forgot that anyone else was in the room. The music had begun and she was swept away in a world of illusion. She imagined he wanted more from her than a mere diversion from his betrothed.

"You don't have any fever," he said, pulling away. She opened her eyes and he was grinning devilishly.

"Would you care to create the scandal of the evening?" he asked.

He had never smiled at her that way. One more battle lost in the war of hearts. God, but he was handsome. She was determined to enjoy his good humor as long as it lasted.

"I have nothing to lose," she replied, her heart picking up a dangerous tempo.

Laughing, he dropped into a deep bow. "Would you care to dance, my lady?"

She laughed and took his hand. They were the first ones on the dance floor. Everyone else was still scrambling to fill out their dance cards.

She was surprised at how easily it all came back to her. She and Bradley had taken dance lessons together as adolescents and fortunately the waltz was one of their favorites. She was stiff and her style was a little different from the other dancers, but she knew what she was doing.

She flushed as she realized that Charles was right. They had quickly drawn a crowd. But she didn't care. Charles was dancing with her - and had claimed every dance that night.

Soon they were surrounded by other couples joining them on the dance floor. Then the music faded as the melody shifted to another waltz.

Charles led her across the long ballroom to one of the six plush window seats. The windows were draped with dark navy velvet portieres. Six huge chandeliers with dozens of burning candles each hung along the center of the tall ceiling.

Charles grabbed two punch glasses from a passing server and pressed one in her hands.

"If your wound bothers you at all, tell me."

She met his gaze over the punch glass.

"And spoil a wonderful evening?"

"I'm afraid I have to spoil it momentarily. I have to see my father. If you wait here, I'll come back for you as soon as possible."

She smiled up at him and he lightly brushed his lips across hers. Then he was gone.

Erika leaned back against the velvet pillows to catch her breath and to steady her pounding heart. She felt just as Cinderella must have felt with her prince.

You mustn't fall in love, she reminded herself. She would

worry about that later, she resolved, pushing aside the thought. Right now, she was enjoying herself far too much to care.

She watched the dancers whisking about the room in all shades of blue, mauve, yellow, brown, and green. One dance ended and another began. She watched eagerly for Charles' return. She was ready to dance again.

Then she saw him. He was on the dance floor with Elizabeth. She wore a deep crimson low cut dress that was impossible to ignore. They waltzed so close to her that Elizabeth's dress brushed Erika's, but Charles never even looked at Erika. He was engaged in a deep conversation, his eyes intent on Elizabeth.

Erika's world careened, then came crashing in a thousand shards at her feet. How could she have been so naive? Fairy tales didn't come true. This wasn't one of her childhood storybook romances. This may be 1837, but this was reality.

She fought hard to hold back the tears and tried to convince herself that Charles was just telling Elizabeth it was over between them. He was a gentleman, and a gentleman would do such a thing. But, no. She had been foolish. A single tear slipped unnoticed from the corner of her eye as the couple whisked by again on the dance floor.

"So, we meet again."

Erika gasped as she recognized the voice and turning, recognized the man. Instinctively she wiped at the moisture on her cheek.

Richard Becquerel sat next to her.

"I trust you've recovered," he said.

"I'm quite well, thank you. I appreciate your hospitality these past few days," she said, managing to keep her voice even. Even if she did earn it by hauling buckets of water and scrubbing walls and floors.

"I assume you'll be moving on, now."

"Moving on?"

"Of course, returning to your own home."

Erika lowered her gaze. Where was Charles?

"I'm sorry, Sir. I have no place else to go."

Richard's face was as red as Elizabeth's dress. She remembered what Charles had said about the Creole's temper. There was nothing she could do about it now.

"He's going to marry her, you know," he said, taking out a cigar, and lighting it.

She felt the all too familiar pressure on her chest. The pressure of despair washing away the last of her hope.

"The date has been set for Saturday, two weeks from today."

"So soon," she said softly.

"Surely you didn't think he was going to marry the likes of you?"

"Me?"

"Is it money, you're after?"

"Money? No. I..."

"You'll find a carriage waiting outside the door for you and a purse on the seat. You should find the money more than sufficient for your needs. You may keep the dress. And I warn you." He leaned close and shook his finger in her face. "I don't want to see your face around my home again."

Erika leaned back and gaped at him. Somehow she had started off without a reputation and it had only gotten worse from there.

"But... But... I can't leave."

He ground his words out through his clenched teeth. "You will do as I say." He stood, glaring at her, before turning and striding away.

Erika glanced across the ballroom. Charles and Elizabeth stood facing one another. Her hand was resting casually on Charles' chest and he didn't bother to pull away. They were laughing.

Richard was right. She didn't belong here. She would have

to take the money and leave. She didn't want the money, but had no choice if she wanted to survive.

Jonathan.

How would she get back to Jonathan if she left the house? Tonight was her only chance. She would have to find a way back tonight. It was the only way.

She got up and blindly slipped out the side door. Charles had promised her an evening and promptly abandoned her. Well, she would forget him just as quickly. Even as she made her way toward the carriage parked in front of the house, she knew she was lying to herself.

She would never forget him.

A darkly cloaked figure sat in the driver's seat. The thought crossed her mind that she should be cautious about getting into the carriage alone with a strange driver.

"Excuse me," she called, "are you Richard Becquerel's driver?"

The man turned his head slowly and she was relieved to see that his face, though unfamiliar, was kind.

"Will you take me to the Becquerel Estate?"

The man frowned. "Mr. Becquerel said for me to take you into town."

She lowered her head and sniffed loudly.

"Please," she said. It was difficult to maintain her composure with her heart breaking. "I have no where to go tonight. Please, take me back to the plantation. Just for tonight. My things are there."

"All right, ma'am. I don't care what Mr. Richard says, I can't abandon you in the middle of the night. Get in, and I'll take you back to the plantation."

Erika thanked him profusely and managed to get inside. There was a purse heavy with coins in the middle of the bench.

Erika didn't know how much money it was, but it was more than she had at the moment. Swallowing her pride, she tucked the purse in the folds of her skirt and leaned back against the leather seat.

Her heart heavy, she stared out into the night at the passing trees and a house now and then. They passed a plantation silhouetted in the moonlight and she recognized it as one she passed each time on the way to visit Jonathan.

She closed her eyes and allowed her mind to wander. She was dancing in Charles' arms. Then a blur of red came between them. It was Elizabeth. The pain of his deceit and desertion was so strong, it hurt physically.

Her eyes flew open as they rounded the corner to the Becquerel Plantation. They stopped and a few minutes later the driver opened the carriage door. He helped Erika struggle out with her wide skirts and she was relieved that the driver had been kind enough to bring her here.

"Ma'am," the man said. "I'll be here waiting for you over there next to the stables in the morning before daylight. We have to do what Mr. Becquerel says."

"Sure."

"We'll both be better off if no one else knows you're here."

"Of course," she said, backing away from him.

He tipped the brim of his hat and before she could reach the front door, he had climbed back up on the driver's seat and was guiding the horse and carriage to the stables.

Erika, finding the front door unlocked, was very quiet as she entered the foyer. She had tiptoed halfway across the room before she realized the unusual silence was not only due to the time of night.

The clock was silent.

Relief flooded through her and the tears she had held back so diligently flowed unchecked down her cheeks.

"Jonathan!" she called loudly, bunched up her long skirts, and started up the stairs.

CHAPTER 9

"The wedding will take place two weeks from Saturday," Richard had said, coldly.

"No. I won't do it," Charles said looking steadily at his father. Even if he did consider marrying her, it was too soon. Love was something that made your heart beat faster when you saw her. It was trust. Trust and passion all rolled into one. It was feeling what he felt when he was near Erika. He didn't feel any of this with Elizabeth. He needed time. Time to think of come up with an alternative.

"Charles," Richard said coming to stand closer to his son and lowering his voice. "You know what Perry has done. We have to get our cotton to the river within the month. He's blocked our access. There's no other way."

"I'm sorry, Father. I need more time," Charles said. Feeling cold inside, he started making his way back to the ballroom. Erika had waited for him long enough. Her eyes, trusting and sincere, tormented him. He had a compelling need to see her - another way to define love. She had disappeared before. He couldn't bear for it to happen again.

Before he could take another step, Elizabeth burst into the room and grabbed his arm.

"Please, Charles," she pleaded. "Just dance with me once." Her lips turned up in a seductive smile and she lowered her lashes primly.

"No."

"But what can it hurt?"

"I'm sure you'll think of something."

At one time, long ago, he would have done anything Elizabeth wanted. Her silver gray eyes had carried him to the depths of his own fantasies. But he had learned. It had taken him awhile, but he had learned quickly enough not to trust her.

He glanced back at his father. Richard wasn't watching him. He was staring into the flames of the fire, chewing on the end of his cigar.

Maybe if he danced with her once, she would leave him alone. He had made the decision to marry her long ago. He had a commitment to fulfill, but he find another way to do it. In the meantime, they had to come to an understanding.

He'd seen Elizabeth with Thomas and Albert as well. In fact, he had encouraged Albert to entertain her. He was counting on that being the way out.

If Perry would leave her alone, Elizabeth would probably find herself surrounded by plenty of suitable beaus and she'd soon forget about him.

He would have to talk to her, he thought irritably. He may as well get it over with now. Then he could spend the rest of the evening with Erika.

His thoughts returned full force to that mysterious young woman who had come into his life. Where was she really from? She came to him with nothing more than the clothes on her back and a bag full of things all of which were strange to him. She couldn't draw water from a well or climb into a carriage without difficulty. She disappeared into thin air. She claimed to be from the future. And everything he had observed about her seemed to support that notion.

Yet, with one touch or even a glance she had the power to take his breath away.

He didn't care where - or when Erika came from. He only cared that she was here. And right now he only wanted to be alone with her. The first thing he had to do, though, was get rid of Elizabeth.

"All right," he said, every fiber of his being protesting. "One dance."

With a genuine smile of triumph, she took his hand and led him out on the dance floor. He saw Erika sitting where he had left her and his heart twisted. She was so trusting. She would be easily hurt. Fortunately, she hadn't seen them yet. Knowing it was only a matter of time before she did see him with Elizabeth, he almost jerked his hand free and backed away.

"I understand Father has tied your hands behind your back," Elizabeth said as she turned to place her other hand on his shoulder.

He groaned inwardly. They were immediately the center of attention. No one there could help but notice Elizabeth's dark crimson dress. If he hadn't known what manner of serpent lay beneath that lovely exterior, he would have been proud and honored to have her in his arms. But he knew. He nearly recoiled at her poisonous touch.

"Why do you insist on doing this to our families, Elizabeth?" Charles asked.

"I'm doing nothing more than any other woman would do."

Charles had tried to keep them away from Erika, but it was next to impossible with the floor so crowded with couples. Even now, Elizabeth seemed to be pulling him in her direction.

"If you force this marriage, both our lives will be ruined."

"I think not. I'll have your name and you'll have my land."

Charles stared hard into her eyes. There had to be a way to get beneath her cold exterior. "Christopher loved you, you know."

Elizabeth laughed elegantly. "I can find love anywhere, anytime."

If she had been a man, Charles would have punched her in the jaw. As it was, he could only stare at her, disbelieving. He'd only been fooling himself. There was nothing beneath the woman's heartless shell.

As they waltzed in front of Erika, he could feel her watching him, but he couldn't bear to look in her direction. They were so close he could have touched her. But he couldn't meet her gaze.

"Will you not be happy until you've taken my name and ruined it?" Charles asked once they were safely back in the midst of the other dancers.

"Why, Charles," she said, dropping the smile for a shocked expression. "After all we've been through together, you don't trust me?"

"Hell, no. I don't trust you."

"If you insist on using such language around a lady, I'll have to tell Papa."

"I'd like to tell your Papa a few things," Charles mumbled.

"What?"

"Nothing. Elizabeth. Listen to me." He tightened his hold upon her hand. "Call this whole thing off. Make up whatever you want. Say you came to your senses and wouldn't have me. There are plenty of fine gentlemen out there with names as good as mine. Look at Thomas. His family is respected and he adores you. You would be happy together. Think about Andre. He's besotted with you."

She looked up at him with hooded eyes. "Perhaps, but I don't think you understand the value of the Becquerel name."

Charles stopped mid stride and threw up his hands. The

woman had but one thought in her mind. He grasped her elbow and led her off the dance floor.

"Tell me," he said, "what are you going to do once we're married? After you've gotten my name, what's left for you?"

"I'm going to dance and dance and visit my friends and travel, too, I think."

It was so preposterous, Charles could do nothing more than laugh.

"What of running the plantation? If you were to be my wife, you'd have to run the household, you know."

"I hardly think so. Your mother does a fine job of it. I certainly wouldn't interfere."

"You're insane," he said as he ran a hand through his hair in exasperation. "If you become Mrs. Becquerel, you will take the load off my mother. You will make candles, nurse the workers, knit their socks, not to mention, curing hams and making pickles. There is little time to socialize or travel when there's a plantation to run."

"Nonsense," she said irritably, tossing her head. "The workers do all that."

"The workers are taken care of by us. I have my hands full with the field work. My wife will do all those things and more."

"It isn't true. You're just trying to get out of the wedding. You will marry me. I'm going to tell Papa." She turned and, picking up her skirts, started off toward the library.

Charles stared after her for a moment and a smile slowly spread across his features. Perhaps he had inadvertently found the way to frighten her away. Relieved to be rid of her, he skirted the ballroom and quickly returned to Erika's window seat. She was no where to be seen. He quickly scanned the room, but she was not there.

Richard.

His father had done something with her. His jaw clenched

in anger, he set out to locate his father. He found Richard standing with a group of friends on the veranda.

"Where is Erika?" he asked, heedless of interrupting them.

Richard glanced at his circle of friends. "Erika?"

"You know very well who I'm talking about. What have you done with her?"

"My son, it isn't respectful to raise your voice to your father."

Charles knew he should apologize and back down. Under normal circumstances, he would not have deliberately embarrassed his father. But then his father would not normally be so unfriendly toward a harmless stranger - especially the woman he was in love with and was going to marry.

"I wouldn't, Father, but you have sent an innocent girl into the night alone."

The men stared at Richard and Dr. Alkin cleared his throat. Richard glanced at their host and shifted uncomfortably.

"Now. Don't jump to conclusions. She said she had a headache and wasn't feeling well."

A carriage Charles recognized as one of their own rumbled down the driveway and Richard's attention was involuntarily drawn to it. Charles studied his father for seconds, no more. Then, with a muttered oath, he hurried to the stables.

He expected Richard to call out after him - to try and stop him. But he didn't. Apparently even his father had a limit as to how far he would push him.

He quickly chose and saddled a horse. He would have it returned in the morning.

Richard had probably sent Erika into town, but he couldn't be sure. He relaxed only when the carriage came into sight in front of him. Following at a safe distance, he wondered what his father could have said to convince her to leave. Then, with distaste, he remembered his dance with Elizabeth. He had brought her here and then deserted her among strangers. There was only one conclusion she could have drawn.

He felt inside his jacket for the music box. He had planned to give it to her tonight. He still would. And he would apologize for the abominable way he and his family had treated her since her arrival.

He would apologize and she would stay with him.

He wouldn't let her leave him.

"MISS ERIKA?"

Erika froze and gasped as surely as if someone had socked her in the stomach. She didn't have to turn around to know that Villars stood at the foot of the stairs.

"What are you doing back so early? Where is Mister Charles?"

Erika turned and slowly retraced her steps. She kept her eyes on her feet. Dropping her skirts, she sat down hard on the bottom step and laid her head on her knees.

Her face wet with tears, she finally looked up into the man's kind face.

"Villars," she choked out and fought hard to swallow the lump in her throat. "What am I going to do?"

"Now, Child, don't cry." Villars went over and instinctively patted her back. Even after he removed his hand, his words continued to soothe.

"Mister Charles will be home directly and he'll know what to do."

"Of course he will," Erika answered absently. She had lost her grandfather and now she had lost Charles. What cruel twist of fate had sent her to a different century, then taken everything away from her? What was the purpose?

Jonathan's absence hit her again, full force. She wanted to

see his dear old face, hear that beloved voice she had known all her life.

Villars held out his flickering candle to her and she took it. Looking into the yellow flame, the only image that burned across her mind was that of Charles holding Elizabeth in his arms. They were a couple, engaged, and she had intruded.

"You get some sleep and I'll tell Mister Charles you're here."

"No," she said quickly. "Don't tell him I'm here. I must leave first thing in the morning. I'll be gone before he gets up."

"Yes ma'am," Villars said slowly.

"What's wrong with the clock?" she asked, wiping her nose with the back of her hand.

"It just needs winding. Here, let me show you."

Erika caught herself just before she told him she already knew how.

She held the candle and watched him wind the clock as she had done so many times before. The only difference being that its face had no scar across its face. It soon resumed its steady ticking.

"That's all there is to it," Villars said, closing the delicately etched glass door. "You go on up, now, and get some sleep."

Erika hesitated. "You won't tell Charles?"

"Don't worry, Miss. I won't say a word."

Erika went upstairs to her room and carefully unpinned the cameo. Thinking, again, of Jonathan, she wistfully laid it safely on the dresser before struggling with the multitude of buttons on the back of her dress.

There was a button hook on her dress, but she had no idea how to use it. Unable to reach any other than the very highest and lowest buttons, she gave up and decided it wasn't worth the effort.

Exhausted and heartsick, she lay down and arranged the folds of the silk and white cotton slips around her. Pulling the blanket up to her chin, she was asleep within minutes, her mind eager to escape.

She thought she heard the door open during the night, but the fogginess of sleep was too thick to rouse her.

When she did wake, several hours later, with the sun across her face, she kicked off the blanket and her feet searched for a cool spot.

She opened her eyes and stared at the blank, empty ceiling and remembered where she was - and wondered "when" she was.

"Good morning."

Erika gasped and quickly turned her head toward the voice. There was no longer any doubt as to "when" she was. Charles Becquerel sat draped across the suddenly small green velvet chair, his feet propped carelessly upon the foot of the bed. He, too, still wore his evening clothes and that familiar evening shadow had once again appeared across his unshaven face. At the moment, he looked more like a river boat gambler than a simple cotton farmer.

"What are you doing here?" she asked, pulling the blanket back up to her chin. She couldn't meet his gaze. There was something odd and frightening about the glint in his eyes.

"I missed you. Why did you leave without me?"

He was angry. Erika did not want to feel his anger. She wanted his love.

"I... I was tired. My leg bothered me," she lied.

"I see," he said and pulled a wad of white tissue from inside his coat. "How is it now?"

"It's better." Her gaze lingered on the bronzed skin beneath his open collar. Then she allowed it to wander down to his hands. Strong hands. She longed to feel their touch upon her skin.

"My father had something to do with it."

She lifted her eyes to meet his. The silence between them was almost tangible. Erika didn't know how to respond to him. She didn't know what to make of his ever changing moods.

"Have I done something to make you mad?" she asked suddenly, unable to stand the silence any longer.

"No. I'm just trying to decide what to do with you."

"Charles, I apologize for coming between you and Elizabeth. That was never my intention. It's just - it's just I have nowhere else to go. You see, I have to be here. In your house."

Why didn't he answer her? Suddenly she realized even his outrage would have been preferable to his silence.

"When I went into town, I brought something back for you," he said finally.

He handed her the wad of tissue. She carefully pushed aside the paper and brought out the little wooden box.

"For me?" After everything that had happened, he had still thought to bring her a gift. When she lifted the lid and the music started to play, she could feel the moisture in her eyes.

"It's nothing much." Charles said lightly. "You just seemed bereft of your belongings and I thought it might amuse you."

"Amuse me? It's beautiful." She felt the urge to go to him. She wanted to kiss him. But something in his expression held her back. "Thank you," she said instead.

"By the way, there's no need to apologize for anything. Everything has been worked out between Elizabeth and me," he said, frowning.

"It did. How did you manage?" she asked, swallowing the lump in her throat. They would be married after all then.

He should have looked happy. He was to be married.

"The wedding is set for two weeks from Saturday."

She nodded, clutching the music box to her.

"Everyone's going to be happy. Elizabeth. Perry. My father."

"And you," she said softly.

"You can't buy or sell what Perry wants. There are only two ways to assure a man's acceptance into the circle of gentry. One is to be born into it. The other is to marry into it. Perry obviously can't do the first since he acquired his land himself and has already been born. And already married, I might add. The only alternative is that his daughter marry me."

"Why does it have to be you? You said yourself that all the guys liked her."

"That has nothing to do with it. My father, as a neighbor is the only person who can justify trading his name for a piece of land. It would be worthless to anyone else because it's surrounded by Becquerel lands."

Since he had decided to go through with the wedding she had no right to stand in his way. There was no guarantee that she would be here anyway. She could be hurled back to her time at any minute. Then she would have disrupted their lives for nothing.

She would simply walk away. She had the money Richard had given her. Surely she could find some job in Natchez. Anyone could wait tables or wash dishes.

She tried to ignore the nagging thought that she had to stay here, at the house. Perhaps there was some other way to get back to Jonathan. If not, she would make what she could out of her life here. She had run out of choices.

She stood up and smoothed her skirts. Her hair had come loose and swirled wildly about her shoulders. She tucked it behind her ears and licked her dry lips. Now, where was her purse?

"What are you doing?" Charles asked.

"I'm leaving," she said, squaring her shoulders.

"Erika. I wouldn't marry Elizabeth because my father wants me to and I certainly don't love her."

"Then, why?"

He turned away and she saw the pain flicker across his face. "I can't tell you." He grasped her arm and pulled her roughly toward him. "Just believe me when I say it's you I want."

She felt his chest hard against her own. His grip on her arm was strong, but he didn't hurt her. His face was so close to hers. She knew all she had to do was look up and he would kiss her.

"No," she whispered.

"Erika." He gently grasped her chin and tilted her face toward his. Their eyes locked and she was lost.

"Let me love you."

"No."

His mouth came down on hers, gently, then passionately. Her body responded and her arms slipped around his neck. Her mind was blank except for the taste and feel of him.Then ever so slowly, a nagging thought crept back into her mind.

Elizabeth. Charles was practically a married man. It seems he had made his choice. She was nothing more than a diversion.

With surprise on her side, she was able to pull away. He let her go. Searching frantically, she located her purse. Someone had tucked it away in the wardrobe along with her slacks, shirt, and gray linen dress. She took all of her belongings from the closet and neatly folded them into a stack on the bed. She could feel Charles silently watching her every move. He didn't try to stop her. Her hands trembled beneath his gaze.

What did he want from her? He'd told her he was getting married. There was nothing left for her here.

Suddenly Charles stood up and, without a word, left the room.

Her resolve shaken, she sat down hard on the bed. He was angry at her. She would probably never see him again. Well, she thought, squeezing back the tears, her life had taken a turn and she would just have to live with it.

She picked up the music box and tucked it safely into her purse.

Charles burst back into the room. With her camera!

"Where did you get that?" she asked, hurrying toward him.

"I believe it belongs to you. I meant to give it to you sooner, but I'm afraid I was neglectful."

She snatched it from his hands and pressed the power button. Here was her proof. Her proof that she had to stay in the house to get back to her own time. Now he would understand.

Only she had no proof. With a groan, she tossed the empty bag aside. Apparently, she had replaced the memory card.

"Damn it," she said.

"Something missing?" he asked.

"Yes... No. I don't know."

"What is it?"

"It's a..." She paused. He would have no idea what a camera was. There was no reason to explain it since she had no pictures to prove her origin. However. In the event that she did get back to her own time, she would have something to prove to herself that he really existed.

"It's a looking glass. You look through it."

She held the camera up and focused it on Charles.

"Smile," she said.

Completely unaware of what was going on, he did smile. Her heartbeat quickened as she snapped the picture and got that wonderfully confident expression in a digital picture.

The flash lit up the room for a split second. Charles leaped backwards, surprise in his face. Erika lowered the camera and immediately knew she had bumbled the whole thing. Now what would she tell him?

"Oh dear," she said setting aside the camera. "I'm afraid it's blown up. Oh well."

Before she knew what was happening, Charles had snatched the camera from her hands and tossed it onto the bed.

"Are you alright?" he asked urgently.

Erika smiled. He did care. Maybe only a little. But he did care. Concern was plastered all across his face. She could see his chest rising and falling with his quick breathing.

"I'm fine," she said.

Suddenly he pulled her into his arms and hugged her tightly, his arms clutching her. As though he would never let her go. Then he lowered his head and pressed his lips savagely against hers. He plundered her mouth, roughly, passionately.

This time she surrendered completely.

"Erika," he said pulling back slightly. "Oh, God, I need you."

Erika blinked. He needed her? No. She wouldn't put them through this. It could never be. She wouldn't be his - or any man's last fling before marriage. He had told her he was getting married. There was no need to drag this out any further.

"I have to go," she said, her voice barely audible.

He released her then. His eyes changed. They became cold. She had hurt him. But he had hurt her.

"I have a carriage waiting to take me home."

"And where is home?" he asked suddenly suspicious.

"I'm going into Natchez," she said, evading the question.

"So, you played me for a fool," he said, sending the chair flailing across the floor. "What were you after?"

She couldn't blame him. He thought she had lied to him. Only she was lying to him now. For his own good.

"I wasn't after anything," she said, gathered up her belongings, and walked past him, her head held high.

He wasn't about to let her go so easily. He grabbed her arm and turned her toward him.

"You're hurting me. Let go!"

"My father paid you off, didn't he?"

She didn't answer. He pushed her away. She stumbled and almost fell.

"Charles."

"Just go away. I don't want to hear your denials. I know what he's done and I know your type. Just go on."

She turned her back and went out the door. She didn't look back.

The rest of the family obviously hadn't returned home last night. She slowly made her way down the stairs. She took in every detail of the house as though for the last time.

She paused in front of the clock and watched the pendulum swing back and forth.

She walked past the drawing room and paused in front of Charles' portrait. Her heartbeat quickened and once again she thought she might burst into tears.

"Miss Erika?" Villars asked and halted at her expression. "Did Mr. Charles find you? I didn't tell him you were here."

Erika blinked the cloudiness from her eyes and focused on Villars. She tried to smile, but the effort was lost. "It's alright, Villars. I'm on my way out."

"Where are you going?"

"I'm going... home." There was no point in having them think she had no where to go.

"I'm sorry to see you go, Miss Erika."

Erika squared her shoulders, and without thinking, extended her hand toward him. "Good Bye, Villars."

Villars hesitated only a moment before he mimicked what he had seen Charles do a thousand times. He took her hand and brushed his lips toward the top of it. His lips didn't actually touch her skin.

"Take care, Miss Erika."

Erika walked back into the foyer and stared up toward the landing. Charles stood there, watching her. His expression was hooded, almost blank.

They seemed to stare at each other for an eternity.

Then Charles became blurry. The clock's ticking seemed to faded until she could no longer hear it. Erika thought she was falling.

The last thing she remembered was seeing Charles leaping dangerously down the stairs, his arms outstretched, his voice, further and further away, calling her name.

CHAPTER 10

$\mathcal{E}$rika opened her eyes. She lay sprawled across the pale cream rug in the foyer of the house.

She carefully stood up, completely disoriented. It was growing dark.

Where was Charles? Villars had been right behind her when she had fallen. Why hadn't he helped her?

Where was Charles?

Erika's gaze wandered around her. Then suddenly stopped, her eyes widening. A telephone sat on the end table in the parlor. She blinked, but it remained.

She turned, slowly until she was staring into the face of the grandfather clock. Its silence was louder than ever before.

"Oh, no!" she cried, in a panic. Her first impulse was to hide. But the man she had killed was gone. She looked quickly around. No one was in sight.

Going quickly to standing in front of the clock, she scanned the dial. The jagged tear was there - between the six and the seven.

She bunched her skirts up above her knees and flew up the stairs, faster than she had ever run up them in her entire life. She ran directly to Jonathan's room and threw open the door.

The room was empty.

The bed was unmade, sheets and blankets tossed carelessly across the bed. It must have been a fierce struggle. Jonathan must have had more strength to fight off Mable than it seemed. But where was he?

She quickly retraced her steps and searched the rooms downstairs. There was no sign of Jonathan in the library, the parlor, or the dining room. Going out back through the kitchen, she halted. Even before Grandmother Vaughn had been in that fatal accident almost seven months ago, Jonathan had continued to pick up after himself. He had never expected his wife to be his maid. Only now, the house was in sore need of one of Charles' workers.

The sink was piled high with dirty dishes. The garbage can stood overflowing in the middle of the room.

Erika's breathing came in short gasps. If Jonathan was here, something was desperately wrong.

She stepped out the back door, and it was then that she heard the riding mower crank up. Rushing around to the front of the house, she saw him.

Jonathan put the mower in gear and started out across the lawn. He was raking leaves the way he did every fall. He had a red plaid bandanna tied around his forehead. He looked healthier, much healthier.

Going to the edge of the barn, Erika stood in his line of vision. He didn't see her at first. Then when he looked directly at her, his expression didn't change.

He looked away. But only for a moment. When he looked back, and she was still there, he almost smiled. He turned off the lawn mower and she stepped toward him.

"Erika?" he asked softly, "is that you?"

With the feel of hot tears running down her cheeks, she

started running toward him. He stepped off the lawn mower and threw his arms around her.

"It is you," he said setting her down so he could look at her. "Where on earth have you been?"

There was a life in his eyes that she hadn't seen in months and he looked ten times more healthy than when she had seen him last.

"I'm not sure."

"We looked for you - for days. The police even gave up on finding you."

"The police were looking for me?" All color drained from her face. They knew. They knew she had killed a man.

He shook her shoulders. "Erika, listen to me. Have you been hurt? Do you need a doctor?"

"No. That man. Mable's son. Did they find him?"

Jonathan released her shoulders and turned away. Smokey rubbed up against Erika's leg. Reaching down to pick him up, she hugged the big gray cat against her, as if he could protect her from all the horrible things that were sure to come.

"Your brother says Mable accused you of stabbing her son. But the boy was alright. He claimed to be a doctor." Jonathan kicked the lawn mower tire. "Bradley sent them away and got me to the hospital. In a couple of days, I was fine."

Pausing, he turned to face her again. "There was only one problem. We couldn't find you."

The pain in his face hurt Erika. "You were so sick," she said. Even now, perspiration had beaded out across his forehead.

"Mable was trying to poison me. She had been giving me small, but steady doses of arsenic. It's a good thing you came along when you did."

Smokey spotted a blue jay and leaped from Erika's arms to pursue it.

"I knew she was up to something. I just couldn't get back," she said, her voice trailing off.

Jonathan wiped his forehead with his handkerchief. "Erika. Where were you?"

Smokey leaped toward the bird just as it spread its wings and flew out of reach.

"You know that her son was in on it?"

"Jeffery admitted to working with his mother."

"Good. Are they in jail?"

"No. I didn't press charges."

"But why not? They tried to kill you!" Suddenly his words sank in. "You said Mable's son didn't die?"

"No. He was fine."

"But I saw him. I... I killed him."

"He didn't die."

Relief washed over like a spring rain. For days, the thought that she was a murderess had hung over her head. Her limbs felt weak and her hands trembled.

"You haven't answered my question. Erika, where were you?"

Almost giddy with relief, she wanted to bound across the lawn and chase birds with the cat.

"Actually, I was here," she said instead.

"Where? We looked everywhere for you."

"See this dress."

Jonathan seemed to notice her dress for the first time. He had been so grateful to see her, he hadn't even seemed to notice.

"It was made in 1837."

"Where did you get it?" There was something in his voice. It sounded like dread.

"1837."

Their eyes locked. She watched the emotions play across his face from disbelief and distrust back to resigned sadness. Erika shivered despite the gentle warmth of the November sun.

Why didn't he say something, anything? She would rather he accused her of being insane than this - this silence.

Then he stepped toward her and put his arms around her. "It's good to have you home." He said hoarsely. "You need to get changed and I have a kitchen to clean up."

Smiling Erika allowed him to lead her into the house. It was good to be home.

Before going upstairs, she called Jonathan into the parlor. Charles' portrait stared down at her with that arrogant expression. But it was the woman in the painting next to him that concerned her now. It was not Elizabeth. Unlike Charles' dark haired, creamy skinned betrothed, this woman had blonde hair, bright blue eyes and a delicately featured baby face.

"Who is that woman?" she asked, pointing to the woman's picture.

Jonathan adjusted his bifocals. "Let's see, this is Charles, I believe."

"It is," she said quickly.

Jonathan glanced at her, but didn't comment. "This would be his wife."

Erika's heart lurched. It couldn't be. Charles was to marry Elizabeth. This was not Elizabeth.

"I believe her name was Sierra."

Erika began to tremble deep inside. "Sierra," she repeated. Charles' cousin really had come and she had married him. *I hope he loves her,* she thought. "And this?" she asked pointing to the portrait of the man next to Charles.

"That's Charles' brother, Christopher. Your great-great-great grandfather, I believe."

Brother? Charles didn't have a brother. Only a younger sister. "Where is Andrea?" she asked.

Jonathan watched her carefully. "I don't know anyone named Andrea."

"But you must. She's Charles' sister. Younger sister."

Shaking his head, Jonathan went over to the bookshelf and picked up the family Bible. The pages were yellowed, but the leather cover had been carefully conditioned. Wordlessly, he turned to the center and began scanning the names.

Erika went to his side and held her breath as she read silently along with him. He turned the page. There it was. Andrea Becquerel.

Born March 1827. Died November 1837.

Erika's breath caught in her throat and she stumbled to the couch.

Andrea was such an adorable child. She thought of the love she had given Mittens. The thought of her life ending made Erika's heart shudder.

"Does it say what killed her?" she asked, staring at Charles' picture.

"No," Jonathan said and opened his mouth to say something else, but with his shoulders sagging, he silently turned and left her alone.

`Going upstairs to change she realized she really didn't want to be alone right now. After removing the corset, she stood taking air deep into her lungs. She had worn the corset entirely too long. Gratefully, she put on a dark gray sweatshirt and sweatpants.

As she headed for the door, her eyes strayed toward the dresser. She froze.

Confused, she walked over and picked up the cameo. It was her Grandmother Vaughn's. Only now, it was tarnished and dull. It was old. Very old.

She had unpinned the cameo from her bodice last night before going to sleep. Last night had been over one hundred fifty years ago. The cameo had gotten left behind in 1837 and now it was an antique.

If there was any doubt remaining in her mind, it was now gone.

Charles had been real.

It had really happened.

ALMOST TWO WEEKS LATER, Erika sat in the office of her four room apartment. The blinking cursor nagged her to complete the report she had started two hours ago. But her thoughts refused to focus.

Her eyes rested on the little music box Charles had given her. She had put it next to her computer so she could see it while she worked. Now, she wasn't sure that was such a good idea. It was impossible to get anything done while her thoughts were in a place where the music was soft and the men gallant.

"Wake up, little sister."

Erika jumped several inches off the chair.

"Bradley!" she cried, her heart pounding frantically. "How did you get in?"

"You left the door unlocked."

"Oh. I've been a little absent minded lately."

She turned to study her younger brother. He had the same black head of hair and green eyes she did. He wore the khaki slacks and green sweater that were the uniform of his fraternity.

"Where have you been?" she asked. "I haven't even heard from you since I came back from Jonathan's."

"School keeps me busy. Just because you didn't have to study to make A's, doesn't mean I don't have to."

"Are you? Making A's, I mean?"

"Of course. I have to follow my little sister's footsteps, don't I?"

"In some ways."

"Hey, why the long face?"

"It's not so long," she said forcing a smile on her face. "Why are you so chipper, anyway? Wait. Let me guess. There's a girl."

Bradley's grin deepened, "You know me too well."

"Well, tell me about her. How long have you known her?"

"Two months."

"Is it serious? Do I need to start planning a wedding?" Her smile faltered with the words. In just three days, another wedding was scheduled to take place. Charles and Elizabeth. Unless, of course, Sierra had changed all that.

"It's too soon to know."

"In two months? You'd know. You'd know immediately if you wanted to marry her."

"There's no chance of that," he said, with a frown. "A girl can't marry two men at the same time."

"Bradley, she's married?"

"Unfortunately. But, hey, with the divorce rate what it is, I figure I've got two years to wait, tops."

Erika looked down. She knew how it felt to love someone who belonged to another. She certainly couldn't condemn her brother for doing something she had considered doing herself. "I'm sorry, Bradley," she said, looking back up at him.

Bradley studied her carefully. "Do you want to tell me what's wrong?"

"There's nothing wrong," Erika said quickly and glanced toward the music box sitting beside her computer.

"What's this?" Bradley asked and reached over her arm to pick up the gift Charles had given her.

"It's nothing, Bradley. Put it down," she said and jumped up, grabbing for it. He easily lifted it high out of her reach.

"Erika's got a boyfriend," Bradley said in a sing song voice.

"Don't be such a child," Erika said, sat down, and picked up her pencil.

"Come on, Erika, lighten up. I'm your brother, for God's sake. What's come over you?"

Bradley was right. There had never been any pretensions between them. She could tell him anything, anything at all, and he wouldn't turn away from her.

She had practically told Jonathan she had traveled back in time and he hadn't seemed to think she was completely crazy. But then, he hadn't mentioned it again, either.

But Bradley would understand. Bradley always understood. If only she weren't afraid to tell him.

Bradley lifted the lid on the jewelry box. He took one look at the sick expression on her face, immediately closed the lid, and apologized.

She looked away and squeezed her eyes tightly against the moisture. The pain hadn't lessened. If anything it was stronger now that she had someone here to share it with.

"It's okay," Erika said, taking a deep breath.

"What did he do to you?"

"He didn't do anything."

"Erika. Tell me the bastard's name. He won't live to see sunset."

"No, Bradley. It's not like that at all. I had to leave to come back to work. It just didn't work out. It was bad timing." She chewed on the end of her pencil. "And I think he's sort of engaged."

"You *think* he's engaged? Sort of? You don't know."

"Well, he said he was. But he also said that he doesn't want to marry this girl. And he didn't marry her."

The muscles in his jaw tight, Bradley set down the music box.

"If he doesn't want to marry her, why is he engaged to her? And what do you mean he didn't?"

"It's his father. His father will cut him out of his inheritance if he doesn't marry her," Erika said.

Bradley raised an eyebrow and frowned.

"The girl's father owns a lot of land," she continued, "that will go to his family if he marries her and Charles' father is a wealthy man to begin with."

"You are making absolutely no sense whatsoever. It all sounds like something out of a romance novel," Bradley said and walked to the open window. A gentle fall breeze ruffled his dark hair. She should never have told him, Erika thought. She had only confused him.

"What's his name?" Bradley asked suddenly.

"Charles."

"Does he love you?" he asked and turn back to face her.

Erika looked up into her brother's green eyes that mirrored her own. "I don't know."

"Do you love him?"

Erika pressed her pencil lead against the desk and slowly slid her fingers down it. Bradley certainly has a knack for cutting to the heart of things, she thought as she rubbed the black smudge from her fingers.

Suddenly she had to tell him. She had to get it out. She was dying a slow death keeping all the longing and confusion bottled up inside her.

"Yes," she said, lifting her eyes slowly back to his.

"Then you've got to tell him."

"I can't," she said, but not from lack of trying. She had wandered around the house for two days trying to do just that. She had cried out her love for him. She had willed her thoughts to him. She had tried and tried until she knew it was time to go back to work. Time to get on with her life.

"If you tell him, only two things can happen. He can turn you away or he can love you back. You have to run the risk. You have to take a chance. Otherwise you'll never know. Don't sit on the sidelines, Erika. Get out there and live."

Erika smiled. He was right, of course. Only this time it was impossible.

"I can't, Bradley."

"Yes, you can," he said coming to sit on the desk next to her. "You can do anything."

"No. You see, I'm here and he's... there."

"Go to him."

"He's too far away."

"If you really want him, take some time off."

"Bradley, I can't travel through time at will."

He sat back and stared at her.

She had told him. She hadn't meant to, but she had.

Bradley lifted the music box lid and took the photograph from it. The haunting music flooded the room and Erika's heart. Then he abruptly dropped the lid and the music faded.

"He's an arrogant fellow, isn't he?" Bradley asked, studying the picture.

"Yes," Erika said, smiling.

"I suppose that explains where you were."

She nodded.

"I knew something had happened to you. Your car was still there and so were your clothes."

"I was there. I was in 1837."

"Are you sure?"

"Bradley. I couldn't be more sure."

"What was it like?"

She sat back and remembered the way Charles had made her clean that house. She remembered the way he had nursed her after the snake bite. She remembered dancing with him. Then she remembered the music box... only minutes later watching Charles fade. She was really the one who had faded. Then she was here again.

"It was... it was just life."

"You want to go back?"

She didn't want to give up medicine and convenience. But she was in love with Charles. There was no longer any doubt about that. She would go anywhere or any time to be with him.

But could she? And if she did, would he want her? Or would he be married to another?

"I think so," she answered.

"You have to be sure."

"How can I give up a way of life, a career, my family, you, Jonathan, for something that may or may not can happen?"

"That's a choice you have to make. If you love him, go to him. You only live once, Erika. You've got to make it your life - not someone else's - not even mine."

He can turn you away or he can love you back.

"When is the wedding?" Bradley asked.

"Saturday."

"Well. That certainly doesn't give you much time, does it? I suggest you get onto this right away. What does that give you? Three days? It's your job to convince this man that he is missing the best deal of his life."

"Thanks, Bradley." Erika said softly.

"Hey, what are brothers for?"

Erika got up and put her arms around her little brother. "I love you," she said, "and no matter what happens, I always will."

Her brother held her tight, and she could feel the sobs between them, though she couldn't tell if they were hers or his. It didn't matter. They had always been close enough that it didn't matter.

He didn't want to leave and she didn't want him to go. She hadn't really consider this, but leaving her brother behind was probably the hardest thing she would ever do. It was a little bit like dying. If this worked, she wouldn't see him again in this lifetime. She could only have faith that she would see him in the next.

By the time he left her, both of them had red-rimmed eyes and heavy hearts. Erika refused to face the finality until she knew whether or not she could even travel back in time again.

Half an hour after Bradley had left, Erika stood packing her suitcase, chiding herself all the while. If she was going back in time, she wouldn't need it. She couldn't take it with her, could she?

"It happened more than once, and chances are it'll happen again," Erika said aloud to herself. "There's got to be a reason for it - something more than mere chance. I'm twenty-seven years old and Bradley is right. I've never taken a real risk in my entire life."

She opened the top drawer of her bureau and took out a snapshot of Jonathan's home. She stared at the picture and imagined she was there. A breeze from the river blew softly against her back and she heard the whistle of a steamboat as it prepared to dock.

Then Charles opened the front door and came out dressed in a black tailcoat. He beckoned to her and she was in his arms. Her body pressed against his tall, hard one as his lips pressed against hers.

Then the phone rang and broke her reverie. It was Bradley. Telling her good-bye one last time.

CHAPTER 11

Charles tossed the smoldering cigar stub onto the grass and ground it beneath his foot. If he was going to do it, it had to be now. He had to do it or get back to work.

Squaring his shoulders, he walked the short distance up to the cottage.

Villars's words echoed in his ears as he knocked on the door.

"It's just not fitting for a white man to go get himself smitten with a ghost. I don't want no part of it. I don't want nothing to do with. No, Sir. I don't."

"Well, Villars," Charles said to himself. "You don't believe she's a ghost any more than I do."

He opened the door and stared into clear, green eyes set in a wrinkled face. Silver streaked black hair had been swept back and secured at the top of the woman's head.

Charles started. He had seen this woman on several occasions in the past few years, but only now did the delicate features of the woman's face spur recognition.

He was staring at an older version of Erika.

"Good evening, Madame Vaughn," he said formally.

"Come in. I've been expecting you," she said, as she led him inside.

Unlike Villars, Charles was not afraid of Vaughn. He went inside and took the seat she offered him.

"What is it you need?" she asked.

"Don't you know?"

"And if I do?" She paused and took up her knitting. "Wouldn't it be more polite for you to tell me?"

His father thought her a witch. But witches didn't knit baby blue scarves.

"Very well," he said, reaching inside his pocket for a cigar. "Tell me about her."

Vaughn laughed. Her laughter was gentle and kind, though, much like his mother's.

"I presume you mean the new girl I've seen wandering about the plantation."

"You know her," Charles stated.

"I have watched her."

Charles put the unlit cigar back into his coat pocket. "You're related to her," he said.

Vaughn paused and her knitting needles lay idle in her lap. "You're a wise man. Like your grandfather."

"A blind man could see the resemblance."

"What do you want to know?" she said as she lit a candle on the end table next to her chair.

The evening was growing late. He'd promised Andrea he would read her a bedtime story.

"Is she from the future?"

"Did she tell you that?"

He didn't answer.

"Why do you ask me that?"

Charles studied the older woman's face. He had seen loneliness before. Vaughn was lonely. His grandfather,

Nathaniel Becquerel had brought her here. He wanted to get married, but Vaughn refused. No one knew why.

Shortly after he had set her up in this cottage only a few yards from their home, Nathaniel had a heart attack and died. Vaughn had not been welcomed as part of the family. Richard had said she was a witch.

Nathaniel had been smitten with Vaughn. He had tried to protect her from the harsh words and actions of Richard and a few suspicious neighbors. Nathaniel had been convinced that Vaughn had been gifted with a special sight. One that could only have been acquired from being in the future.

At the time, Charles had not believed him.

"I believe she is. She's different."

"Good," Vaughn said picking up her knitting again.

"Why has she gone?"

"Do you want her back?"

"Yes. What can I do? What can I do to bring her back?"

Vaughn got up and went to sit beside him on the sofa. She took his hands in her withered ones and gazed into his eyes.

"Only love can bring her back."

"I do love her," he admitted softly.

"But do you love her enough to sacrifice everything for her? Do you love her enough to forsake all others?"

Charles looked down at her fragile hands gripping his own with a surprising strength. "I'm not going to marry Elizabeth," he said. "I can't. I don't love her."

"But are you willing to marry Erika?"

"If she were here, I'd marry her this minute."

"You're so like your grandfather." She gently patted his arm and went back to her chair. She began to knit again and seemed to have forgotten him.

After a few minutes, Charles broke the silence. "How do I get her to come back?" He asked again.

"You wait. If your love is strong enough, she will come to you."

CHARLES RETURNED to Erika's room again, and again he could find no sign that she had even been there. He only knew that it hadn't been a dream. Everyone else remembered her, too.

If only he had something tangible. Something to prove she existed.

He sat down on the bed and a small object on the floor caught his eye. He reached down and picked it up. It was the cameo Erika had worn. The pale ivory sculpture was so unlike Erika in its paleness, yet so much like her in its fragility.

It suddenly occurred to him that he had never seen her without this cameo pinned to her bodice. It must have some special meaning for her. He clenched it tightly. It was the only evidence except his wavering memory that he had of her existence.

It was something tangible that he could hold onto.

LESS THAN TWO HOURS LATER, Charles sat alone in his father's study when Villars handed him a letter. Charles ripped it open absently and the elaborate wax seal crumbled and dropped away unnoticed.

"Charles, can I come in?" Rebecca asked opening the door.

Without reading it, he tossed the note into his top desk drawer.

"Of course, Mother." He went around the desk and sat beside her on the sofa.

"What's bothering you?" she asked, placing a hand on his.

"Nothing. Why would you ask that?"

"Everyone's noticed your silence these past couple of weeks.

Even Andrea wants to know why her big brother makes Snow White and Cinderella sound like tragedies."

"I'm sorry. I guess I have been a little preoccupied." He had been more than preoccupied. He had hardly eaten anything. He had roamed the house, hardly speaking to anyone. He hadn't slept. He hadn't shaved. His eyes looked hollow.

"That girl, Erika, you miss her, don't you?"

"Yes."

"You took a liking to her?"

He nodded and went to the window. A liking. That was one way to put it. She had invaded his every thought. The very fiber of his being. He had spent countless hours standing here since Erika had gone away. It was almost as though he were watching for her.

Yet deep inside, he knew, if she came back, she wouldn't come by way of the road.

"A man in your position has to marry a woman of background. You know that. If nothing else, she has to have a strong head for running a plantation. With your brother gone, it's up to you to keep it running," she said and lowered her head. Almost two years after the battle of the Alamo, she still rarely mentioned her youngest son. None of them were able to face the fact that Christopher wouldn't be coming home.

"Erika is all that and more," Charles said, turning back to his mother. "If you could just spend some time with her..." His voice trailed off. The truth was he may never see her again.

"Who was the message from?"

"Elizabeth, I guess."

"Where did you put it?"

"In the drawer," he said absently.

"I suggest that you put it somewhere safe. Don't let your father see it."

"You're right," he said and strode to the liquor cabinet. He poured a shot of whiskey and quickly swallowed it. "I'll talk to Elizabeth. Father won't know until it's too late."

"You're not going to marry her?

He turned and looked into his mother's eyes. She loved Richard. He knew she did despite the man's sometimes vile disposition. "How can I?" he said, "when I don't love her?"

Rebecca came to stand behind him. "If you truly love Erika," she said, "I hope you find her."

She reached up and kissed her son on the cheek. Then she turned and with only the rustle of her skirts, she left him. Charles was left alone, once again, with his own thoughts.

Remembering the note, he went back to the desk and pulled out the key to the right hand drawer. As far as he knew, no one else, not even his father, had a key to this drawer

He retrieved the note and tossed it inside the drawer. But before he could shut it, something caught his attention. He picked up the small rectangle piece of tin and studied its images. He immediately recognized himself and beside him stood Erika.

What really stunned his mind, though, was the image of his brother, Christopher standing next on the other side of Erika. Christopher had never met Erika. That much he was certain of.

The likeness was far too lifelike to be a painting. The images were in black and white, yet they were so real. Someone had captured their very essence on a piece of tin.

But who else had a key to this drawer?

Just on the chance that it was his father, he replaced the picture and took Elizabeth's note with him.

Except for one detail, he would have been elated to find a likeness of Erika.

Christopher had died in Texas.

CHAPTER 12

Huge oak trees stood guard over the drive as it wound its way beneath them. They stood tall and sturdy, brushing the sky with their limbs. The land belonged to the forest. People came and went, from explorers to high rise tenants; only the trees survived the cruel passage of time.

A dark gray curtain of Spanish moss hung from the tree branches. It walled in and isolated the road. The wind ripped at the sodden curtain, tearing at the fortress. A jagged lightning bolt split the darkness and the inevitable crash of thunder shattered the ensuing tension.

A set of headlights struggled to reveal the lonely country road. Once again, Erika mentally scolded herself for not getting on the road earlier.

She gasped as a limb scraped across the roof of the car and forced her attention back on the driving. A shiver raced up her spine, not only from the damp night air, but from the sense of utter isolation. She paid scant attention to her increased speed on the muddy road.

Suddenly there was a man standing in the road before her.

She slammed her foot on the brake. The car skidded to the

right. She jerked the steering wheel in that direction. The seat belt locked itself into position across her shoulder. The car responded to her quick reaction and somehow stayed between the ditches, but it continued to skid forward out of control.

She stiffened and braced herself for collision with the man in front of her.

He stood there, his arms stretched toward her making no effort to save himself. The wind whipped his white shirt, tearing it from his black trousers.

It was him.

When the car was less than three feet from slamming into the man, he vanished. Almost immediately, the car ground to a halt.

It was him. No, it couldn't be.

"Damn," Erika swore, her hands trembling. She strained to see out the back window. There was no sign of the man.

"Where did he go?" She reached over and clicked the door lock button. Just to make sure.

She exhaled slowly and fell back against the velour cushioning. The seat belt relaxed its hold across her shoulder. She took a deep breath and pressed down gently on the accelerator. The rear wheels spun useless in the mud.

"Great," she said with a groan. Now she'd have to get out and walk the rest of the way, in the storm, with a stranger afoot.

Lightning flashed outside the window and thunder crashed on its heels. A limb scraped against the roof of the car. Erika pressed all her strength against the accelerator and the car somehow broke free and lunged forward. She clung to the steering wheel and kept her eyes glued to the road in front of her. She was afraid to glance in the rear view mirror. Afraid of what she might see. Afraid of seeing him.

As she rounded the next curve, a glow of lights flickered through the trees. She drove around behind the house and turned off the motor. The automatic light clicked on and surrounded her in a safe glow.

Had it been Charles? The image of the man standing in the road was quickly fading. The man had been tall and slim like Charles, but it had been hard to make out his features in the storm.

Perhaps it had merely been a spirit. His spirit. Calling out to her. Beckoning.

No, he wouldn't do that.

He probably hadn't missed her for long.

After gathering up her purse and umbrella, she faced the driving, chilling rain. Before slamming the door with her foot, she pulled her small suitcase from the back seat. The umbrella proved itself useless by turning inside out before she could splash around the house and up the steps.

She lifted the brass door knocker for the second time and pounded it, harder than before, against the door. Pulling her coat tighter, she dug in her purse for a key. The wind whipped around the corner, covering her with a misty spray of cold rain.

At last she heard someone shuffling toward the door. "Who is it?" Jonathan called.

"Jonathan, it's me."

"For Christ's sake." He struggled to open the door. "What are you doing out in this mess?"

"I hope I didn't wake you."

He grabbed her suitcase and ushered her in. Erika was grateful to be inside the warm, dry house.

"I wasn't asleep, but why are you here?"

She looked up into the face of the grandfather clock. It was good to hear it ticking again; to have the hours punctuated by its delicate chimes.

"I had to come," she said.

Jonathan grunted and started up the stairs with her suitcase.

Erika went into the parlor and scanned the muddy lane she had come in on. The rain had slowed to a drizzle, but the storm still echoed in the distance. Puddles of water shimmered in the moonlight.

Suddenly she stood very still and her eyes widened. It was him. It was the man she had almost run over. His white shirt glowed softly in the moonlight. His arms were still outstretched toward her.

"Jonathan!" she cried without taking her eyes off the man. "Hurry! Come quick."

"What is it?" Jonathan asked, coming to stand behind her, his breathing labored after hurrying down the stairs.

"It's that man again. I almost ran over him. Do you see him? There, by that tree."

"I don't see anybody," Jonathan said, squinting into the darkness.

Erika turned her head for less than half a second to determine his viewpoint, but when she turned back, he was gone. No one was there.

"He's gone," she said softly and turned away from the window. "But he was there. Didn't you see him?"

Jonathan went back and collapsed on the sofa. He still hadn't fully regained his strength. "No. I didn't see anybody or anything. Why don't you go upstairs and get some rest?"

Erika turned back once more and strained her eyes, but she couldn't see anything anymore. He was out there. Somewhere. She was certain.

"Good night," Erika said, kissed him quickly on the cheek, and hurried upstairs. She undressed and climbed beneath the blankets, exhausted.

She closed her eyes and almost immediately she was sound asleep. It seemed like only minutes later when someone woke her, pounding on the door. "Breakfast. It's eight o'clock. Are you there?"

"I'm here," Erika said, stretching.

Fifteen minutes later, Erika joined her grandfather in the kitchen. Yawning, she sat down at the kitchen table and buttered a piece of toast.

"There is something you aren't telling me," Jonathan said, tearing a corner off the hot chocolate packet, and pouring its contents into a coffee mug.

"Maybe."

"No maybe to it. You don't drive all the way out here on a Wednesday night if nothing's wrong." He glanced at the microwave's digital clock. "I assume you aren't going to work today."

Smokey rubbed against Jonathan's leg and meowed.

"I think he's hungry," she said.

"Are you going?" Jonathan persisted.

"No."

"You took the day off?" he asked, but it was more a statement than a question.

"I quit."

Jonathan filled the cat's bowl with milk and set it down. The cat eagerly lapped up his breakfast.

"I'm serious," he said, impatiently.

"So am I."

"That's the most illogical thing I've ever heard come out of your mouth."

"Jonathan," she pleaded, reaching across the counter for her mug. She stirred the steaming liquid, studying it intently.

"Okay. What happened? You worked too hard to get your degree to walk away from it. What do you need? Money? Just tell me how much and I'll write you a check."

"No. It's not money. It sounds crazy, but do you remember when I disappeared?"

He nodded. "I couldn't forget."

She put the spoon aside and met his gaze. "I can't tell you. You wouldn't believe me. Even I have trouble believing it."

"Try me." He said with his hand clenching his own mug. "Look." He took a deep breath and tried to speak calmly. "From the time the first word came out of your mouth, I've listened to you - your dreams and the fairy tales you concocted in your vivid imagination. I watched you go to college and achieve what you set out to do."

He tried to still his trembling hands. "You always knew the difference between what was real and what was something you created in your mind. You know it now. If you believe in something, you can tell me, if for no other reason than you always have."

Jonathan knocked his cane from its propped position next to the chair. It echoed as it hit the hardwood floor. He grimaced and placed his hand against his forehead.

"Jonathan!" Erika called and hurried to kneel next to his chair. "Are you okay?"

"I'm fine," Jonathan said, waving her away and trying to straighten up. "I'm alright. But I know something happened to you. You were gone for days. You disappeared. And it has something to do with Charles."

Erika dropped into the chair next to his. "Do you believe that someone could go from one time to another?"

"You mean, like into the past?"

"Yes," she said smiling. "Like into the past."

"Why do you ask?"

"Because I met Charles Becquerel. I danced with Charles Becquerel. It was 1837. I know. I was there. I didn't tell you, but I was snake bitten while I was there. I -"

"You were bitten by a snake?" Jonathan echoed, concern in his voice.

"Yes, right here." She pulled down her sock and revealed two minute red scars, side by side.

"Did you see a doctor?" Jonathan asked, frowning.

"No. Charles took care of me," she said, unable to keep the pride from her voice. "He gave me a music box just before-"

"Do you still have it?" Jonathan interrupted.

"Yes. I do." She got up, retrieved her purse from the living room and brought out the little hand painted wooden box.

"Can you go to him?" Jonathan asked, after studying it.

"I don't know." Erika pulled herself back to the present and closed the lid. The music stopped abruptly and so did the spell that had seemed to envelope her. She carefully placed the music box back into her purse.

"I'm not sure it would make any difference. He's getting married Saturday."

"Married?"

"Yes. It's one of those arranged things."

"To Sierra?"

"No. He's actually supposed to marry a girl named Elizabeth Miller."

"I don't recall that name."

"I know. That's what bothers me. Sierra's the one he married, not Elizabeth."

"I wish Vaughn were here. She'd know what to do."

"Why do you say that?" Erika asked, leaning forward.

"No reason. She'd just know. That's all."

Something about his statement nagged at her. Jonathan knew something and he wasn't telling her.

"Did Vaughn ever go back in time?"

Jonathan glanced at her with an odd expression and suddenly went to the sink and started cleaning the dirty dishes.

"Did she?" Erika asked, going to stand beside him.

"How would I know?"

"She would tell you. She told you everything."

He stopped then, closed his eyes, and took a deep breath. "You're wrong. She didn't tell me everything."

"But Jonathan..."

"No. I know nothing." He said and slammed the dishrag against the counter top.

Erika backed away and kneeled down to scratch Smokey's ears. She hadn't meant to anger him. But it was so important that she know. She had to know.

"Are you going back to him?" he asked softly.

"I don't know."

Bradley's words came back to her. *He can turn you away or he can love you back.*

"But you have to try."

"Yes."

"Then marry him. If he's the one you've set your cap for, then go get him. Don't let anything stand in your way - not even time itself."

ERIKA EASED OPEN the attic door and coughed at the dust. She hadn't been up here since she was a little girl and Vaughn had taken her on treasure hunts throughout the old house. Through all these years, one memory stayed with her. That of a huge trunk filled with a world of treasures.

Using the flashlight as a guide, she quickly found the trunk in a corner of the attic. It wasn't as big as she remembered. Kneeling down, she opened the lid. Tears stung the corners of her eyes as memories of Vaughn came flooding back. Vaughn should be with her now; to help her sort things out and figure out what to do.

She carefully riffled through the things. An old Confederate uniform. Someone's dress from the roaring twenties. A pipe. A baby blanket.

Disappointed, she sat back on her heals. Nothing seemed relevant to the plantation days before the Civil War. She had hoped to find something that had belonged to Charles or his family. Something to get her back to him.

Just as she was about to close the lid, the corner of a book caught her eye. The cover was cracked with age and the pages yellowed. Squinting at the smudged ink, she held the flashlight closer. Then she gasped.

"The journal of Christopher Becquerel. 1837."

Charles' brother.

With a shiver, she closed the book and, clutching it to her, made her way down from the attic.

She closed the door to her bedroom and with a tingle at the base of her spine, began to read.

I have come home. It is with some regret that I realize I should have written my family before showing up on their doorstep. After all, they did think I died at the Alamo. Yet somehow I wanted to tell them face to face. And introduce the newest members of our family.

SEVERAL HOURS LATER, Erika finished Christopher's journal and realized she hadn't looked up or taken a deep breath since she started.

She knew she had to go back. Now she knew why Charles had agreed to marry Elizabeth. And why he hadn't. And more importantly, she knew she could save Andrea from an untimely death.

If only she knew how to get back.

She had no idea how to carry it through. Jonathan and Bradley both told her she should go to him. They must think she had some control over it. She was here one minute, there the next. Nothing she did seemed to make any difference.

She took out the music box and opened the lid. She squeezed her eyes tight as the soft music brought back vivid images of Charles.

What was he doing now? Was he sorry she was gone? Or

was he relieved that now he could get on with his life? If the real Sierra showed up, she was in trouble. History was not something to be tampered with.

A car door slammed outside. She closed the music box, ran to the window, and looked down. An old rusty Ford LTD had stopped in front of the house. As she watched, Mable and her son got out.

She gasped. What could they be doing here? As they walked up the front steps, she noticed that the man walked with a limp. She had done that to him. And from his expression, he wasn't here on a social call.

She did have one advantage. Her car was parked around back and they didn't know she was here. She quickly hid the music box in her wardrobe and tried to think. A weapon. She had to find a weapon. She quickly searched the room, but found nothing suitable.

A knock at the door brought her frantic frenzy to a halt. Jonathan had come to warn her. She flung open the door.

"Villars!"

The black servant stood staring back at her equal disbelief.

"What are you doing here?" she asked.

"Why, Miss Erika, I didn't expect to find you here either." Villars said in confusion. "I was just coming up to dust the room."

Erika threw open the wardrobe doors. It was empty except for the gray linen dress they had given her. Her jeans and sweaters and shirts were gone. This time she had nothing; no purse. She groaned in desperation. She had done it. But why now? Why now when Jonathan needed her?

"Is it still 1837?" she asked.

Villars chuckled. "You ain't been gone that long, Miss Erika."

Erika's eyes widened and she felt a lump in her throat. "What day is it?"

"It's Saturday."

"But that's the day after tomorrow."

"No, Miss. It's today."

"But the wedding is Saturday."

"The wedding is today."

"No, it can't be today!"

"Yes, Miss."

"Why aren't you there?"

"I had to get the house ready for Mister Charles and Mistress Elizabeth."

"But he doesn't marry Elizabeth."

"Excuse me, Miss Erika?"

"Nothing. How long before the wedding?"

"Sometime this afternoon. Mister Charles will be back by sundown with his new bride." Villars said, with an unfathomable expression "I got the house all ready."

"Damn," Erika said and collapsed onto the bed. She pressed her hand over her eyes and took a deep breath.

"It's alright. Miss Erika. You don't have to go. Visitors are always welcome here. I'll bring your supper up and Miss Elizabeth won't even know you're here today."

No, she thought. She wouldn't hide like a criminal. Not this time. Last time she had come here involuntarily, but this time she had planned it.

And she had brought nothing with her.

All the effort she had taken to pack things she would need in the past and she had left them all behind. Including the medicine. Well, she would just have to go back for them. And find out what Mable and her son wanted from Jonathan.

When she looked back at a bemused Villars, her face was set in determination. "I can't stay here. I have to leave."

"Yes, Miss Erika. I'll get a carriage," Villars said and reluctantly started for the door.

"No," she said putting her hand out to stop him. "I have to leave on my own."

"I don't think it's a good idea to go out on foot. You might get hurt again. Besides, it's been raining all day and it's not looking to let up."

Erika glanced toward the window. She hadn't even noticed the steady rain. "I don't intend to go outside," she said.

"How do you plan to leave, Miss?"

"I think you know," she said softly. It was a gamble, but she was almost certain Villars had seen her disappear more than once.

She refused to think of the possibility that she might not could leave even if she wanted to desperately. "You do know, don't you?"

Villars fidgeted, but met her gaze bravely. "I know. And some of the others would say how you're an evil witch."

"Do you think I'm an evil witch?"

"I know you're not evil, Miss Erika."

Erika laughed shortly. But he did think she was a witch.

She sat back down on the bed. She had not thought about being viewed as a witch. No one must know - not even Charles - ever. The Salem witch hunts hadn't been that long ago. "Villars. Promise me you won't tell anyone I came back."

"I wouldn't tell, Miss Erika. I wouldn't do nothing to get you into trouble."

"Not even Charles."

Villars grimaced "No, Miss. If that's what you want."

"That's the way it has to be. I'll have to stay in this room. Will you bring my meals up here, like you said? I'll leave just as soon as I can."

Villars left and Erika went to the window, pulled back the heavy navy curtain and pressed her cheek against the cool glass. Rain drops splashed onto the glass, then crept downward to fade into the puddle on the window sill. The gusty wind shook the few brown pine needles from the evergreens and tossed them against the glass before they fell away into the darkness. Erika pressed her forehead against the cool window and gazed unseeing into the blackness.

CHARLES LEANED against a tall oak and blinked the rain from his eyes. The house was shadowed and barely visible in the darkness. The guest room window he stared into was dark and lifeless. Turning away, with no shred of hope remaining, he wiped at his cheeks, but the rain had already washed away the tears.

CHAPTER 13

*L*ater that evening after Erika had finished her supper of fried chicken, corn, peas, and fresh baked bread, Villars returned to pick up the tray.

"Have they made it back yet?" she asked.

"No, Miss. That must be some real celebration over at the Miller's."

Erika winced. Every time he mentioned the wedding or Elizabeth, it was a stab in her heart. "Could you bring me a book up from the library? It doesn't matter which one."

"Of course," Villars said, gathering up the tray.

Now what? Erika thought, going over to stand in front of the window. The evening sun had come out and reflected off the puddles. For what seemed like the hundredth time today, she looked expectantly down the lane. Only this time, it wasn't empty. Clutching the window pane, she stared hard. Squeezing her eyes tightly shut, she looked again.

A Conestoga wagon pulled by six horses lumbered toward the house. She had seen nothing but the finest carriages since her arrival in this century.

A bearded man sat proudly on the seat and beside him, a women clutching an infant.

"Villars, someone's coming."

"It must be Mr. Charles. I better get downstairs."

"No. Wait." She stepped aside. "It's someone else."

"Looks like somebody on their way west. I'll feed 'em some vittles and they'll be on their way," he said, then paused, a frown on his face.

"What is it? Do you know them?"

He continued to stare a moment longer, then shook his head. "Of course not. It's just someone passing through."

Villars hurried downstairs and she watched as the man stopped his conveyance in front of the door and stepped down. Something about the self-assured way he moved reminded her of Charles. He gently took the child and helped the woman down. The woman was thin and dressed plainly, but looked healthy and strong. She smiled at him nervously before they stared toward the front door.

Erika glanced down at herself and sighed. She couldn't very well go downstairs dressed in blue jeans and a sweater. Making a quick decision, she went to the wardrobe and quickly pulled on her gray wool dress, stockings, and leather boots.

Edging down the hallway, she could hear a commotion downstairs. Someone was laughing. At the door to the parlor, she came face to face with the stranger. And looked into a familiar pair of smokey blue eyes.

But even beneath the beard, she knew it wasn't Charles. His eyes were the same, yet his features were subtly different. His smile was definitely different. He was smiling kindly at her.

"Christopher," she said to herself.

"Don't tell me my little brother has gone and taken himself a wife."

"No. I - I..."

"Come on in, I want you to meet my wife."

Erika had never seen a man so proud of his family. He introduced his wife as Milly and their daughter as Rebecca.

Erika felt she knew this man through his journal, yet now that he was here, standing in front of her, he seemed so full of life and vigor.

"Have we met before?" She heard him ask.

"No. I'm a friend of Charles'."

Christopher and Milly stared expectantly at her. Millie absently bounced the baby on her knee.

"I'm Erika," she said, purposively avoiding her last name. Where was Villars anyway?

"Where is everyone?" Christopher asked, seeming to echo her thoughts.

"Didn't Villars tell you?"

"No. He ran off to get a clean diaper for the baby."

Erika swallowed hard. She wasn't sure she liked having the advantage. From his journal, she knew Christopher wouldn't like what she had to say. But apparently it had become her job to tell him.

"They all went over to the Miller's."

Christopher frowned. "Elizabeth Miller's? Whatever for? Mother despises those people."

"Not any more, I'm afraid. You see, Charles is getting married to Elizabeth."

Christopher stared at her, speechless. The baby cooed and Villars rushed back in with a clean white diaper.

"Here you go, Mister Christopher. Miss Andrea's things were all put away, but they'll come in handy with a little one around again," Villars said, then stopped and looked from one to the other of them.

"Villars, is this true?" Christopher asked.

Villars glanced at Erika. She shrugged.

"Is my brother marrying Elizabeth Miller?"

Villars shifted the weight on his feet and lowered his eyes. "Yes, Sir."

"Why on earth..."

"He thinks you want him to," Erika said. Maybe this was the reason she was sent back in time. She had to tell him. "He doesn't love her."

Christopher sprang to action. "I have to stop them."

He quickly brushed a kiss across his wife's lips, and ran out the front door and down the stairs toward the stables. Hearing Erika behind him, he looked over his shoulder, but didn't slow down. "Is there something else you need to tell me?" he asked.

"I'm coming with you," she said running to catch up with him.

He frowned and she lifted her chin in determination.

"Very well. Go get the stable boy to saddle your horse. And hurry."

"There isn't time. I'll ride with you."

"Jeez." He swore as he threw a saddle across the horse's back. "Why do you have to go?"

Erika tore away from his probing gaze and looked down at her booted feet. "I don't want Charles to marry Elizabeth either." Taking a deep breath, she braved a glance at his face, but he ignored her and continued to saddle his horse.

"All right. If you must go. You can ride with me."

Erika exhaled raggedly. She wanted to go, yet she wasn't sure she was doing the right thing. Bradley's words came back to haunt her.

He can love you or he can send you away.

CHARLES STOOD at the front of the church. On the outside, he was calm, but on the inside, he was a mess of clashing emotions.

In a few minutes he was supposed to take a bride. He was to promise to love, honor, and cherish a woman he felt nothing for. It was because of her that his brother went to Texas and never came back. He almost bolted from the church, but held his ground as he remembered his last conversation with Christopher.

"You have to watch over her for me, Charles." Christopher had said.

"I know you love her, but Father isn't going to let you marry her."

"How is he going to stop me?"

"You're the oldest son. You get the plantation after Father's gone. He can disinherit you."

Christopher laughed. "Do you really think I would be so fortunate? You're the one the land belongs to. You're the one who followed Father around in the fields since you could toddle. I only learned the land because he insisted. I'm a scholar, not a farmer."

Charles had worshiped Elizabeth until that day. Once Christopher turned his back and walked away, Elizabeth had shown her true colors. He had watched as she completely destroyed her reputation, cavorting with all the single beaus in the county - and a few married ones.

What did it matter anyway? Erika was gone and with her, she had taken his heart.

There was one thing he was certain of - if Erika had stayed, he would not have gone through with this wedding. When he had seen her disappear in front of him, he had lost his will to fight.

The music changed and all eyes turned to the back of the room. Elizabeth entered. His stomach twisted. She really was beautiful. Like a porcupine. Time seemed to stretch on forever as she made her way toward the altar.

A late guest stepped through the back door. Charles stared

at the bearded man. He knew those eyes. No. It couldn't be. He stared harder. It was! It was Christopher!

Christopher smiled and stepped aside.

Charles blinked hard. Erika? He'd seen her in his dreams so many times, he couldn't believe she was actually here this time. There was such misery and pain in her face. Elizabeth reached the altar and, turning, followed his gaze. She looked like she might be sick.

Charles started down the aisle, ignoring the gasps and whispering that followed in his wake. Reaching his brother, he hugged him close. Then he turned to Erika. He longed to take her in his arms, but something in her expression held him back.

He followed his brother and the woman who was almost his wife into the clergyman's office. And for the first time in weeks, he smiled.

For fifteen minutes, Erika waited tensely. Had they arrived too late? She didn't know if the wedding was beginning or ending. Either way, Charles had obviously been happy to see his brother. But what about her?

It was at that moment that Elizabeth burst from the office and marched back down the aisle. "What are you doing here!" she cried, her face streaked with tears.

"I came with Christopher," Erika said, but despite her guilt, her spirits were rising. If Elizabeth was unhappy, it was a good sign that the news would be good.

"Where is your husband?" she asked following Elizabeth outside.

Elizabeth's face was flushed and her hands trembled. "He's not my husband," she said in a high pitched tone.

"Really?" Erika fought the smile that threatened to spread across her face. "I thought you just had a wedding."

Elizabeth slammed the door to the church and collapsed on a wooden bench. Her delicate ivory wedding dress swirled around her. A bride this beautiful shouldn't be in tears.

"He didn't want to marry me. I forced him. Now Christopher's come back and I've made a mess of everything."

In a sudden burst of sympathy, Erika put her arms around Elizabeth in an effort to comfort her. As her hand brushed beneath the veil, across her back, she realized several of the buttons gaped open.

"Elizabeth," Erika said, "your dress is undone." Before Elizabeth knew what she was doing, Erika had tried unsuccessfully to pull the two sides of the dress together.

"Get away from me," she cried.

"But your dress isn't fastened."

"I am aware of that. It won't fasten." She stood up and pulled the long veil around her shoulders and clutched her stomach.

Realization dawned on Erika and she felt a tug in her chest as her heart began to shatter around the edges. Elizabeth was pregnant. "Does Charles know?"

Elizabeth looked up in confusion. "Of course not. Though it apparently doesn't matter."

Seeing the sick expression on Erika's face, Elizabeth's expression changed and she began to purposely twist the dagger she had unintentionally planted. "How could he know? You really don't think he'd leave me at the altar if he did?"

"Of course he wouldn't," Erika said softly and sat down weakly next to her. Then a tiny spark of hope ignited as she realized Charles wasn't the only man Elizabeth was seeing. "Is it Charles'?"

"Why wouldn't it be? We are engaged," Elizabeth said confidently.

"Well, what about that other man? Thomas."

"You are mistaken, of course," Elizabeth said, but some of her confidence seemed to have subsided.

"I suppose it's rather awkward, not knowing who the father of your child is."

Elizabeth's face turned crimson. "Why, you little spoiled brat. It's none of your business, but I know full well who the father is."

Erika didn't believe her completely, but had no choice. "What are you going to do?"

"What do you mean?"

"Are you going to have it?"

A trace of fear crossed Elizabeth's face. "I don't seem to have a choice, do I?"

"You could have an abortion."

Elizabeth's eyes widened. "You mean, kill it?"

"I suppose. An abortion."

"No. I would never kill my child."

"If you have it, your reputation will be ruined forever."

"I'm going to have it. And it is going to have a father. I will see to that."

"I suggest you choose its father quickly. You can't go around dressed like that much longer."

"Erika," Elizabeth said grasping her arm. "Charles is the father and he will take responsibility for his actions. You stay away from him or I'll - I'll tell my father."

Charles and Christopher burst through the door.

"Did you tell them?" Charles asked.

"Not yet," Elizabeth said, looking down to her hands folded in her lap.

"You've got to," Charles said, grasping her arms.

"Charles. Stop it," Christopher said, pulling his brother away. Kneeling in front of Elizabeth, he took her hands. "Do you want me to tell them?"

"Christ! You can't do it, Christopher. She has to."

"Charles. Let me handle this."

"It's alright. I'll do it," Elizabeth said and got to her feet.

With a glance at Erika, she opened the door and went back into the church. Christopher followed.

"Where the hell have you been?" Charles asked, running a trembling hand through his hair.

"I had to go to my grandfather."

"I thought my father had finally gotten to you."

"Are you going to marry her?"

"No."

"Did you notice anything different about her?"

"Like what?"

"She seems to have put on a little weight."

"It happens to women her age."

Erika winced. She was probably five years older than Elizabeth. She hadn't put on any extra weight.

"Charles..."

"She did it. She called it off." Christopher said, coming back outside. "Let's go. I want you to meet my wife."

The three of them hurried out to Charles' coach before the crowd could descend upon them. Christopher tied his horse to the coach, but didn't join them inside.

"You two go ahead. I'm going to find Mother and Father and ride back with them.

Now that they were alone, Erika could feel the tension between them. Wordlessly, Charles reached out and touched her hair.

Before she knew what was happening, he had taken her in his arms. With a deep groan, he kissed her. His hands moved down to unbutton her dress and with a start she felt his hands against her bare flesh.

Then her dress was in the floor and he pressed her down on the leather seat. All the pain and longing of being apart propelled their passion to new heights.

She felt his hardness against her thigh and strained against him.

"I've missed you," he breathed against her ear. "Don't ever leave me again."

Erika's heart swelled. She belonged to this man.

"I want you," he murmured against her ear.

With those words, Erika was lost in sensation. His lips were soft and demanding against hers. His hands tangled in her hair and ran gently along her back.

His tongue sought hers and plunged deep inside her mouth.

She was exactly where she wanted to be.

CHAPTER 14

"*Y*ou've got to be putting me on," Christopher said.

"No," Charles said, "You do remember making me promise, don't you?"

After a tearful welcome, the two brothers had escaped to Charles' garconnaire. Christopher was happy to leave the baby with the women and enjoy the late afternoon with a good cigar and even better whiskey.

"Of course I do, but it's been so long, I thought surely you wouldn't stick to it."

"I promised you, Christopher. I was going to carry it out even though it would have ruined my life. Why the hell didn't you write?"

"I wanted to see you in person. I never thought you'd be about to marry the little witch."

"I wouldn't have, except for Father."

"The land."

"Yes. He'd sell his soul for that piece of land."

"Well, it's taken care of now."

What do you mean?"

"He won't be bothering you about it any more. I explained it all to him on the way back from the Miller's."

"What did you tell him?"

"I just told him how it was."

"Christopher, what did you tell him?"

"I just told him how Elizabeth was and all."

Charles laughed. "He always did listen to you. I don't know why. You never spent any time with him. He seems to think you're the smart one in the family."

"I am."

Charles threw a pillow at his brother and they dissolved on the floor in a wrestling match.

"All right. I give up," Charles cried after his brother had him pinned to the floor. "What did they do to you out there? You've got the strength of an Indian."

"You have to," Christopher answered seriously. "You never know when your life will depend upon your strength. It's a wonderful place. But it's a hard life."

"Will you go back?"

"We'll go somewhere. Maybe to California. After living in the wide open spaces, I couldn't stay here for very long."

Charles had been as far east as West Point, but he'd never been out west. He'd always known he would be responsible for running the plantation.

"What about you," Christopher asked, "tell me about Erika."

Charles smiled. That was a topic he could get into. "What about her?"

"Is it serious?"

"It could be," he said thoughtfully. "She's a lot like Vaughn."

"Grandpa's Vaughn?" He asked, incredulously.

He nodded.

"You boys sure can pick 'em."

"Father despises her." Suddenly he remembered the likeness he'd found in the study desk. He thought about telling

Christopher, but it was too odd. That was something a man had to keep to himself. He wondered how it would turn out.

"Despite the fact that she's strange," Christopher said, teasingly, "is it serious?"

Charles smiled. "I didn't say she was strange, but yeah. It's serious. I'm gonna marry her."

"Come on."

"No, really. She's the woman I can't get enough of."

"That exactly why I married Milly. But then Milly really is plain. Erika is anything but plain."

"She's gorgeous, isn't she?"

"Yeah, it's a good thing I'm already married, little brother."

ERIKA PICKED at the egg on her plate and broke her biscuit into bite-size pieces. The grandfather clock chimed eight times. She had waited until the rest of the family had finished breakfast and gone about their business before she had put on her gray dress and come downstairs.

She hadn't seen Charles since he'd helped her out of the carriage. She assumed he'd been with Christopher, as he should have been. Still, she felt neglected and a little lost.

She had worried over Elizabeth and her unborn child. She claimed Charles was the father and Erika had no reason not to believe her. She wasn't concerned about her threat that Perry would come after her if she didn't stay away from Charles. She was worried about what Charles would do. He would very likely see it as a matter of honor and marry Elizabeth.

But what if he married her and wasn't the father?

And there was still the matter of Sierra. According to history, she was the one he would marry and she hadn't even shown up.

"Miss Erika," Sadie said coming into the dining room. "Why aren't you eating your breakfast?"

"I guess I'm just not hungry." Her head was throbbing from the confused thoughts that ran rampant through her mind.

"You should eat your breakfast."

Erika dipped a spoonful of strawberry jam onto the pieces of biscuit. "Have you seen Charles today?"

"No. But he'll show up. Don't you worry none about Mr. Charles."

"I sure was looking forward to having another woman around the house to do this kind of stuff. Mistress Rebecca has her hands more than full," Villars said coming into the room with basketful of fall flowers. He set it down on the table next to a row of empty vases.

"Let me do that," Erika said, jumping at the opportunity to do something.

"I meant the mistress of the house, Miss. You're a guest."

"Nonsense," she said and went around the table and separated the flowers into the two vases. "It looks to me like I've moved in. I can do this just as well as Elizabeth could have."

"Elizabeth wouldn't have lifted a finger," Sadie mumbled.

Villars grumbled about something not being proper, but nonetheless he seemed pleased that Erika wanted to help.

After she finished putting the flowers in the vases, Erika wandered into the library. She was in the process of choosing a book to read when the front door slammed.

She froze. She didn't want to see Richard and she didn't know how Rebecca and Andrea would respond to her return. But there was a possibility that it could be Charles. Her heartbeat quickened, she hurried to the library door and peeked around the corner.

Villars, too, had heard the door and come into the foyer.

Albert! What was he doing here?

Erika jerked back from the door and went quietly back to the sofa. She grabbed a book from the bookcase and opened it, but stared at the door. Her pulse pounded in her ears. She wiped her sweaty palms on her skirt and realization struck her. Without Charles here to intercede, she was afraid of Albert.

She clenched her eyes shut. When she opened them, Albert stood leaning against the door casing, watching her. His expression was bold as he smiled at her. The smile was not friendly.

"I see you made it back," he said. "Charles was worried about you."

She bit her lower lip, but didn't say anything

"You're the talk of the town, you know. Showing up here like this."

He stood up straight and took a step forward.

Her eyes darted right and left, but there was no where to run.

"But then I'm sure you know that since you're the reason he didn't marry Elizabeth."

"No," she said, shaking her head.

He reached behind him and slammed the door shut. Then in two short strides he stood over her and grabbed her wrist.

"What did you do to make him leave her? A little sway of the hips. Maybe a lowered bodice."

His hand reached out for the front of her gray dress.

"Stop it," she shrieked and twisted away. If this dress was ruined, she would have nothing to wear but her blue jeans and sweater.

He grabbed for her again, successful this time, and wrapped his fingers around the neckline of the dress.

"Charles thinks you're just an innocent girl who wandered off from home. But I know better. I can see the lies written across your face. You're a runaway bond servant. You're somebody else's property."

He jerked his hand back and the dress ripped down the front, revealing her thin chemise.

"You'll be going back to your master soon because I've

reported you. Soon you'll be claimed by your rightful owner. But first I'm going to borrow you."

Suddenly his large hands were all over her. They slid over her chemise, riding it up, roughly fondling her breasts. Then a hand slipped between her legs.

"Villars!" Erika screamed, fighting him.

"He won't come. He won't come to rescue you. Nobody will. The family's gone into town and the workers won't intercede the actions of an old friend toward a bond servant."

"Stop it," she cried again, trying to grab his hands. "I'm not a bond servant."

He captured both her hands in one of his and ripped her chemise. Then he was straddled on top of her. Albert was a big man and she was powerless beneath him.

His lips were wet and sloppy against hers. She turned her head away and immediately wished she hadn't. His head dipped to her breasts.

"No!" she cried, tilted her head back, and screamed a horrible scream of terror.

Suddenly the door burst open and bounced off the wall. Charles was in the room and had hauled Albert away by the neck in a split second.

Erika clutched her torn clothing together, trying to cover herself.

Charles drew his fist back and slammed it into Albert's face. Albert fell back against the floor, his nose crushed.

"What the hell do you think you're doing?" he asked with anger seething from every pore.

He didn't wait for an answer. He pulled Albert back and pummeled him again wildly in the face and stomach.

Suddenly Richard was in the room. "What's all the commotion?"

He took one glance at Erika's flushed face and torn clothing and hauled his son off a now semi-conscious Albert.

"What's gotten into you?" he asked, holding Charles' arms and glaring into his narrowed eyes. "What are you doing?"

Charles didn't answer, but pulled away from his father, straightened his shirt, and assessed Erika.

"Are you alright?" he asked gently.

She swallowed and nodded quickly.

Albert groaned audibly.

"You could have killed him," Richard said. "Apologize and get him upstairs so your mother can clean him up."

Charles turned his piercing eyes on his father, his fists clenched at his sides, and his jaw clenched dangerously.

"Father, I will not apologize."

He stepped next to Albert and placed one black booted foot in the center of his previously best friend's stomach.

"I demand satisfaction."

CHARLES URGED HIS HORSE ONWARD, ignoring the foaming lather on its skin. The dogs had fallen back some time ago. Only then did he notice the paddle wheeler chugging along with him. He had followed the river road for several miles and didn't know how long he'd been racing the steamboat.

He slowed the horse to a trot and several passengers aboard the *Natchez* who had gathered to watch him waved as they passed him and continued up the river. He didn't wave back. They were too far away to see the scowl that lined his features.

He rode down to the river's edge and allowed the horse to drink the murky water. At least he would be able to think coherently now that he had outrun some of his frustrations.

His best friend had betrayed him. His best friend for all of his thirty-one years. He laughed, a hollow sound without humor. He had ended their life-long friendship without hesitation over the honor of a woman he had met little more than a month ago.

Perhaps he was a fool as his father had yelled accusingly after him. He may be, but he had never felt so alive as he did when he was with Erika. She was his. And no one on this earth was going to hurt her.

Thank heavens he had gotten back to the house in time. If he hadn't, Albert would have raped her, right there in his own home. What could have come over Albert? Charles shook his head. He really didn't care. The memory of Erika helplessly struggling against Albert still made Charles irrationally angry.

Reasons didn't matter. Tomorrow at dawn Albert would pay for what he had done.

His best friend had betrayed him.

It was late into the evening before Charles went home. The house was quiet. The family had no doubt gone on up to bed in preparation for an early morning tomorrow.

He went straight up to Erika's room and was a little relieved to find no light beneath her door. He wouldn't have known what to say to her anyway. Going down to the dining room, he found a full plate of leftovers waiting for him.

He had just begun to devour the seasoned fried chicken when his father came into the room and drew up a chair beside him.

Charles watched him warily. Richard would want him to call the whole thing off.

"Feeling better?" Richard asked with surprising calmness.

"I'm still going through with the duel, if that's what you mean."

"I expected no less from my son."

"You aren't going to try to stop me?"

"I couldn't if I wanted to."

Charles studied his father. If he didn't know better, he would have said that was pride in his eyes.

"You love her," he stated, "don't you?"

He had since the first time he'd seen her. It hadn't mattered then who she was or where she came from and it certainly didn't matter now. After yesterday in the carriage, his desire had only increased. He thought about her constantly.

"Charles, I want to be your second."

Charles' sterling silver fork clattered to the floor.

"Christopher has already asked."

"Then you'll have two. I'm too old to care about protocol."

He studied his father and for the first time wondered if he had made the right decision. What if something did happen to him? If Charles were to die, there would be no one here to carry on the family name or run the plantation. Christopher didn't want it. He was already making plans to leave again.

It took all the will power he possessed not to say he'd apologize and call it off. His parents couldn't stand to lose another son. Even though Christopher had come back, his parents had mourned for a year. They couldn't take that again. He took a deep breath.

"I'd be honored," he said.

IT WAS STILL DARK when Erika woke the next morning. She put on an emerald green day dress Rebecca had given her last night. A couple of tucks in the waist and it fit almost perfectly. Charles' mother had been aghast that Erika still had nothing to wear. Charles had assured his mother that he had been taking care of her. She wouldn't have understood about her taking the pink gown with her to another time where it had been left.

In a couple of hours, a duel would be fought over her honor.

Charles had warned her about the anger of the Creoles. She had been almost as frightened of him as she had been of Albert. The last thing she wanted was for Charles to think she had done something to bring on Albert's attack. To her relief, he never even brought it up.

Thoughts of Albert sent a shiver down her spine. She had never expected Charles' best friend to behave so dishonorably.

Honor.

It hadn't taken her long to begin to think like these people.

She had been glad to see Charles. Now she was frightened. They had hardly even spoken since her return. Of course, that episode in the carriage spoke volumes. And he had nearly killed his best friend over her without even stopping to ask questions. She almost smiled. He must care about her a great deal to have fought so fiercely for her.

For her or for honor?

Albert believed she was a bond servant, another man's property. He claimed she had run away from her master.

Suddenly she remembered something he had said. He had reported her to the authorities. Someone could try to claim her. What would Charles do? Would he let her go? She knew Richard would be glad to see her go. He hadn't seemed at all surprised to find her half naked on his couch.

Charles was the one who protected her. If he should be killed, she would have no reason to be here in this time. She would probably even be cast out on her own if not collected by someone claiming she was his bond servant.

She had come here to be with Charles. He mustn't die. She couldn't allow him to fight the duel. She had to stop him.

Her honor wasn't worth his life.

CHAPTER 15

Charles blew on his fingers and rubbed his hands together. Flexing his fingers, he studied the dozen men, half of whom were gathered to watch him die.

"They'll be disappointed," he said aloud to himself.

Richard and Christopher huddled together, whispering. It was comforting to have their support. Albert had no family left and only a few friends hung around. Probably more to see a good duel than in concern for Albert. He hadn't really noticed that Albert didn't have a lot of other friends other than himself.

"I thought you had better sense than this."

Charles turned at the unexpected voice behind him. A man about the same age and a couple of inches shorter than Charles stood watching him.

"Alexandre!" The two men clasped hands and roughly embraced.

"It's been so long. What are you doing here?"

"I only got in last night. I'd planned to ride over tonight, but then I heard the unfortunate news."

Charles frowned and glanced back toward Albert.

"Only a woman can come between friends, *non*?" Alexandre asked.

"I am merely protecting my reputation and defending the honor of a lady."

"According to the rumor, she is a runaway servant."

"That's Albert's rumor. Actually she's..." *She's from the future.* "not a servant, I can assure you. She's merely been separated from her family"

"I see. And you've taken it upon yourself to take care of her."

"It's not like that."

"Don't you know that no one fights duels anymore?"

"Maybe nobody does, but I'm about to."

His father was speaking quietly to Albert's second. Charles needed to be alone. He needed to prepare himself.

"Won't you join us for dinner tonight?" Charles asked as though they had met on the street. A casual observer wouldn't have known that he was about to kill his best friend or die himself.

"Of course."

Charles turned his back and began to concentrate. He had to put everything but the gun out of his mind. He was a good shot. Always had been.

"Charles. Albert." The short, stocky Dr. Alkin moved with his little black bag so that he could see each of the men. "I implore you to call off this foolishness. No good can come of either of your deaths. Your quarrel can be settled sensibly."

No one seemed to notice the sun hadn't actually come up, but kept its face hidden behind the clouds. Perhaps it, too, wanted to avoid watching the scene below.

Albert continued to stare into space and made no response.

The doctor turned to Charles who merely nodded. As the two men took their places back to back, Albert met Charles' eyes for a brief instant. Charles sucked in his breath. There was no remorse in his friend's eyes. Only a deep hatred. Where had it come from?

Albert was a large man, tall, as well as broad, but Charles was a couple of inches taller with a trimmer figure.

"Make your peace," Albert said over his shoulder.

"You're making a mistake," Charles said calmly.

"That remains to be seen."

The doctor began to count off the ten paces. The two men walked slowly away from each other. An owl hooted somewhere in the groove of trees. A raindrop hit Charles in the eye and he blinked it away.

"Ten!" As the doctor's voice echoed across the field, Charles raised his right arm and turned slowly and steadily. In less than a second he was in firing position.

But he didn't fire.

Albert made a sloppy turn and waved his gun unsteadily. He squinted and tried to line up the pistol with some part of Charles' body. His nervousness was evident in his clenched jaw. Even as children, Charles had been the better shot.

Still, Charles did not fire. His gaze never wavered from Albert's face.

"You've got him, man. Do it!" Alexandre's voice broke the silence but only increased the tension as his words hung on the air like shots themselves.

A galloping horse came closer and closer until it ground to a halt in the trees only yards away. No one dared glance away from the two men standing face to face. Then it was silent again.

Charles watched Albert down the barrel of his gun. Suddenly he pitied Albert. He also pitied himself because he knew their relationship could never again be the same and he would miss the friend he had once cherished.

Albert's position changed. He relaxed the grip on his gun and squinted toward his opponent.

Still, Charles did not fire.

Without warning, Albert squeezed the trigger. The shot rang out across the clearing. Neither man moved. Everyone's eyes searched back and forth between them, no one really quite sure which one of the men had fired.

Then Albert dropped his gun and fell to his knees. "Shoot me," he demanded. "I want to die."

"What makes you think I would hit you?" Charles asked softly, barely heard even in the silence. He could feel himself fading.

"You're a perfect shot. You never miss. Please..." Albert put his hands together over his face and put his head down on the ground.

"Your murder isn't worth burning in hell for, Albert." Charles whispered and shot his gun straight up into the air. He glanced at his right shoulder and noticed the dark stain spreading across his white shirt. Then he felt his knees buckling and it was getting darker and darker. He fell unconscious onto his stomach.

"No," Erika cried and slid from the horse's back.

Albert lifted his head and glared at her. "You killed him," he said pointing in her direction.

"No." Erika cried again and felt one foot touch the ground. The other one was hung in the stirrup. She slipped and the next thing she felt was the ground slapping her in the face.

Forcing her chin up, she saw Dr. Alkin rolling Charles over. Her bottom lip started to quiver and tears started to roll down her dusty, scraped cheeks. She jerked her foot out of the contrary stirrup and brushed the hair out of her damp face.

She couldn't bear to look at Charles lying there helpless. The image of the two men standing there face to face with pistols pointing at each other was too much of a shock.

After the shot rang out, she had known something was wrong. Charles had slowly become deathly pale and she seemed to have been the only one to see the growing stain on his shirt. She wanted to cry out, to reach him, but it happened so fast. She couldn't make her body move.

"He's not dead." Doctor Alkin said impatiently. "Now get back and give him room to breathe."

She jerked her head up as Charles opened his eyes. The doctor tore open his black bag and pulled out a bottle of whiskey and a pair of forceps. He ripped open the blood soaked shirt and gently lifting Charles' head, forced him to drink.

He followed the bullet's path into the flesh of Charles' shoulder and, after rummaging around a bit, pulled out the bullet. Charles hadn't uttered a sound, but had passed out cold again.

Dr. Alkin rummaged in his bag for several strips of cloth which he then wrapped around Charles' shoulder and tied in a knot.

Erika looked away and winced. Something was wrong. But she couldn't think clearly with her face stinging from the fall and her leg pounding. Dr. Alkin had done something wrong. If that wound became infected, Charles could die.

That was it! Infection. He had to wash the wound and put on a clean, sterilized dressing. But then this was 1837. Doctors were often more harmful than helpful. She had to tell them. Had to make them do it right.

"Doctor. Wait," she cried and tried to get up.

She was surprised when Richard appeared at her side and helped her up.

"Thanks," she said, watching him suspiciously.

"Are you alright?" he asked.

"Yes, but we've got to help Charles. We've got to kill the germs."

He backed away from her. Whatever kindness had passed between them, suddenly dissipated.

"What are you?" He asked, his face turning red. "Have you

come here to cast evil upon my family? We've had nothing but ill fortune since you first appeared in our house."

"Most of it's been my misfortune," she said below her breath as she dusted herself off and began picking the dirt and leaves from her hair.

Casting him a warning glance, she strode toward Charles. The doctor stood back admiring his work.

"Dr. Alkin," she said, taking the bottle of whiskey from him. Fortunately Charles had passed out again. Before anyone could stop her, she had untied the bandage and plied the cloth from Charles' wound.

She tilted the whiskey bottle and poured it over his shoulder. Charles groaned.

Richard grabbed her arm and pulled her away. "What are you doing, trying to kill him?"

"No," she said, suddenly angry at the knowledge that they wouldn't even bother to listen to her. She had probably just saved Charles' life.

Two other men Erika didn't know approached them and took Erika from Richard's hold. They each held one of her arms gently, but she could feel the threat beneath their grasps.

"We've got to get him home," the doctor said, quickly rewrapping his patient's wound. "Does anyone have a coach?"

Dr. Alkin scanned the men's faces, but each one stood in silence, between watching him and watching Erika.

"Very well. We'll have to get him up on his horse and move slowly."

It had begun to rain in earnest now. Black clouds had halted the coming dawn.

At first Erika didn't notice the man watching her. But as she stood here, held in place between the two men, with the rain washing her hair into her eyes, she was drawn to his kindly face. He was a tall man, almost as tall as Charles. He was handsome, too, with light brown hair, but his skin was much paler than Charles'.

Dr. Alkin, Richard, and the other men managed to bring Charles to consciousness and put him unsteadily upon his horse. Once again Erika had reason to doubt the doctor's wisdom. Charles' mouth was set in a grim line and his face had lost a great deal of its color.

The man who had been standing aside, watching Erika, approached her now.

"Release her," he demanded.

Erika felt her arms released. The two younger men shrugged and walked away.

"Thank you, Sir."

"It is my pleasure... Miss?"

"Erika Becquerel."

"Ah, so you're Erika."

As she brushed back her drenched hair, she noticed Albert sitting on his horse. He glanced in her direction, then rode away. She shivered.

"He just rides away," she said.

"Yes. It's a duel. A ridiculous affair. But here, you're going to catch your death. I'll take you home. I assume you're still staying with Charles."

Was that a frown of disapproval that crossed his face. Why did she care?

"Yes... But I wouldn't ask you to do that."

"I insist."

He retrieved their horses and after looking at her strangely, helped her mount the horse astride. Of course, all ladies rode side saddle and the battle with the stable hands had been enough excitement for one day. She was grateful that Alexandre didn't comment on her choice of saddle.

Except for the fact that she had probably saved Charles from infection, she wished she had stayed home. The wind had picked up tossing the tree limbs about and she was reminded of the night when she had nearly collided with that man in the road. Was that just two nights ago? She couldn't keep up any more.

Thunder rumbled overhead and a feeling of foreboding settled over her.

"Have you studied medicine?" he asked, interrupting her thoughts.

"A little."

"I thought as much. Back there, you seemed to know what to do."

"It's really just common sense," she said flatly, not bothering to look at him. He left her alone the rest of the way home. Erika hardly noticed the silence.

After he had dropped her off at the front door and was leading her horse toward the stables, Erika realized she hadn't even asked his name.

Once inside, she immediately started up the stairs to locate Charles.

"Good Lord! What were you doing out in that storm?" Rebecca asked from the head of the stairs.

"I... I -"

"I'll order you a hot bath. Get to your room and get out of those wet clothes."

"But, Charles?"

"He's asleep. Now off with you."

Erika went to her room and waited while the tub was filled with steaming water. When she settled into the tub she realized she was chilled to the bone.

Who was the man who had so gallantly brought her home?

She had been inexcusably rude to him. She felt a tinge of regret that she would probably never see him again. After her experience with Albert she could have used a good friend.

What on earth had come over Albert? She couldn't help but

smile at the way Charles had attacked his best friend in her behalf without even waiting for an explanation.

The smile disappeared as she remembered him falling wounded to the ground. He had almost died for her.

If Charles had died, she didn't know what she would have done. She had to talk to him. She had to tell him the way she felt before something did happen to prevent it. That was the problem. Neither knew how they felt about each other.

But what if he didn't feel the same way about her?

He can turn you away or he can love you back. You need to know one way or the other.

With determination, Erika stepped out of the now cool water and wrapped the towel around herself. After he had a few hours rest, she would tell him.

WHEN CHARLES AWOKE a couple hours later, he felt much better. Making it home was one of the hardest things he had ever done. The only thing he remembered about the ride home was the storm, the cold, wet storm. The instant they had grasped him to pull him off the horse, he had collapsed again.

He hadn't really expected Albert to shoot him. He knew Albert could have killed him if he had wanted to. He just didn't think his best friend would shoot him.

Former best friend, he corrected, as he sat up on the edge of the bed. He had spent days trying to sort out his feelings for Erika and to make sense of her disappearance. Thank heavens he had come to the house when he had. Villars had burst into the garconnaire, pleading with them to help her. Charles still didn't know how he got to the house so fast, but he knew he would have killed anyone who harmed Erika. He probably would have, too, if his father hadn't intervened.

What would Richard do now, he wondered. After pulling on a clean white cotton shirt, he started down the stairs.

Suddenly, he jammed his hand into his pocket. With a sigh of relief he pulled out the cameo. He had put it there for luck. He went out the front door and collapsed on the bench. He knew he would eventually have to give the cameo back to Erika, but until then he would hold onto it.

Charles didn't hear the coach until it pulled into sight. He watched it with growing apprehension. Elizabeth was not the person he wanted to deal with after all he had been through today.

He didn't recognize the white driver who jumped down and opened the door. First came tiny feet, then a glimpse of white petticoat followed by folds of blue. His mouth dropped when he saw the vision that stepped out before him. She was petite with long blonde curls falling loosely around her shoulders. Her features were delicate and her skin a smooth creamy white. She was beautiful.

And she was walking toward him.

"Good afternoon," the young woman said sweetly.

"Good afternoon," Charles echoed.

"You must be my cousin, Charles." She held out her hand, palm down. "You don't recognize me, do you? I'm Sierra. Your cousin from Memphis."

CHAPTER 16

Charles realized Sierra held her hand out to him. He gently took it in his and kissed it lightly.

"Really, Charles. You mustn't gape. Now, I haven't changed that much, have I?"

"You're Sierra? Sierra Becquerel."

She nodded and smiled sweetly.

"Little, scrawny Sierra?"

"Well, I hardly think I'm scrawny, now do you?"

"Yes, hardly."

"You were expecting me, weren't you?"

"Yes. But I thought... I thought..."

"It's okay, Cousin. You look a little different yourself. But aren't you going to invite me in?"

Charles regained his senses and stepped aside. "Of course, I am. Do come in, Cousin Sierra. You are always welcome in our home."

"You do have a lovely home. I've always thought it was."

"Thank you. How is your family?"

"Very well. Thank you. Father's ague seems to be on the

mend. He swears he's going to stay away from New Orleans, but I don't believe it for a minute."

Charles laughed. "Villars, I'd like you to meet our guest," he said, his eyes never leaving Sierra.

"Welcome to Becquerel Estate, Miss."

"Why thank you, Villars. You remember me, don't you?"

"This is my dear cousin, Sierra," Charles said.

Villars' smile faded into a look of confusion and finally into the same expression Charles had worn when she stepped from the coach. "God help us," he murmured, looking heavenward.

"My goodness. Have you fellows forgotten what a woman looks like?"

"Come now, Villars. Let's not make our guest feel uncomfortable. This is my cousin and we'll treat her as one of the family."

"Yes Sir."

"Now you take Miss Sierra on upstairs to her room and see that she's made comfortable. Then I'll be needing you down here."

Villars didn't move. A young lad came into the foyer with one of Sierra's trunks.

"Well, go on."

"Mister Charles, should I put Miss Sierra in your old room?"

Charles started to say no, but then he remembered that Erika was in the guest room. That would have been a catastrophe.

"Yes. Of course," he hastily answered, smiling at Sierra.

Villars swallowed and led Cousin Sierra up the stairs.

Charles went into the study and poured himself a drink, spilling as much sherry beside the glass as in it. He suddenly wanted to be back upstairs in bed, but he barely made it to the sofa before he collapsed in weak exhaustion.

. . .

WHILE ERIKA DRIED her hair in front of the fire, Villars brought her a breakfast tray.

"Is Charles alright?" she asked, pouncing on him for any information.

"He's fine, Miss Erika. He's sleeping downstairs on the sofa."

"On the sofa? Why isn't he in bed?"

Villars chuckled. "Nothing can keep Mr. Charles down for long. He's done been up and went outside on the porch."

"Can I see him?"

"No ma'am," Villars said seriously. "If you wake him up, Mistress Rebecca will have your hide."

"All right. I won't wake him up, yet," she said, sitting in front of the fireplace to eat the eggs, bacon, biscuits, and hash browns Villars had brought her.

Before Erika had finished her breakfast, Sadie came in to curl her hair. She then pulled back her thick hair and tied a bow high at the back of her head.

Erika surveyed the results in the mirror. She had put on one of Rebecca's simple ecru gowns and her own sneakers. She was growing accustomed to wearing the long dresses and nothing more than a little rice powder on her face. She felt almost at home in this perplexing year of eighteen thirty seven.

She quietly made her way downstairs. She wouldn't wake Charles. She just wanted to see for herself that he was okay. Stopping at the parlor door, she gazed at his face. Asleep, he couldn't hide the pain. His breathing was heavy and his forehead deeply creased. She had probably risked her welcome here in pouring that liquor on his open wound. But she would risk anything, even her life, to save his.

Erika slipped quietly out the front door and started down the path leading to the cemetery. She paused in front of the white guest cottage. The old woman was there, sitting on the porch. She stood up and started down the steps toward her.

The woman's face was in shadows from a hooded cape

pulled low over her eyes. Erika's heart began to pound frantically. Her palms were damp.

She knew this woman. She was certain of it. That knowledge frightened her near to death.

Standing face to face with Erika, the woman slowly pushed back the hood.

It was Vaughn.

Erika staggered blindly to the picket fence and leaned weakly against it, her eyes never leaving her grandmother's face.

"No," she said. "It can't be."

"Erika," Vaughn said, holding a hand out toward her.

"It can't be. Yet, you're here. In 1837."

A single tear rolled slowly down Erika's cheek. Her feet didn't move.

"You aren't the only one it's happened to. I just planned mine a little better, that's all."

"Planned?" Erika asked, suddenly jolted out of her silence. "You can't plan to have an accident and die."

Vaughn dropped her hand and turned to the side. "You're right. No one can plan an accident. But with a little help, you can fake it."

Erika couldn't believe what she was hearing. Vaughn had feigned her own death in order to leave her husband and family to come back in time? But why?

"Charles' grandfather, Nathaniel," Vaughn said as though in answer to her thoughts. "I was in love with him."

"But Jonathan."

"Oh, I loved Jonathan, too. I still do. But I also fell in love with this time. It's so peaceful here."

"You chose this as a way of life?"

"Didn't you?" Vaughn asked.

Erika flushed with guilt. She, too, had made the decision to come here. Only she'd carried it out by accident. Was that different? She didn't know.

"Who helped you?" Erika asked.

Vaughn closed the distance between them and took Erika's hand. "Let's go sit down on the porch."

With a sob, Erika threw her arms around her grandmother. She cried freely now, all the events and emotions of the past few weeks breaking free from their dam and gushing forth. And she felt a certain relief - relief that someone was here who understood - who knew.

Vaughn gently patted her back, then led her up the steps. She went inside and quickly returned with a handkerchief for Erika to dry her eyes.

"Vaughn, I missed you so much. I grieved for you. Why didn't you tell us?"

"Would you have believed me?"

"I don't know. I could have been given the chance."

"Would you have forgiven me?"

Erika knew that wouldn't be as easy to answer. Vaughn had chosen to end her way of life. She had walked away from her family.

"I didn't want to take that chance," Vaughn said. "I would rather have you grieve for me than to hate me."

"Where is Charles' grandfather now?"

"Just a few weeks after I... moved here permanently, he had a heart attack. He didn't suffer much and he made sure I'd be taken care of."

"You didn't marry him?" Erika asked hesitantly.

"No," she answered quickly.

"Why not?"

"Jonathan," she said simply.

"Have you told Charles?"

Erika gaped at her grandmother. "You know about Charles?"

"He came to me. About you. He recognized that we were related somehow."

"I did, but I don't think he believed me."

Vaughn carefully removed the scarf from her neck and folded it neatly. "If your positions were reversed would you believe him?"

Erika knew it would be impossible. It would take an inordinate amount of faith in someone to believe something like that.

"But how did you carry it out? Who else knew?" Erika asked, changing the subject.

Vaughn unfolded her scarf and placed it back around her neck. She studied Erika's face several minutes before answering.

"Jonathan."

"Jonathan knows! Oh, God, no wonder he's been so depressed." She immediately wished she hadn't said the words as soon as they were out of her mouth.

Vaughn's face turned pale. "Has he taken it hard? He promised me he wouldn't. We talked about it for hours."

"He loves you more than life." Maybe she could convince Vaughn to go back to him. "It's almost killed him to have you gone. He's the saddest person I've ever known. He's aged years in the past seven months."

Vaughn stood up and walked to the edge of the porch. She looked down and studied her fingernails before she answered.

"If I could go back to him, I would."

Erika fought the panic that threatened to overwhelm her. They were trapped. Trapped in a time that didn't belong to them. Then she took a deep breath and voiced the question that had to be answered.

"How do you know you can't go back?"

"I don't know."

Erika watched in silence as Vaughn returned to her chair and sat down.

"It's just a feeling," she said. When she turned to Erika, her eyes were filled with a deep sadness. "I think the torch has passed on to you. You're the only one who can go back and forth now. I only hope we've made the right decision." She placed her hand over Erika's and squeezed gently.

There was one thing that just didn't fit. Vaughn had planned to go back in time. She had planned it and carried it out. "How did you know you could do it? How did you know when it would happen again?"

Vaughn's eyes glazed over with that far off, dreamy look. "At first I didn't know when to expect it," she said. "Until about seven months ago, I thought it was random. But now I think you can will it to happen?"

"Will it?"

"Yes. I thought about where I wanted to be and who I wanted to be with so hard that my mind was completely focused on that time period. The next thing I knew, I was there."

"I don't know. I've thought a lot about where I wanted to be and then when I wasn't thinking about it at all, I traveled."

Vaughn laughed. "You're still new at it."

Erika didn't find it amusing at all. "I hope I don't become proficient at it. Much more and I would go completely crazy."

Vaughn sobered. "I've given it a great deal of thought over the years, to say the least. If the old Indian's theory is correct, then the tear in time should be healing itself. I'm eighty years old, so it's been about sixty-six years since it happened," she paused and studied Erika. "Hopefully when you get where it is you want to be, you'll stay there. Do you know where you want to be?"

"No... Yes... No... How could I? I thought I did , but so far I haven't been given a choice. It's the hardest decision I'll ever make. I only know that I want to be with Charles."

"You must decide."

Erika shivered. Choosing when she wanted to live was no minor decision. It wasn't even one she felt capable of making. "Did you tell Nathaniel you were from the future?" she asked.

"No. I told him I was from the past."

"But, why?"

"Because I am."

Erika had opened her mind to a lot of new information today. She had, however, a little trouble assimilating this latest revelation. "No," she said slowly, "You're from the future."

"I was born in 1700."

All right, Erika thought. Anything was possible.

"I came to America when I was fourteen years old. I was one of the casquette girls who came across from France seeking a husband."

"You were born in France?"

"Oui. Very much."

"My traveling companions were set upon by Natchee Indians not far from here. My best friend, Mary, was butchered by them."

Erika hardly breathed as Vaughn paused in her story to wipe her eyes.

"I managed to hide in the bushes, but one of them found me. He was old, with a long, gray beard. I thought he was going to kill me. In a way, he did kill the person I was. It seems the man was not an Indian at all, but rather a Frenchman living among them.

"He said there was only one way to save me - he had to send me through time. He warned me that a tear would result and not only me, but also my descendants would be susceptible to falling through it. Little did I know how right he was," she said, smiling wistfully.

"My first stop was with Nathaniel in the late seventeen hundreds. He was a young man then and we fell quickly in love and were married. I had a son.

"Two years later, I found myself in 1930. You can imagine what a shock that was. And a disappointment. Ten years went by before I could accept the fact that I was never going back to Nathaniel.

"Jonathan was the most patient man I've ever known. He waited for me to come around. I finally began to consider myself widowed and agreed to marry him. I loved him, mind you, it just wasn't the same as the passion I'd shared with Nathaniel.

"We went on to have your mother. She and I were never close. I don't think she ever felt the pull with history like you did. Or maybe it was me. I never completely forgot about the dark headed son I bore Nathaniel. His name was Zachery and I never saw him again. He was killed in the War of 1812.

Erika remained silent, waiting for Vaughn to go on.

"Then, about a year ago, it started again. I finally told Jonathan about it. He believed me of course. He always believed me. He loved me so much. But the pull from Nathaniel was too strong. Even with both of us being married, we couldn't stay away from each other."

Erika waited several minutes, and finally decided Vaughn had finished her tale. "Where is his wife now?"

"She went to live with her married daughter in Virginia. I think she knew I was here, but she didn't know about my time travels. Richard's family never understood why he kept me around and I can't blame them."

Erika stayed with her grandmother for another hour, filling her in on everything that had happened since she had left. As the minutes passed, a weight began to lift from Erika's heart. The realization that her grandmother hadn't really died, but was alive and well, gradually began to sink in.

Knowing she would see Vaughn again that evening, she returned to the house with a lightness in her step. When she opened the front door, she heard Charles' laughter. Andrea must have come downstairs and woke him.

She reached the door and peered around it. Andrea was not the cause of his laughter.

"Of course he did. How could anybody say no to such a lovely creature as you." Charles was saying.

"Now, you're trying to flatter me."

Erika immediately recognized the woman as Sierra. She looked exactly the same as she did in the painting. Sitting on the edge of the bed, she wiped Charles' face with a damp cloth, touching him tenderly and easily. Charles' arm was wrapped casually around her waist. Erika felt as though someone had stepped on her chest.

"Well, it's true. You're the most beautiful woman I've ever seen. Any man would do absolutely anything for you."

The woman must have sensed someone watching them, because she suddenly looked up at Erika. Charles, too, quickly looked up and pulled his arm away. He was unable to hide the guilty expression that clouded his features.

"Erika. Come on in," he said.

"Good morning," Sierra said , with a bright smile, rinsing the cloth in a porcelain basin next to the bed.

"This is my cousin, Sierra Becquerel," Charles said.

Erika looked at them numbly.

"Your father and my father have a mutual cousin. I believe that makes us third cousins, doesn't it?" Charles asked looking into the angelic face that hovered over him.

"Yes. I believe it does. But that doesn't matter, does it?"

"No. I think I'm rather fortunate to be able to claim such beautiful kin folk."

Sierra Becquerel was indeed the most beautiful and wholesome girl Erika had ever seen. She was dressed in a baby blue dress with bows on her sleeves and a bow in her hair. Erika suddenly felt like yanking the bow from her own hair. She felt silly, like she was trying to be younger than she actually was.

"I was just checking on you," Erika said, managing to keep her voice even. "You seem to be doing fine, so I'll leave you two alone." She hoped Charles didn't recognize the bitterness that no doubt had crept into her voice.

"You don't have to go," Charles said beneath Sierra's hands and the damp cloth.

"It was nice to meet you, Mrs..." Sierra said pleasantly, completely unaware of the tension running between Erika and Charles.

"I'm not married."

"Oh, I'm sorry," Sierra said putting away the cloth and meeting Erika's eyes with pity.

Erika looked from one to the other and suddenly she couldn't stand it any longer. She turned and fled out the front door. She didn't know where she was going, but she didn't care.

By the time she reached Charles' garconnaire, she was exhausted. The tight corset squeezed the air from her lungs. She went inside and closed the door behind her. She didn't know how she managed to manufacture so many tears in one day, but as she leaned against the thick wood, her body shook with sobs.

She would end up just like Vaughn. There was no way to change history. Charles would marry Sierra. It had already happened and it couldn't be changed.

She would be left here alone, heartbroken, just like Vaughn. Then, in a few years, when Vaughn had really died, there would be no one but her. No family. No children.

She wasn't sure when she had decided she wanted children. But she did. She wanted a family. She wanted to make up for all the heartbreak her own father had caused her,

her mother, and Bradley. He should never have walked out on them.

Erika wanted a husband who would make them a family. Someone who would spend the weekends with them. Go to the park. Go on a picnic. Go to the mall.

Maybe it wasn't too late for her to get back to her own time. Surely she could find someone there who would be willing to be her companion for life - a father to her children.

She would never love anyone again. Not the way she had loved Charles. That was a once in a lifetime thing.

She curled up in a chair next to the fireplace. She would stay here until everyone had gone to bed tonight. Then she would find a way back. A way back to her own time.

Vaughn had said she could will it. She would will it.

THAT EVENING CHARLES slowly made his way downstairs to join the others. His father insisted on holding his elbow.

"Really, Father. I can make it on my own. You people are making entirely too much fuss over me."

"Nonsense. You should be in bed right now."

When Charles reached the parlor door, he was surprised to find Alexandre there waiting for him.

"You did invite me," Alexandre said, reading his expression.

"In the light of things, I never expected you to take me up on it."

"In other words you forgot." Alexandre said good naturedly. "But that's perfectly alright. Your lovely sister, Andrea, has kept me entertained."

Charles glanced at Andrea. She was much too young to be entertaining men, much less older men. The memory of Albert's attack on Erika was far too fresh in his memory.

"He's been listening to me play the pianoforte," Andrea said cheerfully.

"Wonderful," Charles said, deciding to dismiss the matter. Alexandre was nothing like Albert.

"Alexandre has come not only to see you, but for more important reasons as well," Richard said, pouring three glasses of sherry.

Charles turned his attention to his friend. His father's continued cheerfulness made him apprehensive. He worried that Richard might have something up his sleeve. Where was Erika anyway?

"Ah, there she is," Richard said and they all turned to the door. Sierra stood smiling, her gaze directed toward Charles.

Charles wondered if Alexandre had come to call on Sierra, but his friend paid no more than cursory attention to her.

Sierra immediately took her seat on the sofa next to Charles.

"Alexandre has asked permission to call on Erika," Richard said.

Charles looked at him sharply. Richard sent him a warning glance. "I assured him we would all be delighted."

"Where is Erika?" Charles asked, trying to keep his voice calm. He hadn't seen her since just before lunch. He would have gone after her then, but he just hadn't had the strength.

"I assume she's in her room," Richard said, pulling the bell cord. Villars appeared moments later. "Villars, ask Erika to come to dinner."

Villars glanced at Charles and lowered his gaze to his feet.

"I'm sorry, sir. Miss Erika's hasn't been in her room since this morning."

"Where is she?" Charles asked, coming to his feet.

"I don't know."

"Did anyone see her... leave?" Charles asked. What he meant was did she disappear again. He knew Villars would understand.

"No sir."

Charles glanced at Sierra and knew what had upset Erika. The question had been nagging at the back of his mind all afternoon. What with the loss of blood, he wasn't thinking clearly. Erika thought he was attracted to Sierra. What a preposterous thought. Sierra was a child and his cousin to boot - his real cousin.

He studied Sierra and knew how Erika could have made that mistake. Sierra was beautiful. But then so was Erika and he was in love with Erika.

He had to find her.

Richard called after him as he went out the front door, but Charles had been convalescing too long already.

A PAIR of strong arms wrapped around Erika and her eyes fluttered open briefly.

"Charles?" She murmured.

"It's me." Charles' familiar voice whispered against her cheek.

Erika closed her eyes, wrapped her arms around his neck, and snuggled against his warmth. She had been so cold. But Charles was here now. Everything would be alright.

She drifted back into that nebulous world of dreams where everything had a happy ending and if it didn't, it wasn't real anyway.

When she woke again, she found herself in Charles' bed, with a warm fire in the fireplace.

Yet she was alone. She felt lost, empty. Then the door opened and Charles came back into the room. Suddenly, she felt whole again.

CHAPTER 17

The lawn was littered with colored oak leaves. The storm had passed quickly during the night leaving the ground glistening with moisture in the early morning sunlight.

Charles stood in front of the window, buttoning his cuffs. Pausing, he leaned against the window frame to watch a pair of squirrels scampering up the trunk of the old oak tree.

A movement beyond caught his attention. He watched as Erika came out onto the lawn and started down the path. After last night, he hadn't expected her to be up until much later in the morning.

He didn't understand her, but he didn't have to understand her to love her.

Even the way she walked was different from the other women he knew. She walked with a purpose, with confidence. There was nothing coy about her movements. Though, he quickly reminded himself as he watched her, she was entirely feminine. Only it was an innocent feminism, sort of like Andrea.

Yet she was a woman. He was physically aware of that

obvious fact each time he saw her or every time he even thought of her. It seemed he'd been in a constant state of arousal for the past weeks, he thought wryly, because Erika Becquerel had hardly left his thoughts at all.

If only he knew why she had come to their home.

If only he trusted her to stay with him.

He set a tray of food on the bed beside her and handed her a mug of hot tea.

ERIKA SILENTLY ACCEPTED IT AND, studying him over the rim of the glass, quickly drank half the warm liquid. Chilled inside and out, she welcomed the burning sensation of the hot tea as it warmed her insides.

"I'm really not hungry," she said, handing him the mug.

"Nonsense. You haven't eaten all day."

He watched her with a strange expression and she couldn't fathom his thoughts. There was a determined set to his jaw. Whatever was on his mind, he wouldn't be denied. She pulled the blanket up to her chin.

Charles brought a hand up and gently swept away a stray lock of hair from her cheek. His thumb lingered against her skin. His touch was gentle, almost reverent.

She shivered, but not from the cold.

He stood up and went to stoke the fire in the fireplace. Although he was gone for less than a minute, Erika missed him from her side. It isn't normal to feel this way, she told herself. She wanted to be a part of him. She desired him, but she not only wanted his body, she wanted all of him - his heart and soul. She was in love with him.

The thought jolted her, but didn't come as a surprise. She did love him - down to his very soul. That was the reason she had traveled over one hundred fifty years to be with him. Had his soul called to hers? She didn't know. If only he would tell her how he felt. If she had some clue that he loved her, too. She knew he wanted her, but that wasn't enough. She wanted to be everything to him.

He came back to her side and took her in his arms. She turned her face to him and met his dark smokey blue eyes. All she needed was some word from him - some assurance that she was more than a fleeting passion.

His head lowered to hers and he pressed his lips against hers, gentle at first, then he increased the pressure. She went limp with sensation. He forced her lips apart and she began to kiss him back, their tongues entwining passionately.

He tasted of brandy and cigars and she was almost drunk with the feel of him. His hands caressed the back of her head and her neck. All the passion and fire for each other they had suppressed, suddenly ignited into a flame they couldn't deny. Theirs was a powerful love; powerful enough to bring them together in the first place; powerful enough to withstand the test of time.

Her arms slipped around his neck and she entwined her fingers in the silky hair at the base of his neck. She gave in to him, holding nothing back.

Then his hands moved lower and caressed her back. His thumb moved painfully close to her breast. She wanted him to touch her, yet she was afraid for him to.

Suddenly his hand covered her breast. She arched toward him for a moment, then tensed, pushing his hand away.

Charles' lips grew still upon hers, then he drew back and studied her face. She wasn't being coy. He'd had enough women to know when they were playing hard to get. There was uncertainty in her eyes and perhaps even a touch of fear.

He, too, felt fear. Fear of the emotions she could wring from him. She had no idea what she did to him. Intrigued by her innocence, he wanted her. But he not only wanted her body, he wanted more. He wanted her love, her trust, her very soul. She was from the future. What kind of men had she known there? Did he stand up to comparison?

What would she think if she knew how much he cared? Perhaps after all, it didn't matter.

"Erika..." He began.

"Wait." She interrupted. "This is wrong." She lowered her eyes.

Elizabeth haunted him even at the most intimate moments. "I belong to no one," he said. "However I give my heart to whomever I choose."

She lifted her eyes and met his gaze directly. "And who do you give your heart to?"

Lowering his head, he nuzzled her earlobe. "You have it. I gave it to you the first time I saw you."

She trembled against him and pulled him tightly to her. "I'm so afraid. You're to be married soon and I will be no more than another of your many conquests."

"Who exactly do you think I'm going to marry?" he asked, leaning on one elbow, amused.

"I don't know. Sierra, perhaps."

Charles laughed. "I must be quite a lucky man to have two women lined up for marriage. Especially since I have proposed to neither of them."

"Then you aren't getting married?" she asked with a shade of hope to her voice.

"Who would you have me marry?"

"I would - I would have you marry whomever you choose."

"Good. Because I choose neither of them. At the moment, I have thoughts only for you." *At the moment, and for the rest of my life*, he added silently.

Erika looked up at him with trust in her eyes, trust he had so longed to see. Not here, not now. He would marry her. He wanted to wake up every morning for the rest of his life and have her by his side. Charles Becquerel had fallen in love with this woman from the future.

He wrapped his arms around her and lay down next to her. In a few minutes, he heard the sounds of her even breathing and knew she was asleep.

They had a life-time before them to fill with passion.

Deep in the night, Erika woke and felt strong arms wrapped around her. Though she knew it was Charles, she turned to see his face. Bathed in moonlight, his strong features were softened. Unable to resist, she reached out and caressed his cheek.

Charles stirred with her movements and his dark blue eyes met her green ones.

"Are you all right?" he asked.

"Yes. I'm sorry I woke you."

"I'm not," he said, pulled her closer and wrapping his leg around hers.

"Charles?"

"Hmm," he murmured against her cheek.

"Do you know where I'm from? Really?"

Charles was silent for a full minute and when he answered, his tone was grave. "From the future," he said.

"I know. But do you really believe me? I'm not sure I would believe it if it were the other way around."

"I admit I didn't believe you at first. Not because I didn't want to. Just because it was so improbable."

She watched his face, his eyes. She watched for the meaning behind his words.

"Since then," he continued. "Certain things have come to my attention. And though it's hard, I do believe you."

"What things?" she asked, propping her head on her elbow.

"Your grandmother, Vaughn, for one thing. I know that she's from the future, too. Then there's the photograph."

Erika tensed. Charles had never seen the photograph she

had taken of him. It had gone to the future with her. If Charles had seen it, something was wrong - very wrong.

They both jumped, startled, as Villars pounded on the door and cried out. Charles sprang from the bed and threw open the door.

"Come quick. Miss Andrea has taken ill."

Erika gasped. This was it. This was the day Andrea was to die.

"What's wrong with her?" Charles asked, rushing out the door.

"I don't know, but she's powerfully sick."

"Did you send for Dr. Alkin?"

"Yes, sir."

Erika rushed out behind them, running to keep up. She forgot all about her own problems. A child's life was in danger here. Damn! Her medicine had been left behind.

Andrea's bedroom was silent when they entered. The room was lit with candles. Rebecca leaned over her child holding a damp cloth to her forehead. Richard stood by the door, with his hand across his eyes. Christopher and Milly stood in front of the window, holding each other.

Andrea was buried beneath a mountain of blankets, her eyes closed. Her doll, Brahe, lay beneath her cheek.

Charles kneeled beside the bed and Erika stood next to his mother. When Rebecca turned to rinse the cloth, Erika placed her hand upon the child's cheek.

Her body was raging with fever. Just as Christopher had written in his journal, she was burning up inside.

Erika went around the bed and leaned down to whisper in Charles' ear. "I can help."

"No," he said abruptly. His face was wrought with concern. The hardships these pioneers faced on a daily basis made them realize how fragile life was. Unlike those in the twentieth century, they lived without the hope of medical breakthroughs.

Even Dr. Alkin's arrival did little to alleviate their concerns.

"How long has she been this way?" the doctor asked.

"She was fine up until a couple of hours ago,"

"Hmm," Dr. Alkin replied.

Erika frowned. That was medical language for "how odd."

"She definitely has a fever," he said. "I think we should bleed her."

Erika gasped. Not leeches. Surely they didn't still use those things.

He went to his black bag and pulled out a jar.

"Get me some milk," he said.

Rebecca reached over and pulled the bell cord. A servant opened the door almost immediately and was sent for a glass of milk.

The doctor chose a short, thin, leech. Erika had a stiff stomach. She had to. But the thought of what this man was about to do made her queasy.

When he received the milk, Dr. Alkin applied a drop to Andrea's neck.

"Stop!" Erika cried.

"Excuse me?" Dr. Alkin responded, incredulously.

"What's the meaning of this?" Richard asked.

"He's going to kill her."

Dr. Alkin smiled condescendingly. "Doctors bleed patients all the time. It gets the bad blood out of their systems."

"She doesn't have any bad blood. She has a fever. She needs to keep all her blood."

"My, dear, you're wasting valuable time," Dr. Alkin said. "I have to bleed her quickly before it's too late."

"No. Charles, please. Let me tend her. I know what to do."

"Get her out of here," Richard said.

Christopher moved closer to the bed and stood quietly watching the confrontation.

Erika took Charles' sleeve and stood close to him, looking deep into his eyes. She could see him wavering.

"I can save her life. I know what to do."

"Bleeding never hurt anybody. It's a routine procedure."

Erika glanced swiftly at the doctor and returned her attention to Charles. If only looks could kill...

"If he attaches that leech to her neck, she is going to die. Charles, if you ever even thought of trusting me, do it now. Trust me to save your sister's life. I can do it."

"Dr. Alkin," Charles said quietly.

Erika turned her back and felt defeat wash over her. She didn't matter. She couldn't change what had already happened.

Andrea would die.

"Dr. Alkin," Charles repeated. "Please leave. Mother, Erika has studied medicine. She can help Andrea. Please allow her to."

Erika suddenly felt new life surging inside her. She only hoped she was right about how to help Andrea. If she failed...

Dr. Alkin shook his head sadly and turned to leave.

"No," Richard said. "I'll not trust my daughter's life to this strange woman. Dr. Alkin is a doctor. He can help her."

"Let her try, Richard," Rebecca said, moving to stand in front of her husband. "Erika is Vaughn's granddaughter."

Richard's face turned red. "That's all the more reason to keep her away."

"Do you remember when Vaughn cured little Brodie?"

Erika didn't have time to worry about how Rebecca knew who she was. She and Richard went into the hallway and continued to speak in hushed tones. She yanked the bell cord. She had a daunting task before her.

She sent for a tub of cool water and any ice that might be left over from the fall dance. Someone remembered that Standly Jones, just outside Natchez, had an ice house and a wagon was sent to fetch a load.

She opened the window and removed all the blankets from atop Andrea. When the bath arrived, she had Charles assist her in undressing Andrea and placing her gently inside the tub of cold water. He held her beneath the shoulders and kept her head safely above the water.

The child shivered and moaned softly. Erika did her best to keep the rest of the family back. She took what ice Villars located and dropped it in the water. It wasn't enough to do much good. She could only hope it would be enough until the wagon arrived.

After a few minutes longer, Erika had Andrea removed from the bath, dried off, and dressed. Her fever was still too high. She needed the ice.

She allowed them to nestle her back beneath the blankets for the time being. She paced to the window and listened for signs of the ice wagon.

Milly left to tend her own baby. Charles held Andrea's hand and spoke softly to her.

If Andrea died, Erika knew she could forget about Charles ever trusting her again.

Eventually everyone except her and Charles left the room to tend to other matters while Andrea slept. Charles laid his head on the side of the bed. His shoulders shook gently. Erika's heart went out to him. He was trusting his sister's life to her and she wasn't even sure she could save her. So far, she'd seen no evidence that she had any influence on history.

She kneeled beside him and put her arms around him. She could feel his shoulders trembling beneath her hands. He wiped his face on his sleeve and lifted his head.

"It's so futile," he said. We bring people into the world, we laugh, we love, then we die. What is the purpose?"

"She's not going to die," Erika said firmly, allowing none of her self doubt to show. "I won't let her."

"There's nothing you can do. Feel her hand."

Andrea's skin was scalding. If the ice didn't arrive soon, it may be too late. Hugging Charles quickly, she went back to her post by the window.

Just when she was about to go insane, the wagon arrived with the ice.

Moving quickly, Erika had chopped ice dropped into the tub. Once again, Andrea was disturbed from her comfortable bed and placed in the tub. Erika ignored the child's shivering and lowered her into the ice water. Andrea's glazed eyes opened and she moaned miserably. The room quickly filled with concerned family members.

"Charles, try to keep everyone away. They're not helping," Erika said. Andrea started to cry. Erika felt her forehead. Was it cooler? Maybe just a tad. Maybe.

Rebecca kneeled beside her daughter and spoke soothingly as she stroked her hair. Andrea continued to cry.

"Are you sure this will work?" Rebecca asked.

"It has to," Erika responded.

From the corner of her eye, she saw Richard watching her curiously. He held something in his hand.

Erika went to the window, closed her eyes, and counted slowly to one hundred. Going back to the tub, she placed her wrist against Andrea's forehead. Her eyes met Rebecca.

The seconds ticked slowly past. They stretched into minutes. It was the longest two hours she had ever spent.

The fever was going down.

Erika was crazy and he was insane for allowing her to do this. He couldn't watch his sister any longer. Andrea sat in that tub of ice water, shivering and moaning. Her eyes were open now and she watched him accusingly.

He supposed somewhere deep inside he believed that Erika

was from the future. If she was, maybe she could save Andrea. If she wasn't, it really didn't matter anyway.

Her fever was too high. If they didn't do something, she wouldn't make it. At least she was conscious again.

Andrea was the most important person in his life. She was almost like his own child. If she died, he swore he would never speak to Erika again.

But Erika was doing everything she could. Andrea stood a chance. He'd never believed leeches did any good anyway.

"Charles," Rebecca called urgently. Andrea had quieted.

Charles wanted to go outside and shoot himself. Without his sister, he couldn't bear to live.

"The fever's broken."

Charles felt weak with relief. Andrea would live.

They removed her from the ice water, dried her off, and got her back into the warm bed. This time, she slept peacefully.

Erika curled up on the daybed and fell asleep.

Charles took up vigil beside the bed to make sure the fever stayed down. Richard startled him with a hand on the shoulder.

His expression was odd. "I want to show you something," he said.

Charles recognized the life-like painting he'd found earlier in the desk drawer. "I've seen it," he said, expecting his father to be angry.

"But look at it now," he said.

Charles studied the tin. It had changed. He was certain of it. Andrea had not been in the picture before. Now, she sat on the steps smiling.

"My God," was all he could utter.

"Then I haven't lost my mind," Richard said.

"Where did you get this?"

"I found it in Vaughn's things many years ago. Did you see the date on the back? 1837. That's why I thought she was a witch. And when this one showed up," he gestured toward Erika, "I thought she was, too."

"How long have you had this?"

"About six months."

"I checked in New York last June at several shops. No one has ever seen anything like it. Other than that, we're the only ones who've seen it."

"What are you going to do?"

"Nothing. Perhaps I'll give it back to the old woman. I don't care if they're both witches. That girl just saved my daughter's life."

Charles smiled to himself. Erika was no witch, however, she was very much from the future. Just like her grandmother.

"When she wakes up, I want to apologize to her. She can stay here as long as she likes."

Charles studied the picture again. Yes, his sneaking suspicion had been correct. There was a wedding ring on Erika's hand.

"I have a feeling she's going to be here a very long time, indeed," Charles said.

CHAPTER 18

$\mathcal{E}$rika woke to find herself in her own room with the curtains pulled shut. The grandfather clock announced the arrival of noon. Noon!

She had to check on Andrea. Leaping from the bed, she realized she was wearing a nightgown. Grabbing a robe tossed across the end of the bed, she ran into the hallway and burst into Andrea's room.

The little girl's laughter greeted her. Milly was there with the baby tugging playfully at Andrea's hair.

Erika went to the bedside and felt Andrea's forehead. It was cool. She sent up a silent prayer of thanks. A greater power than she had intervened last night.

"Miss Erika, you have a visitor," Villars said, coming into the room.

"Me? Who is it?"

"Yes ma'am. Mr. Alexandre Alkin."

Erika excused herself and hurried back to her room to get dressed and freshened up. Why would Alexandre be coming to see her?

She rummaged through her now packed wardrobe.

Apparently Rebecca had finally realized her trunks were never coming and seen fit to supply her with the necessary items.

She struggled into the unfamiliar garments and pulled the ivory lace-trimmed dress over her head. After having no success with the tiny hook and eye closures, she pulled a shawl around her shoulders and stepped into the hall.

Charles met her halfway to the stairs. Her pulse skipped a beat at the sight of him.

"I wanted to thank you for what you did for Andrea. You saved her life."

"I'm only glad I was here to help," she said.

"She's doing much better."

"Yes, I know. Would you do something for me?" she asked.

His eyes brightened and he grinned. "Anything."

She removed the shawl and turned her back to him.

"How can I be of assistance?"

"You know perfectly well," she said, trying to sound indignant.

"Well, it looks like someone has beat me to it. You're already unhooked."

"Charles! Fasten me, please."

"Very well. But I have to warn you, I don't have much experience in putting clothing on ladies."

"You've done it for me before."

"Have I? Then I suppose this will be the second time I've gone against my instincts," he said, deftly fastening the dress.

"And what would your instincts suggest you do?"

He finished her dress and, placing his hands on her shoulders, turned her gently toward him.

A warmth spread over her as his slate blue eyes locked onto hers. Bending his head, he brought his lips against hers.

His kiss was gentle at first, then the pressure increased and he forced her lips apart. His tongue swirled around hers as he brought her hard against him. His lips were soft and firm and ever so delicious.

She wanted it to go on forever. Her arms found their way around his neck and she caressed his silky hair.

His hands moved along her back and his fingers tangled in her hair. Their bodies were pressed tightly together. Despite the layer of cotton petticoats, she could feel his desire against her.

"Good afternoon."

Erika and Charles broke apart quickly, startled by the interruption.

Sierra, dressed in a navy riding habit, stood watching them, her expression unreadable. Erika had completely forgotten about Charles' young cousin.

Charles was equally flustered. "I was just ah... helping Erika with her dress."

Erika glared at him.

"I see," Sierra said, smiling.

"Thank you again, Charles. I have to go. I have a guest," Erika said and started down the hall.

"A guest? Who?" Charles said stepping around Sierra.

"Charles," Sierra said, grabbing his arm. "You promised to go riding with me."

"I can't now," he said tearing away from her. "Erika, wait. Where are you going?"

Erika paused at the top of the stairs, thoroughly enjoying watching Charles' flustered state. Smiling, she lifted the hem of her skirts and disappeared downstairs. She could hear him coming after her.

Alexandre smiled and stood up when she entered. He was a handsome man with dark hair and smooth skin. His thick lashes shaded a pair of friendly eyes. She hadn't paid much attention to him the day of the duel, but now she was impressed.

"Erika, I hope I didn't disturb you," he said, sweeping his hand toward the sofa for her to sit.

"I'm sorry I took so long getting downstairs," her lips still tingled from the feel of Charles' kiss. "Is there something I can do for you?"

He looked confused for a moment. "Richard didn't speak with you about me, did he?"

"No. Should he have?"

"I asked to call on you."

"To call...? You want to date, I mean court me?"

"Yes," he said, reaching for her hand. "I think you're the most enchanting and intriguing woman I've ever met."

"Surely you've not met many women."

"I have. But you're different. Please, allow me to see you. I won't rush you. Although... I hope that we can eventually be married."

Erika swallowed and counted to ten. Married? Her thoughts were constantly of Charles. This man deserved better. "I don't know what to say."

"Just say, Alexandre, I'd be delighted if you'd come to call on me."

Erika laughed. Alexandre was a very sweet man. If it weren't for Charles... At any rate, he could make a wonderful friend. "Okay. I'll think about it."

"Alexandre," Charles said, coming into the room. "How's my old buddy?"

Alexandre rose to shake hands with Charles. "I'm fine and you seem to have recovered quite nicely."

"Yes, give my thanks to your father."

Alexandre sat back down beside her. Charles perched on the arm of the sofa next to Erika.

"Erika has just agreed to allow me to call on her."

"Then I suppose she didn't tell you."

"Tell me?"

"Yes. You may call on her if you wish, but you would be wasting your time."

Erika and Alexandre stared at Charles.

"You see, we're to be married."

"Who?" they both asked in unison.

"Erika and I."

Erika couldn't believe she had heard him correctly. "What are you talking about?"

Charles kneeled on the floor in front of her and took her hands. "Erika Becquerel, will you do me the honor of becoming my wife?"

Erika still couldn't grasp what he was asking her. She heard him, but thought surely she'd misunderstood.

"This is so sudden. I -"

"Just say yes," Charles demanded.

"Yes."

"Good," he said, standing up and going to the liquor cabinet. "Will you have a brandy Alexandre? To celebrate my engagement."

Erika felt sorry for Alexandre. Excitement was running through her veins, dampened only by his crushed expression. In that instant, if she could have, she could have married both of them in that instant. But Charles was the one her heart yearned for. The man she wanted to spend every day for the rest of her life with.

"I'm sorry, Alexandre," she said, taking his hand.

"That's alright, my dear," he said patting her hand gently. "I understand completely. I should have come home earlier, that's all. I wish you both a lifetime of happiness."

He took the drink Charles handed him, tipped it to his lips, and swallowed until it was gone. Taking his hat from a chair, he turned and went into the foyer - where they heard him introduce himself to Sierra.

Charles and Erika looked at each other and smiled. It seems his infatuation with Erika was short-lived after all.

"Did you mean it?" Charles asked, after the Sierra and Alexandre had gone outside together. It seems Sierra had found someone to go riding with her.

"Mean what?"

"Will you marry me?"

"Yes."

Setting his own drink aside, he grabbed her up and twirled around the room with her. Her feet never touched the ground. Laughing they collapsed on the sofa.

They hardly noticed when a horse pounded into the front yard and someone stomped up the front porch steps and threw open the door. Elizabeth pushed past Villars into the parlor, her hair hanging wildly about her shoulders. She shakily clutched a pistol in her hands.

"Erika Becquerel. You have taken everything away from me. You're a witch. I have to kill you before you harm others."

"What? What did I do?" Erika grasped Charles' arm. Her back was to the door. He wrapped his arms around her and protected her head with one hand.

"Ha! What did you do?" Elizabeth's hand trembled wildly now on the gun. "You broke my father. He doesn't come out of his study now. Not to eat. Not to sleep. He drinks all day and all night. He hasn't been sober since the wedding. You took away my betrothed. Then you said I should get rid of my child. Well, my child is dead."

"Child?" Erika heard Charles whisper in surprise against her hair.

"How do you know it's gone?" Erika asked carefully.

Elizabeth cocked her head to one side. "When something is dead, my dear little innocent, it ceases to exist. Perhaps you'll understand once you've experienced it."

Erika tensed against Charles. Without warning, he pushed

her back on the sofa and threw his body over hers. The shot echoed throughout the house. It hung in the silent air for what seemed like forever. Then there were people rushing down the stairs and into the room. Elizabeth collapsed.

Erika struggled to get out from under Charles' heavy weight.

She was soaked in his blood.

CHAPTER 19

*V*illars had stood by watching the whole episode. He had mashed his hat into a flat piece of cardboard and stood there nervously balancing from one foot to the other and back again.

"Villars," Erika called as she freed herself from Charles. "Send for Dr. Alkin. Do it now. Call for Rebecca. Then boil some water. Hurry!"

Villars dropped his hat and hurried off to do as she had said. Rebecca was the first one in the room. She stood looking from Elizabeth to Erika and Charles.

"Sadie. Get me some clean cloths. Run!" Erika said.

Erika stretched Charles' unconscious figure out on the sofa and pulled his legs up onto it. His face was pale so she placed pillows beneath his feet to get some blood back to his head. Sadie came back with the cloths and quickly left the room.

Erika took them without glancing back. "Make sure someone went after the doctor." Then she forced herself to examine his wound. Just as she had feared, the shot had pierced his skull. She placed a cloth around his head to stop the bleeding.

In the next twenty minutes, Rebecca kneeled next to her son, holding his hand. While Erika held the cloths to his head, Richard and Christopher paced the floor, watching for Dr. Alkin. They sent Sierra up to her room out of the way. The heap of bloody cloths was growing on the hardwood floor.

Villars came in with a kettle of steaming water.

"Set it down over there," she instructed. "Did you send for the doctor?"

"Yes, Miss," Villars said and placed the kettle next to the sofa. "But I reckon it'll be awhile. The stable boy jumped on a horse as soon as I told him, and sped out of here, but I just don't know if he can get there and back before... before..."

"Hush."

"Get Elizabeth up to one of the bedrooms." Rebecca told him. "And take these bloody cloths away and see if you can find some more clean ones."

"Make sure they're clean." Erika added. "We can't let him get infected."

Villars turned and walked away in a daze. Rebecca went to stand next to Richard. As he held her, she sobbed onto his shoulder.

"Oh, Charles," Erika whispered. "Don't do this to me." Her hand went back to his chest and she agonized over each interval between his shallow breaths.

Villars came back with an armful of clean cloths and went back to pace in the hall and wring his wrinkled hands. Erika stood up and went to the window. There was no sign of life, much less a doctor rushing to their rescue. It would be too late before he got here - if there was anything he could do anyway.

She sighed and turned away from the bright sunlight and her gaze brushed past the adjacent wall. Her blood ran cold. Charles was going to die. She had saved Andrea and now Charles was going to die in her place.

She looked at his long, lean figure stretched out on the sofa.

She stared unblinking until his chest rose and fell. Then her gaze moved to his face. His chiseled features were so vulnerable. His mouth was slightly parted and how she longed to feel those tender lips against hers - against her warm and eager flesh. She watched his chest gently rise and fall once more before turning back to the window.

She went back, kneeled beside him, and took his limp hand between both of hers. She bent over until her forehead touched their hands and a single tear dropped down and splashed against his white cotton shirt.

She was still there, as though she could connect her own life force with his through their skin when Dr. Alkin pulled his foaming horse to a stop in front of the house. He rushed in without knocking.

"Out. Everyone out." He dropped his black bag to the floor and removed the cloth from Charles' head. He frowned as he examined the wound and placed his hand against the man's chest much as Erika had done for the last two hours.

"Didn't I say to get out?" he said gruffly.

"I won't leave."

"Fine. I don't have time to deal with you."

"What are you going to do?"

"What? Do you think I want you swooning and passing out too? Leave."

Erika stood up and went as far as the hallway. She looked at Villars pacing up and down the foyer, his face blank. She heard Sadie whimpering from somewhere in the back of the house. She took a deep breath.

Dr. Alkin had pulled out a leech. Leeches, again!

This man was not only misinformed, he was a quack.

"No!" Erika cried suddenly, rushing back toward them. "You can't do that. I can save him. I can." She stood behind Dr. Alkin and pushed against his back with all her weight. He stumbled forward a couple of steps. Then stopped and turned around.

He started to push her away, then looked into her sincere face. "What can you do?" he asked.

"I can't tell you." She said straightening up and looking away. "You've got to trust me."

Dr. George Alkin scratched his beard and looked down at the damp leach.

"He's going to die," Erika said. "At least give me a chance. We've got nothing to lose. Let me try," she finished softly, her eyes pleading.

"Very well," he said and returned the leach to its jar. "I'll give you ten minutes."

"Ten minutes?" she echoed. Then nodded. "Alright. It's better than nothing. But I want the door locked. And I want everyone to stay away until the time is up, Okay?"

"Agreed," Dr. Alkin said and put his things back into his black bag. "Do you need this?" He asked, motioning toward it.

"No," Erika said and smiled a little.

She followed him to the door and slipped the lock into place. Then she was alone with Charles. At least what was left of him. She climbed on top of him, stretched her body out along the length of his and placed both arms around his waist and locked her hands together. Placing her head against his chest and closing her eyes, she felt the rise and fall of his chest.

She began with an airplane. She watched it in her mind - listened to it - smelled the fuel. Her jet landed in a city. It landed in a city the size of New York. She envisioned the high rise buildings, then moved her thoughts to the interstates and thousands of cars, honking and screeching through the streets. She walked past a store and saw a washing machine and dryer. Then she moved on and watched a computer, a television, heard herself talking on a cell phone.

Then she switched to thoughts of Jonathan. She concentrated on him, seeing every line of his face. She brought Bradley into the picture. Listened to him chide her about being a wimpy sister. Beads of perspiration popped out on her forehead as she forced herself to concentrate - to vividly picture anything from the twentieth century.

"ERIKA. Come out. Your time is up." Dr. Alkin pounded on the door. "Let me do what I can." There was no response. "Open the door!"

Villars reached into his pocket and pulled out a large ring of keys. He flipped through them familiarly and stuck a long silver one into the door lock. The door opened and he stepped back for Dr. Alkin to enter.

Charles was alone in the room.

ERIKA THOUGHT she heard someone calling her name. Then she heard nothing but the rain pounding against the window pane. A loud crash of thunder echoed around them. She sat up and looked around her. Rain? But it was a beautiful day.

She looked down and for a moment her face was completely blank. She had come forward in time, but Charles had not come with her.

CHAPTER 20

"*D*r. Alkin?" Charles asked opening his eyes. "What are you doing here?"

"Well, Good Evening," the doctor said placing a wrist against the man's forehead. "It seems you were grazed by a gun shot. You're going to be fine, but you lost a lot of blood."

"Erika. Where is she?"

Dr. Alkin looked at Villars. "I don't know. She was here, but when we opened the door, she was gone."

Charles closed his eyes and for a moment he seemed to have passed out again. "You must find her," he said softly.

"Why did Elizabeth shoot you?"

"She wasn't aiming for me. She said she was pregnant and lost it."

"Good God," Dr. Alkin exclaimed, getting to his feet. "Where is she?"

"She's upstairs in the guest room." Villars said moving out of the man's way.

"Villars," Charles murmured.

"Yes Sir. I'm right here."

"Is he gone?"

Villars looked around just as Dr. Alkin started up the stairs. "He's gone to find Miss Elizabeth."

"Has Erika disappeared again?"

"Yes sir, I believe she has."

"Damn."

"I didn't tell you anything, Mister Charles. I didn't say a word."

"You knew?"

"I promised not to tell."

"Where does she go?"

Villars scratched his head. "I don't know. But I know she'll be back. She's in love with you."

Charles sat up against the cushions. "We were going to be married. Send Dr. Alkin in before he leaves."

"Yes Sir," Villars said and went to occupy himself in the foyer until the doctor came back downstairs.

"How do you feel?" Dr. Alkin asked.

"Awful."

"Good."

Charles glanced at him sideways. "Did Elizabeth lose the baby?"

"Yes."

"It wasn't mine."

"How can you be sure?"

If Charles hadn't lost so much blood, he was sure that this man wouldn't have asked him that question. As it was, Charles could barely answer him, much less knock him off his feet. "I'm sure."

"Well, she says it was."

"She's crazy. We need to get her away from here - far away before she kills somebody. I have never touched Elizabeth." He closed his eyes for a moment. "You might let Albert know."

"Albert Fortier?"

"Yeah. There's a very strong possibility that it could be his child."

"I'll see what I can do. Now you get some rest. We'll try to find Erika."

"Thank you," Charles said and closed his eyes against the room spinning around him. They could search, but no one would find Erika. She had gone home.

"Damn." Erika said, collapsing on the sofa. "Damn. Damn. Damn." She beat her fists against the soft cushion and broke into tears.

"Lady, is something wrong?"

Erika looked up and wiped absently at her wet face. "Who are you?" She got up and grasped the arm to hold her balance. "I'm Caroline, Jonathan's nurse."

Not again. She couldn't go though it all over again. She just stood there staring at the stranger. Her thoughts whirled crazily, making no sense.

"How is Jonathan?" she asked.

"He's fine. I mostly just do the housework."

"He isn't sick?"

"He'll probably outlive me."

"I'm going for a walk." Without explanation, Erika walked past the woman and stepped outside in the driving rain.

She walked away from the driveway toward the river. Her shoes splashed in the mud puddles and she kept tripping over the hem of her dress.

She stopped on a grassy knoll overlooking the river. She was close enough to see the deceptively gentle current that hid the dangerous eddies and swiftly flowing undercurrents. She watched as a leaf was left behind on the bank only to be swept up moments later by a seemingly still river.

She wiped the hair from her eyes and let the rain wash over

her face. She felt like the leaf in the river, swept uncontrollably from time to time. She was numb. Nothing seemed to matter.

Her life seemed futile. She hadn't been able to save Charles. He would die in his time and she was stuck back here in hers. It was as though it had all been a dream. The memories would fade, but she would never forget him.

The rain stopped and the sun came out from behind the clouds. Her soaked hair started to dry in the heat.

Her eyes wandered to the horizon and she watched as a tiny speck drew closer and took shape in the form of a ship. The ship became a paddle wheeler churning up the murky water and splashing water on the distant banks behind it. They were too far out into the river for her to make out their faces as they passed, but as she watched, someone waved to her. Absently, she waved back and looked closely, but all of the dozen or so passengers were dressed in either long dresses or tail coats. She couldn't find anyone at all wearing shorts or blue jeans.

Erika's heart pounded in her chest and she jumped up, tripping over her skirts and started to run toward the house. A wagon was coming down the road toward the dock. A wagon pulled by mules, a man carrying a long stick walking along beside it.

The wind picked up and howled around her. She blinked. Suddenly standing before her was a white bearded, very old Indian.

Dear God, was this the man Vaughn had told her about? He wasted no time, but came straight to the point.

"Where do you want to live out the rest of your life?" he asked, lifting his arms to the sky.

"What?"

"Do you want to live in your own time or do you wish to remain here in the past with Charles?"

She didn't hesitate. "I want to be with Charles."

"I am about to mend the rip in time. You must be certain."

"I am. I want to be with Charles - if he lives. Does he live?"

The Indian nodded. "Very well," he said, beginning to chant. Thunder crashed, but there were no clouds. He yelled at the sky.

Then he disappeared.

Erika got to her feet and ran. Her lungs struggled to take in air beneath the tight corset. She half ran, half fell up the front stairs, and pushed open the door. The clock was chiming the three o'clock hour as she rounded the corner into the parlor.

"Charles!" she cried falling beside the sofa and laying her head on it as she struggled to catch her breath. "You're okay."

"Erika," Charles said, smiling broadly. "I knew you'd come back. Villars told me you would." He took her hand and squeezed it as though he would never let go.

Once Erika had slowed her breathing, she looked up and he bent over and kissed her hard on the mouth.

"I thought you were gone," she said.

"Never. Not with a future bride as pretty and sweet as you."

He took in her muddied gown and damp hair. "What happened to you?"

"I got caught in a rain storm."

He pulled her to him as though to fuse their bodies together. Leaning back just enough, their eyes locked and held for what seemed like an eternity.

TWO DAYS later Erika found herself dressed in a white wedding gown standing in the parlor. There was a toast to Charles and Erika - to a lifetime of happiness.

Christopher, Andrea, and Charles stepped out on the front porch. Erika followed closely behind. Richard was already outside speaking with a man Erika had not seen before. He was introduced as Mr. Baldwin, a photographer. The brothers helped him haul his heavy equipment out in front of the house.

Vaughn came outside and gave Erika a hug. "I'm so happy for you. It makes my life a little easier to bear knowing you were able to marry the man you love. Not that I didn't love Jonathan."

Erika laughed, "I know you did. But I understand. If Nathaniel was anything like Charles, then..."

"He was. Very much. I think they're ready now. I'll go back inside."

"Why don't you stay? If you're in the picture, and Jonathan finds it, he'll know you're alright."

"I wish I could, but you see, I'm not supposed to be in this one."

Charles came back and wrapped his arms around his new bride. "Have I told you how beautiful you are?"

"Yes."

"I haven't told you enough. You're the most beautiful bride in all the world - ever."

"I love you."

"And I love you." He placed a finger beneath her chin. "Don't ever leave me again."

"You don't have to worry about that. My fate is sealed."

EPILOGUE

$\mathcal{B}$radley walked through the house one more time. A streak of lightning darted ahead of him through the window. The lights blinked and for an instant darkness surrounded him. He flinched at the deafening roar of thunder, like a volley of cannon fire, that followed.

At the parlor door, he froze as his eyes locked onto his sister's familiar face. Erika smiled at him from a portrait on the wall. Bradley had never seen this painting. She was dressed in an ivory dress with Vaughn's cameo pinned at the collar.

As he moved closer to study it in more detail, he realized there was a portrait of their grandmother, Vaughn, in her younger years, next to it.

"Geez, they look alike," he said, looking back and forth between the two women.

He studied the pictures, wondering when they could have been done, when suddenly his heart lodged in his throat. Erika's picture was dated.

1837.

He squinted, but there was no mistaking it. This painting was dated 1837. His mind rebelled at the notion. Sure, he'd said he believed her, but saying it and seeing proof were two different things entirely.

He smiled to himself as tears welled in his eyes. She had done it. She had gotten back to her Charles and made a life for herself. Her absence left a hole in his heart that would never heal - but knowing that she was happy and in love made it somewhat tolerable. Unbelievable, but he would get through it.

On impulse, he took it from the wall and took it with him as he hurried out the front door, carefully locking it. Jonathan would have to see this for himself.

Bradley placed the key in the ignition and started the car. He could still hear the haunting siren of the ambulance that had pulled out ahead of him.

Jonathan was going to be alright. Mable and her son, Jeffery, had been taken away by the police. If it hadn't been for Erika's warning, Bradley would never have suspected Jonathan was in danger in the first place. To see Mable and Jeffery here a second time had chilled him to the bone. They were serious about getting rid of Jonathan.

When he arrived, Bradley had found Jonathan barely conscious with a phoney will put together by Mable clutched in his hand. She was a descendant of Perry Miller, a neighboring landowner back in the early nineteenth century. Generation after generation had harbored a grudge toward the Becquerels for some long forgotten reason.

Glancing back one last time, Bradley flipped on the windshield wipers and started down the drive.

A flash of lightning darted down and slammed into the house. As Bradley rounded the corner and disappeared down the road, a wisp of smoke drifted up from a corner of the house.

Want a glimpse at the Becquerel's future? How about a bonus short story?

GET MY BONUS SHORT STORY
https://BookHip.com/XBATLFH

Keep Reading for a preview of When the Stars Align...

WHEN THE STARS ALIGN
PREVIEW

Chapter 1

Bradley Becquerel hated Mardi Gras.

But here he was, crushed among the throngs of people, most of them staggering with intoxication as the darkness of an early evening storm settled over the city of New Orleans.

His new client, Ian McGregor had insisted he stay for the three-day weekend. Male bonding, he'd said. There wasn't much male bonding going on when Ian and the other two associates had gotten lost in the crowd over an hour ago.

Bradley had spent the first thirty minutes of that hour looking for them, then decided to make his way back to the hotel. Unfortunately, he could barely walk without literally stepping on someone's toes and being elbowed with every step. Besides, the Pat O Hurricane he'd had earlier had left him needing a drink of water.

With the noise of people and discordant jazz music, he couldn't even hear his own thoughts.

Lightening flashed above the crowd causing the din to increase with screams of surprise, but it was the thunder that thinned the crowd. The thunder that sounded more like an explosion than a mere storm.

After weaving his way through the moving crowd to the sidewalk, he passed the doors of the Place d'Armes hotel, and, after dodging a particularly loud trio of singing drunk college students undaunted by the sudden flood of raindrops, ducked through the next large wooden door. The establishment's name, Le Bon Temps Roule, was engraved at eye level on a bronze plaque on the heavy oak door.

Stepping inside, he was immediately struck by the quietness of the bar. It must have state of the art insulation to block out the cacophony of noise from the street. Other than the faint notes of a piano drifting from a back room, there wasn't even any loud music inside. There were only men sitting around in groups at small tables. Cigar smoke created a haze that prevented him from seeing only a few feet in front of him. He wiped his eyes with his sleeve, but the quietness provided enough relief that he could handle the discomfort of the smoke.

Perhaps he'd stumbled into a private party. Or a smoker's club. Like most places in the country, New Orleans had only a few public places left to enjoy a cigar and most of those were outside. Had he wandered into a private home?

Only a few glanced up as he passed. Some of the men were intent on their private conversations, others engrossed in the cards they held in their hands.

Bradley spotted the outline of the bar toward the left and navigated his way there. Only two other men sat on the row of barstools, huddled together in conversation to his left. He sat at the first stool he came to, near the center of the bar and, squinting through the smoke, examined his surroundings.

The men were all dressed in formal attire. A one hundred eighty degree change from the t-shirts and jeans on the street. Though he was wearing his uniform of black slacks and white oxford shirt, he was sorely underdressed.

A young male server, dressed all in white, carried a tray to one of the tables.

"How can I help you, Sir?"

Brad jerked his attention back to the bar. And his pulse quickened with surprise and immediate...intrigue. Her accent was soft and... French.

He stared into the greenest eyes he had ever seen. Her lips were plush, curved into a pleasant smile – her teeth perfectly straight and white. Her skin, smooth and pale, was framed by long ebony hair swirling around her shoulders.

It was all he could see of her features. She wore a Mardi Gras mask, covering just her eyes and the top of her nose. It appeared to be crafted from delicate white lace, tied around her head with a ribbon.

She lifted one elegant eyebrow and tilted her head to the side. "Perhaps you've had too much," she observed.

"Yes," Bradley managed to croak. "Water."

She poured water into a glass, a secret knowing smile on her lips.

Bradley wanted to see the rest of her face. Her voice and her eyes beckoned to him like a siren's song, but would she be as beautiful without the mask?

His gaze glued to hers, he gulped the water.

She watched him quizzically, that secret amusement playing about her lips.

"You're not from here," she whispered.

"No," he said, keeping his voice low to match hers. "Is this a private club?"

Her gaze skittered around the room. Back to his. "Yes," she said with a shrug.

"But I can be here?"

"We welcome everyone," she said, her smile confused.

"You just…" He swallowed a bubble of laughter. Perhaps he had had too much.

"Miss Lafleur?" A man to his left called out.

She held his gaze another moment, then turned and, retreating into the haze, walked several feet to stand in front of the man who had summoned her.

Lafleur. An old name. Old money.

While she opened a bottle and poured their drinks, he noticed that she wore a floor-length dress in a deep green, matching her eyes. As she worked, he studied the room's reflection in the mirror lining the wall in front of him.

The haziness created by the cigar smoke created an otherworldly atmosphere. For merely a moment, he experienced a flash of vertigo. It was gone so quickly, he decided he must have imagined it.

CAMILLE LAFLEUR HAD her father wrapped around her little finger. It was the only explanation for him letting her work in the tavern during Mardi Gras.

As long as you keep your mask on.

Nonetheless, the men knew who she was. This was well illustrated by the fact that they didn't hesitate to call her by name.

She wouldn't tell her father.

Since this was Friday, she had four more days to work. He'd agreed only to let her work through Mardi Gras, then the masks would come off and she would go back to being a proper young lady. Under normal circumstances, a lady never went into the tavern after dark.

She sighed. At least here she had something interesting to do. She kept the books during the day. It was natural to want to see actual business taking place.

Besides, she hated the mundane balls. Always the same handful of men vying for her hand.

Men she adamantly turned away. Despite her father's insistence that at age eighteen, she needed to take a husband and have a child to carry on the bloodline. In the four years that had passed, he had all but given up on getting her wed.

Though she had two brothers, it was unlikely either of them would be married soon. Both of them had saddled up and went to Texas to fight Comanches. If she could have found a way, she would have gone with them.

Instead, she was forced to stay behind. Needing something to occupy her time, her father allowed her to take over the bookkeeping. The tavern during the winter months and the plantation during the summers.

All three of her father's children, it seemed, had a rebellious spirit.

According to her father they took after their mother.

As she uncorked the French wine, she watched the stranger from the corner of her eye. He wore odd clothes. No jacket. His shirt was white, but he had a narrow silver cravat tied tightly round his neck. It looked, to her, a bit uncomfortable.

And he wore no mask.

The whole point of Mardi Gras was to wear a mask to conceal one's identity.

It only worked, she thought sardonically, if the people didn't know who you were to start with.

Take this man sitting in front of her. He had absolutely no idea who she was – mask or no no mask.

And... even though he didn't wear a mask, she didn't know him.

She sighed.

If wearing a mask was what it took to give her permission to do something exciting and keep away from the interminable balls, wear the mask she would.

She went back to stand in front of the stranger. "You look hungry," she said.

"Do I?"

"Yes." She turned and pulled on a cord. Marcus appeared from the back in less than two minutes. "Bring this man something to eat."

"Yes ma'am," the boy said and rushed through a door behind the bar.

"Where are you from?" she asked, staring into his blue eyes. He looked different from the other men – and not just his clothing. His dark brown hair was short. He was clean-shaven. His teeth were white…and perfectly straight.

"Monroe," he said.

She'd not heard of Monroe, but no matter. Many people visited New Orleans from small settlements. What was it that was so different about him? She couldn't quite sort it out. He looked… out of place.

Marcus returned with a plate of catfish smothered in piquant sauce - one of her favorites, and set it in front of him.

She poured a glass of red wine into a glass and slid it next to his plate. His eyes widened with the first bite. "Spicy," he said, picking up the glass.

"Do you like it?"

"It's wonderful. I've never had anything like it."

She smiled and he froze, his fork in mid-air.

Perhaps it was the mask. She reached up to remove it, but remembered her father's words. *As long as you keep the mask on, you can work downstairs in the tavern behind the bar.*

She had quickly agreed.

I'm serious Camille. If the mask comes off, I'll pull you out of the tavern.

She lowered her hand. Kept the mask on.

She hadn't bothered reminding her father that she was the best barkeep he had. And… he didn't even have to pay her. She and her brothers had spent countless hours during the day playing barkeep. Then, when she was old enough, she had memorized all the drinks.

Her father was a pushover for her, but only as far as her safety went.

Besides she was having more fun than she'd had since her brothers left.

Marcus barely had time to get upstairs and back down before he reappeared at her elbow. "Mistress Camille, your father said it's time for you to come upstairs."

Keep Reading When the Stars Align…

Kathryn Kaleigh is the author of sixty-eight novels, over one hundred short stories, and many collections.

kathrynkaleigh.com